Intellect had never ruled him

All Owain could respond to was what he felt at sharing this moment with his son, knowing that he wouldn't be sharing the future ones. He swallowed hard—pride, pain and pleasure mingling in the smile he gave Hugh.

"See!" Hugh thrust the patch at Owain, his eyes bright with pride at his accomplishment. He proceeded to give Owain a rundown of all the patches he was expecting to receive as his swimming ability grew. His gestures grew more expansive, his whispers louder.

It was like watching himself in miniature, Owain thought. He remembered that feeling, that same sense of endless possibility, of limitless horizons. Of dreams. Owain leaned a hand on the chair, feeling old and tired. He wished he could think of a way to change things, a way to begin again.

He couldn't think of a single one.

ABOUT THE AUTHOR

For Anne McAllister, ideas for stories are everywhere. She has found inspiration from a variety of sources—a childhood memory, a phone book, even a fortune cookie. In all her stories she writes about relationships— how they grow and how they challenge the people who share them. Now the author of eight books, Anne makes her home in the Midwest with her husband and their four children.

Books by Anne McAllister

HARLEQUIN AMERICAN ROMANCE
89—STARSTRUCK
108—QUICKSILVER SEASON *
132—A CHANCE OF RAINBOWS *
186—BODY AND SOUL*

   *THE QUICKSILVER SERIES

HARLEQUIN ROMANCE
2721—DARE TO TRUST

HARLEQUIN PRESENTS
844—LIGHTNING STORM

Dream Chasers
Anne McAllister

Harlequin Books

TORONTO • NEW YORK • LONDON
AMSTERDAM • PARIS • SYDNEY • HAMBURG
STOCKHOLM • ATHENS • TOKYO • MILAN

To my grandmother, Mae Fasel,
with love and thanks for all the memories . . .

And to Courtney and David, with love

Published June 1987

First printing April 1987

ISBN 0-373-16202-2

Chapter One

The sharp autumn wind blew from the north right down the back of Owain O'Neill's neck. He hunched his shoulders inside the navy-blue down vest he wore and moved beneath the shelter of a golden-leaved maple tree to avoid the first spatterings of sleet.

There was warmth in the rental car he had left by the side of the road, also a good heater and a thermos of coffee. But neither interested him now. His eyes were riveted on a group of young children dashing across the playground.

There were five of them, all about five to seven years of age judging from the size of them—about the same as Dougal's Annie—their gender indistinguishable in their jeans and bright-colored parkas. Not that it mattered, he thought as he shoved his fists deeper into the pockets of his fawn-colored needlecord jeans. He had no idea if he was looking for a boy or a girl.

Why was he looking at all? What did it matter? And what would he do if he saw him? Or her? The questions battered him. But he had come too far to turn back now. So he forced himself to ignore the questions, walking instead across the playground, angling toward the white shingled house on the edge of the park, so he could watch the children without seeming conspicuous. Two of the children sprinted toward a wood-framed swing set, and his gaze followed them, wondering if either was the Williams child.

His ears were frozen and his stomach growled. The child he was seeking might not even be here, for heaven's sake. It was insane really. If he had told his friend Dougal or anyone else what he was doing they would have thought he was crazy.

"Owain's gone round the bend," they would have said, laughing. "Write us a song about it, Owain. Can't you write us a song?"

But the music wasn't in him any longer, hadn't been for several months. Now there was only this crazy dream—an obsession almost—that had come upon him ever since he had found out what had happened to Meg.

One of the children on the swings had lost her cap. She had golden hair, tangled and curly. The same color as Meg's? He squinted, trying to mesh reality and memory, but he couldn't. In some ways, he realized with growing self-recrimination, he could scarcely remember Meg. Blond? Yes, of course. With a thin face and wide eyes that had trusted too much and seen too little. He compressed his lips in a thin line, dredging up his few remaining images of her. Then his eyes flickered back to the girl on the swing, and he sighed.

How would he ever know?

The door to the shingled house opened and a woman wearing a coat came out. She glanced over at him, her gaze resting on him long enough to let him know that she realized he was a stranger and wondered what he was doing in the park on such a miserable day. Then she whistled shrilly, and three of the five children looked up and ran over to her. The golden-haired girl was among them. Was she the one?

Owain rested his palm against the rough bark of the tree and watched as the woman waved to someone standing in the doorway, then herded the children into the car and drove away.

"Is that it then, old man?" he asked himself under his breath. "Have you found what you were looking for?"

He meant the question to be self-mocking. In his more rational moments he deplored his present quixotic behavior. He had done some impetuous and foolish things in his life, but this was undoubtedly one of the worst. But—and his mouth twisted wryly at the realization—all the deploring in the world didn't seem to be able to stop him. Drawing in a deep breath of cold air and shaking the accumulation of sleet off his hair, he was turning to head back toward the car when a small body came crashing headlong into his legs.

"Hey!" He stumbled, losing his balance against the tree, his hands going down to catch and steady the child. "Watch it! Are you all right?"

Flashing brown eyes and wind-reddened cheeks turned up to meet his gaze. "Oh! Sorry! I didn't see you. Hugh's chasing me," the girl added by way of explanation. Then she took off again, scattering the leaves in her wake as she darted across the park.

Owain stared after her, frowning, his memory pricked by a pair of smoky brown eyes. He watched as the boy called Hugh raced after her, tackling her beneath the swings, the two of them rolling over and over in a tangle of arms and legs, red and blue jackets. The girl's hair was as dark as his own.

He felt a quickening inside him, a tingle of awareness. This girl had none of Meg's fair hair or light hazel eyes. But did she have to? Of course not. "Elementary genetics, O'Neill," he muttered, his eyes never leaving the child, studying with whole-minded intensity her every move.

She scrambled to her feet and took off again, Hugh chasing her, whooping at the top of his lungs. Owain followed them, drawn by a pull stronger than gravity. His frozen limbs, his gnawing hunger were forgotten as he crossed the playground when they did, shadowing them, entranced.

"Bronny! Hugh! Time to come in!"

Bronny? Owain went white.

The children turned and raced back past him without a second glance as they headed for the same shingled house, two voices chirping, "Coming, Mom!" to the tall, slender woman silhouetted in the doorway. Before he knew it, they had vanished inside.

"Bronny?" he whispered, his voice whipped away by the sleet-bearing wind that pierced him, body and soul. *Bronny?*

For a full minute he didn't move, turning the name over and over in his mind, seeing the child's lustrous brown eyes, thinking of another pair just like them. And another name the same as hers.

Then he scuffed his way slowly, mindlessly, through the fallen leaves toward the car he had left on the verge of the road.

He got in, started it up, listened to the hum of the heater and the gentle purr of the engine turning over. He rested his hands limply on the steering wheel, but beyond that he didn't move. Instead he stared at the white house across the park, its lighted windows a welcome beacon in the waning Wisconsin afternoon.

"Now what, O'Neill?" he asked himself hoarsely. "Walk away from that if you can."

HE COULDN'T.

He told himself he had seen the child. She was a girl, she was alive and she was well. What more did he want?

To see her again. Just once. More than for just a few fleeting seconds.

But how?

He went back to the dingy motel and paced the floor of his room. Then, when it became too confining for the emotions that assailed him, he went back out into the dusk, turning up his collar against the beginning of the snow, and began to walk.

His wandering took him up and down most of the hills of the small Wisconsin college town. He walked across the campus, went up Belle River's main street, past the Methodist church, the cemetery, the elementary school, the feed store, the cheese factory. But he saw none of it. He barely registered where he was.

His mind was filled with the image of the child. *His* child. *His daughter.*

Bronny. Short for Bronwen? Probably. He couldn't imagine anything else it would be short for. Bronwen. His mother's name. How pleased she would be if she knew.

But she wouldn't know.

No one knew now, save himself.

And no one would know. He wouldn't disrupt her life. That wasn't his intention at all. He would just see her once more—and then he would go.

His feet took him back toward the park where he had seen her before. The ground was turning white now, the snow sticking as the temperature fell. His loafers, well-worn and run-down, suited California perfectly. But they were no match for this. His feet were freezing.

There was one light in the small bungalow. And the warm golden glow of it drew him. Before he even realized what he was doing, he was standing on the front porch, scuffing his feet, kicking the snow away, and—God help him—ringing the doorbell.

He knew a moment's panic after he had done it. An urge to cut and run almost choked him. And if the door hadn't opened at that very moment, he might well have done it.

"Yes?" An owlish young woman peered out at him.

"I...Is...Mrs. Williams in?" he stammered at last, wondering even as he did so if this was Mrs. Williams facing him.

"No, sorry, she's gone out right now. If you have typing you can leave it, though."

Owain blinked, confused. "Typing? Er...no."

The girl gave him a curious look. "Well, did you want to leave a message then? Shall I tell her you came by?" She gave him an assessing look. "I'm sure she'd like to know," she added after she had given him a once-over that made him blush.

Owain scowled, embarrassed, thinking that however many times it happened, he would never get used to it, and thanking God it didn't happen often anymore. "No...it's not that important...uh...thank you." And without another word he bolted off the porch and walked briskly back toward the campus through the park.

He knew the girl was watching him go. The light from the doorway spilled into the darkness until he was well across the lawn.

"Idiot!" he muttered, clenching and unclenching his frozen toes as he walked. His fingers were trembling and he jammed his hands into his pockets. "Just forget it."

But he didn't.

Bronny haunted his dreams. And when he dragged himself out of bed in the morning, no more rested than when he had fallen into it the night before, he found himself staring into the mirror and seeing Bronny's hair, mussed and wind-ruffled, so like his own. He shut his eyes, but she didn't go away.

He went out for a walk to clear his head and ended up at the elementary school again. Without thinking he found himself standing by the fence trying to pick her out of the scores of children running around. Finally one of the playground supervisors came over and asked if he was waiting for someone.

"No," he mumbled and walked away. Probably, he decided afterward, he made the woman even more nervous by doing that. But he couldn't help it, any more than he seemed to be able to help himself when it came to forgetting the whole thing. Any more than he seemed to be able to stay away from the park after school was out.

The weather had changed, turning milder. The snow had melted, leaving soggy piles of leaves dotting the grass. The breeze was southerly this afternoon, a far cry from yesterday's snapping wind. It was a good day, Owain thought, for flying a kite.

There was an idea! It had been years since he had flown a kite. Until now, he had never had the time—correction, had never *taken* the time. But why not? And what better reason for being in a park.

Kites, though, he discovered, weren't easy to come by in October.

"A kite?" The clerk at the Benjamin Franklin looked at him as if he had lost his mind. But when Owain insisted, he went off and unearthed one in the back room.

"Have fun," the man said to him with a hint of sarcasm in his voice. But Owain was undeterred, and when he dusted it off and assembled it, he was delighted. A shimmering, brightly colored rainbow, it was, he decided, a good-luck sign.

And he might have been right, for when he got back to the park Bronny and the boy she had been playing with yesterday—an adopted brother perhaps?—were already there playing on the swings.

Owain sat in the car watching them. His fingers fumbled with the kite string, his eyes straying out the windshield instead to watch his child as she swung high as the tree boughs, shrieking and laughing when the boy grabbed her swing and ran under it, pushing her even higher.

Owain dropped the end of the string, picked it up again and reknotted it, tying it and pulling it tight with his teeth. There! Then, opening the door, he got out, holding the kite gingerly in one hand and the spool of string in the other.

He carried them to the center of the park, farthest from the trees that bordered it, then let out a bit of string and began to run, playing the spool out behind him. A gust of wind caught the kite, lifting it, swirling it, then dashing it to the ground.

Owain scowled, rewound the string and tried again. At every second he was aware of his audience. The boy stopped heaping leaves in a pile and watched as Owain took another run with the kite. Bronny swung high and low, but silently now, watching him as he ran, trailing the kite behind.

The fifth time he attempted it—just when he felt he had been acting like a fool long enough—the kite caught in the wind and began to lift.

"Whoo-ee, you did it, mister!" the boy shouted, waving his arms in triumph.

Owain, his ego soaring with the kite, grinned back. He stopped running and turned, beginning to play out the string a bit at a time, feeling the tug and pull against his hand as the rainbow kite lifted higher and higher. When he glanced down again, the boy was standing beside him.

"You got a lot of string," the boy said matter-of-factly. "Bet it could go clear to the moon."

Owain laughed. "I wish it could." He grinned down at the blond head next to him. "Want to hold it?"

"Could I?"

"Sure."

The boy looked from Owain to the kite, then toward his house, clearly weighing things in his mind. "I don't know you," he said finally. "I'd better ask my mom."

Owain nodded. "Good idea."

The boy scampered off in the direction of his house. Owain glanced over at Bronny. She had stopped swinging and was sitting quietly, watching him, her legs dangling, scuffing the leaves underfoot.

She met his gaze with a blatantly curious one of her own. Her brown eyes were wide and serious as they looked him over. This unblinking assessment was even more thorough than the one the owlish woman had subjected him to the evening before, and even more disconcerting. What did she see in him? Could she know?

No, of course not! She could have no idea who he was. But he still felt a shiver run down his spine, and he was almost relieved when the boy returned out of breath and panted, "She'll be lookin' out the window. She says it's all right."

Owain broke the gaze that locked his eyes with his daughter's, and glanced over at the window. An indiscernible face and a flash of golden hair appeared momentarily. A hand waved. He waved back, feeling awkward, as if he were deceiving her somehow.

Somehow? *Oh, come on, O'Neill! Somehow? What do you think she'd say if she knew who you were?*

"Well, can I?" the boy asked, and Owain nodded, giving him the string, helping him wrap it around his fingers. "Wow! It really pulls."

"Yes."

The kite did a somersault, then went higher. The boy laughed delightedly. "I'm glad you came," he told Owain. "We only remember to fly kites in the spring."

"Yeah, I'm glad, too." Owain tucked his hands into the pockets of his vest. "What's your name?"

"Hugh. What's yours?"

"Owain. Is that your sister?" Owain asked, sneaking another glance at the girl. She had got off the swing now and was standing under the tree, watching their every move but not getting involved. Yet.

"Uh-huh. Bron," Hugh agreed, never taking his eyes off the kite.

"Bron?" Owain probed, his tone curious but casual.

"Bronwen. It's Welsh."

"So's Owain. O-W-A-I-N, like Owen, just a different spelling."

"Well, I don't know how to spell Bronwen," Hugh said. "That's her problem, not mine."

Owain laughed. "How do you spell your name?"

"H-U-G-H."

He nodded. "The Welsh spelling would be H-U-W."

Hugh looked disappointed. "But I am Welsh," he insisted. "Or part Welsh. Just like her. I gotta be, don't I, if she's my sister?"

Owain didn't know. He could hardly say, *Well, if you were natural brother and sister, yes. But since your sister is adopted*... Because he wasn't supposed to know any of that.

"My mom says so," Hugh went on stubbornly.

"Then you must be," Owain agreed.

"Can I have a turn, too?"

He spun around at the small voice that had piped up suddenly behind him. Bronwen was staring up at him, her eyes bright and expectant. Owain swallowed hard.

"Uh, yeah. Just as soon as...as your...brother is done. Five more minutes, maybe," he offered. He smiled at her; she smiled back. His mother's smile on a six-year-old. His heart lurched.

"Okay." She waited patiently while Hugh, determined to wring every ounce of pleasure out of his remaining five minutes, raced up and down the park, towing the kite that bobbed along overhead, a rainbow twisting in the wind.

She watched the kite, but Owain watched her, continually fascinated at this incredible human being he had had a part in conceiving. The reality of it still stunned him.

Finally Bronwen tapped Owain's wrist. "My turn?" she asked at last.

He blinked. "Huh? Oh, yeah. Your turn."

On Hugh's next pass, Owain called him over. Then, kneeling, Owain eased the string out of Hugh's grip and wrapped it around Bronwen's small fingers. He took his time, his own fingers trembling as he did it. *His daughter.* And he was touching her at last. He marveled at the soft skin, the perfectly formed fingers, the well-chewed nails. They made him grin even as his throat constricted and his fingers fumbled with the string.

Bronwen looked at him impatiently. "I've got it," she announced and, wrapping it twice around her fist, she gave it a jerk, making the kite bob as proof. Then she took off running, too.

Owain's eyes followed her, watching her jean-clad legs flying over the uneven ground. Her dark curls bounced in the wind and her cheeks approached the berry hue of her jacket. The kite dipped, edging closer to a towering pine tree.

"Watch out!" Hugh shouted, and his sister saw the danger and let out more string.

"Can't catch me!" she yelled at the tree, and she and the kite danced away to the far end of the park.

Owain stood and watched, enchanted, his heart being tugged like the kite on a string as he stored up the moments, tucked away the impressions, hoarded the memories. The strong smell of wood smoke teased his nostrils. A vapor trail from a high-flying jet cut behind the kite, leaving a plume of white across the sky.

"My turn yet?" Hugh demanded, running up to him.

Owain consulted his watch. "One more minute."

Hugh hopped from one foot to another. "C'mon, Bronny! Bring it back now!"

But Bronny was running now, beyond hearing. And Hugh took off after her, while Owain leaned against a tree and wished the afternoon would never end.

"I hope they're not being pests," a voice said beside him, and he turned around quickly.

"They're mine," the woman next to him said with an apologetic smile. "I hope they haven't been too much trouble."

"N...no," Owain assured her, hoping that she thought it was the wind that was leaving him breathless. His eyes flickered from their mother to Bronwen and Hugh, then back again.

Whenever Owain had thought of the mother of his child—which hadn't been often actually—in his mind he had, quite naturally, envisioned his own mother. But the short, well-rounded lady who had patched his own knees and tucked him up at night bore no resemblance at all to the mother of Bronwen and Hugh.

He had known her name was Cara, but that was all he had known. And Cara as a name meant nothing to him. He had never known a Cara. But this one he would never forget, no matter whose mother she was.

Cara Williams was tall—almost as tall as he was—and slender. Her figure was outlined quite nicely by the pair of snug, faded jeans she wore. Her eyes were not the soft doe-brown of his own mother, but the startling green-gold of a lioness. And her hair reminded him of a lion's, too. Full and thick and glossy, gold and brown interwoven, it was pulled straight back and anchored at the nape of her neck with a leather thong. Loose, it would, Owain guessed, have tumbled halfway down her back.

She wore a man's flannel shirt over a navy blue turtle-neck, and it suited her very well. The words "earth mother" popped into his head, and yet, as soon as he thought them, his mind taunted him with an image of her wearing a silky black sheath, gold earrings dangling from her ears, and the golden mane of hair knotted elegantly atop her head.

The direction of his thoughts dumbfounded him, as did the quite inappropriate stirring he felt deep within. *Stop it,* he told himself savagely. *This isn't some groupie, she's your daughter's mother, for God's sake!* And stop it he did. But he couldn't completely squelch the pang of envy he felt for Cara Williams's husband, Martin. He had not only Owain's daughter but a perfectly stunning wife as well.

"Are you at the college?" she asked him politely.

"Er, no." He dug his toe into a pile of wet leaves. "I . . . I'm doing research in the area." Well, it wasn't really a lie.

"On what?"

Caught, he fell back on at least a half-truth. "On the immigration experience. I'm working on my doctorate."

She looked impressed. "From where?"

"UCLA."

"You're a long way from home."

He scratched his head. "Yes."

She gave him a surreptitious glance out of the corner of her eye. "That accent isn't entirely California."

"Not entirely, no. I emigrated myself. From Britain with my parents when I was thirteen."

"Ah, so the immigrant experience lies close to home."

"Very."

The more so recently, though he didn't go into that. He couldn't quite explain it to himself yet—how after years of phenomenal success at the top of the musical heap with Cardiff Connection, for which he played lead guitar, he had felt cut off from his past and how, just as vividly, he had seen that if he didn't do something, his future was going to be what he didn't want either.

He hadn't put it all together yet and been able to make sense out of it himself. He couldn't imagine telling Cara Williams, but damn, he was tempted. She seemed to inspire that sort of confidence.

He cast a sideways glance at her now. She had tucked her hands into the pockets of her jeans and was rocking back and forth on her heels as she watched her children darting about on the far side of the park. Then, when Hugh seemed just about to dash into the road, she pulled a hand quickly out of her pocket and put her fingers between her teeth and let go with an earsplitting whistle.

Owain jumped.

"Sorry," she said, obviously embarrassed. She waved to the children. "That's far enough! Come back now!"

Bronwen, who still had the kite string, slipped in a pile of leaves and Hugh was on her in a second, wrestling the kite away from her.

Owain watched, grinning. Cara clicked her tongue in exasperation. "Those two," she sighed as Hugh succeeded in wrenching the string from his sister's hand. He scrambled to his feet and began to run for all he was worth. "Talk about competition."

Owain grinned. "Anything you can do, I can do better?"

"Precisely."

"I remember that. My brother and I were fierce about it. But we were only a year apart. How about your two?"

"They're twins," Cara said, then covered her mouth as Hugh ran, unlooking, full tilt into a tree.

Owain didn't even notice.

"Twins?" The words echoed in his head. He was certain he had misheard. But what else could she have said?

Cara was running toward Hugh by that time, and didn't answer him at all.

Twins? Owain stood, poleaxed, feeling as if he were the one who had hit the tree. Not his son.

His *son*? Hugh?

His *daughter*, Bronwen, and his *son*, Hugh?

God Almighty!

He began to run, too.

"Is he all right?"

Cara was kneeling on the ground, Hugh's head in her lap. His hand was over his nose, blood seeping through though he tried to pinch it shut.

"Trust you," Cara was saying to him, hugging him close. "What have I told you about looking before you leap?"

"Ah buzzn't leapin'," Hugh protested dazedly.

"The principle is the same." Cara brushed dirt off his forehead where Owain could see the beginnings of a bruise coming up. "Here, lovey, can you stand up?"

Hugh met Owain's stricken eyes and lurched to his feet. "S...sorry aboud your kide," he mumbled, still holding his nose.

"Forget the kite," Owain said. "Are *you* all right?" He turned to Cara, feeling frantic. "Is he all right?"

"He will be," Cara assured him. "It takes more than a nosedive to daunt old Hugh. But," she added with a smile, "I do think he may have had enough kite-flying for one day."

"So have I," Owain said fervently.

"I haven't." Bronwen spoke from above them, and both Owain and Cara looked up to see her standing on a branch of the oak tree Hugh had smacked into. "An' I caught the kite string, too. So can't I fly it a little longer, if Hugh's gonna be okay? Please?"

She looked from her mother to Owain beseechingly.

Cara reached down and pinched Hugh's nose tighter. "Would you mind if she did?" she asked Owain. "I mean, it would be easier. Bronny's not much of a Nightingale, I'm afraid. I'd probably be patching her up from fainting over Hugh's blood."

Owain managed a faint grin. "I don't mind. Shall I bring her over to your house in a few minutes?"

"Give me ten." Cara smiled and held out her hand to him. "I suppose, given that I am imposing on you, I ought to introduce myself at least. My name is Cara Williams."

Owain took her hand, feeling in it the same warm strength he could see in her every movement. "Owain O'Neill."

He held his breath to see if she would recognize it. Some people did. Mostly the members of Cardiff Connection were known by their group identity, but there had been times when he had wished for more anonymity than he had. Lately though, since he wasn't actively performing anymore, most people who knew had forgotten. He preferred it that way. But he still always felt a moment's trepidation when he said his name. Cara's reaction was simply to raise her eyebrows.

"An Irish Briton?" she asked.

Owain breathed easier. "Only half. My mother's Welsh."

"My husband's family is Welsh. Hence, our Bronwen..." She glanced down at Hugh, whose nose was already dripping on her tennis shoes. "But now isn't the time for family history, is it?" She gave him a bright smile. "See you in a few minutes, Mr. O'Neill." And putting her hand on Hugh's shoulder, she hurried him into the house.

Owain watched her go, the faint yearnings he had suppressed earlier beginning to surface again. But this time he didn't have to distract himself. Bronwen did it for him.

"Can you get me down?" she asked him, inching back on the branch toward the trunk of the tree.

"Look before you leap, isn't that what your mother said?" Owain teased even as he moved to help her.

"I don't want to leap," Bronwen protested. "I just want to get down. I was gettin' your kite," she reminded him.

"So you were." Owain lifted his arms and his daughter slipped into them, still clutching the kite string. He didn't set her down at once, just stood there feeling the solid warmth of the small wiry body pressed next to his. Then she wriggled, and he eased her to the ground.

"We'd better move away from here," she said, looking from the string, which so far had not got tangled in the branches, to the kite that fluttered beyond.

"Yes," Owain agreed, and started to walk toward the center of the park. A moment later he was astonished to feel a small cold hand grab his. "Are..." He cleared his throat and tried again. "Are you and Hugh really...twins?"

"Yup." She bounced along at his side. Though she had been slower to warm up to him than her brother had, she seemed to have decided to trust him now. "He's bigger, but I'm older. Ten whole minutes, my mom says."

"You don't look much alike."

Hugh was, as Bronwen had said, bigger. He was taller by half a head. He also had blond hair and blue eyes. Bronwen's brown eyes and brown curls were a definite contrast.

"We got the same noses, my mommy says," Bronwen informed him frankly. And, now that she mentioned it, Owain saw that they did. Noses like his Uncle David and his cousin, Rhys.

He also realized something else. Two children were the reason Meg had sent—or meant to send—him two baby pictures. The baby pictures he had received out of the blue just a few months ago were not, as he had always assumed, two photos of one child, but one picture each of two!

But as rational as it all was—Owain's mind still reeled. *Twins!*

He was still recovering from the shock when the back door of the Williams house opened at last and Cara waved to them. "Disaster quelled," she shouted. "It's safe to come home now."

Owain helped Bronwen reel in the kite, then walked with her toward the house. "Here you are," he said when they reached the back steps. "One daughter. Safe and sound."

Cara gave him a warm smile. "Thank you for watching her."

"No problem. How's Hugh?"

"Bloody and battered, but unbowed."

"I'm glad." Owain shifted from one foot to the other, reluctant now that the time was at hand to say goodbye. "Well, it's been a pleasure." He took a step backward and trod on someone's toe.

"Ouch."

He turned to come face-to-face with the girl who had answered the door the night before. She brightened at once when she saw him.

"Ah, you found her!"

"Found who?" asked Cara.

"Found you," the girl said. "This is the guy I was telling you about. The one who was looking for you." She tossed her long dark hair. "I wish he'd been looking for me."

Owain and Cara looked at each other. Then, embarrassed, their eyes skidded away.

"I thought he was bringing you typing," the girl went on. "But he said no."

"I didn't have it with me," Owain fabricated quickly. "I just wanted to, er, talk about rates and such."

Cara seemed to take that at face value, making him feel like even more of a heel. What would she think when he declined eventually? That her rates were too high?

"Sure. Hang on." She disappeared back into her house a moment and came back with a sheet of paper. "This has all my rates on it. I do tax work, bookkeeping and five thousand other things as well." She gave him a wry smile. "Anything you can do with a computer, actually. Is it your dissertation you're talking about?"

He nodded, not meeting her eyes.

"Well, you look around and get some comparative prices," Cara advised him. "You might get it done cheaper in L.A., if you intend to go back soon." She looked at him expectantly, as if she thought he might tell her when he planned to leave.

"I...might." He creased the paper in his hands. "I...thought about interviewing some of the older immigrants to this area...but..." He let his voice trail off.

"If you do, my grandmother would love to meet you," Cara said easily. "She's always got a good story to tell."

"Thanks. I'll...think about it." He didn't want to think about the flight he had booked from Madison to L.A. the day after tomorrow. It was a flight that he suddenly wished he didn't have to take.

But that was utter nonsense, he reminded himself. His goal had simply been to meet his child—children!—and be assured that they were well.

Obviously they were fine. So he ought to be on his way.

"Well, thanks," he said awkwardly. He looked in the door and waved to Hugh, then touched Bronwen's curls lightly with his hand. His throat felt tight, and he bit the inside of his cheek to keep down the wave of emotion that threatened to engulf him. "It . . . was fun."

"Sure was!" Bronwen agreed enthusiastically. She swung around the porch support, then scrambled up onto the railing. "Can we do it again? Tomorrow?"

Owain turned to watch her, a rueful twist to his mouth. "I probably won't be here tomorrow."

"But—"

"But you can still fly it." He held out the kite to her. "Here. You and Hugh can have it. Think of me when you fly it, okay?"

Bronwen took the kite, her eyes shining. "Thanks. Thanks a lot. Will you fly it with us, Mom?" she asked her mother.

"Oh, I think so." Cara smiled down at her daughter, then ruffled her curls. "Or maybe Suzy will," she said, giving the baby-sitter a nod.

"See," Owain said to Bronwen, "there are lots of people around to help you fly it. Your mom, your baby-sitter. I'll bet even your . . . your dad . . . would like to sometime."

Bronwen's smile faded. "My daddy's dead."

Chapter Two

Serves you right, Owain told himself savagely.

Had he really thought that finding his child was nothing more than a mystery to be solved—a puzzle that, once completed, he could walk away from?

Or, he asked himself as he drove carefully along the narrow hilly streets of Belle River, had he really thought at all?

Probably not.

Thinking ahead—planning—had never been his long suit. The opposite, in fact, was true.

If it weren't, he asked himself, would he have suddenly discovered this afternoon that he was the father of twins? God, the very thought was mind-blowing!

To have the faceless, nameless, sexless child he had been pursuing over the past few months suddenly metamorphose into living, breathing, six-year-old twins—namely Bronwen and Hugh Williams—was almost more than he could handle.

Whatever he had thought he was expecting, it wasn't that.

When the smudged, obviously well-traveled envelope had finally caught up with him in Montana to tell him that Meg Chandler had died in a car accident, and that among her effects was this smaller envelope addressed to him, he had had trouble for a moment even remembering who Meg Chandler was.

When the baby pictures tumbled onto the table in front of him, he had remembered at once.

He had picked up the photos with suddenly cold fingers, the evidence of one night's passion there in his hand.

He had never known much about Meg. She was a graduate student at UCLA, doing something in the arts, if he remembered correctly. But he didn't think he had ever known exactly what. She had also worked part-time as a gofer at the recording studio.

And she had thought that a night out with the lead guitarist and principal songwriter for the phenomenally successful trio, Cardiff Connection, was a coup indeed. He could have drowned in the hero worship he saw in her eyes.

But Owain saw it in most female eyes in those days. He would never have had to spend the night in an empty bed if he didn't want to. Usually though, all publicity to the contrary, he did. Sleeping around took too much energy. And music was, at the moment, the most important thing in his life.

If there was anything, though, that he wanted less than the continual distraction of groupie after groupie, it was commitment to one woman. He certainly wasn't ready for that. So thank God, he thought—then and now—even when she turned up pregnant, Meg Chandler had felt the same way.

She had cornered him in the studio two and a half months after their one fateful night together. He hadn't seen her since, hadn't even really given her a thought. He, Dougal and Mike had been on tour. Twenty cities in twenty-seven days. And they had just arrived back in town to cut a single when Meg zeroed in on him the first day he showed up at the studio.

She was paler than he remembered, her eyes wide and almost defiant when she asked him to have a cup of coffee with her. She didn't look as if she would take no for an answer.

Owain didn't bother to try it. Meg was a nice kid, and if she wanted a cup of coffee, fine. But he was too busy this trip for another roll in the sack. He would have to make that perfectly clear.

But the question never came up.

They sat facing each other over a Formica-topped table in a tiny room populated by vending machines and spare extension cords, and people walked in and out, buying yogurt and stale ham sandwiches. Meg had waited until he had taken his first sip of scalding coffee before she said baldly, "I'm pregnant."

It was as if the world had tilted on its axis. He spilled the coffee all over his pants.

Pregnant? God in heaven! And no doubt she meant it was his since she was telling him about it! He could just guess what she would say next.

"I won't marry you," she went on firmly, confounding him. "I don't want to get married. But I'm not going to have an abortion either." She was glaring at him as if she had already decided what *he* would say next, too.

"Good," he said, and she looked at him as if he had startled her. He supposed he deserved the look. His behavior having been not overly responsible up to that point, Meg could hardly have been blamed for imagining that he would just suggest that she get rid of the baby.

Still, he couldn't do that. Even *his* sense of irresponsibility didn't extend that far.

"So do you want it, then?" she asked him.

"Want it?"

She shrugged. "I didn't know," she said awkwardly. "I thought you might. I don't really know you very well, do I?"

Owain certainly couldn't dispute that. "You mean, *me* take it? Raise it?"

Meg nodded, her eyes skewering him over the coffee cups.

"What about you?" he asked desperately.

She shook her head. "I'm going to grad school. It wouldn't be fair to any baby, saddling it with me. I won't have time. And I don't think, for now at least, I'd be a very good mother."

Owain wanted to ask why she hadn't thought of that before. What had happened to the protection she had assured him she was using?

But she looked terrible, thin and pale, with dark smudges under her eyes. And he suspected that she had already been over those questions without him. Besides, even knowing the answers wouldn't help them now. The baby was on its way.

Baby! God, he couldn't even fathom it. Hadn't even tried. Didn't want to. The less he thought about it, the better. But obviously, some thinking, some planning, had to be done.

"I don't think I'm cut out for fatherhood right now either." He tried and barely succeeded in smiling. Meg looked as if she needed some sort of reassurance desperately. Perhaps knowing that he shared her feelings of inadequacy would help.

"So you don't want it either, then?"

She made it sound like a parcel that neither of them knew what to do with. Like the birthday gifts his Auntie Sophie used to give him. But maybe it was better that way. If he thought of it as a person, it would be harder to reject.

But at the same time, visions of himself trying to raise a child alone, dragging it from town to town, leaving it with strangers, being responsible for its welfare when he was so obviously irresponsible, made him drop his eyes to his hands wrapped around the Styrofoam cup. He tried to envision them cradling an infant, supporting a small body, sheltering a life wholly dependent on him.

He couldn't see saddling any child with a father like him either. Not then.

"I can't," he said, feeling as though his guts were being wrenched out.

"We can put it up for adoption, then." Meg sounded calm, matter-of-fact.

Probably she hadn't been, he realized later. Probably she had been just as upset by what they were doing as he was. She had simply had longer to get used to the idea.

"Adoption?"

"It would be best for the child. A *wanted* child, a chosen child." She smiled for the first time that afternoon. "I was."

Owain started. "Adopted?"

Meg nodded, her eyes dropping to her stomach as if she were considering the child and its future and how similar they would be to her own past.

"How did you feel about it?" The notion made him curious.

"I didn't mind. I was happy actually. I would much rather do that for this baby—" she nodded at her abdomen "—than make it miserable living with me. It is a person, after all. And it deserves some happiness, too."

"Yes." Owain shifted uncomfortably in the molded fiberglass chair, his mind still trying to grapple with the events of the past half hour. "But what about your natural parents?"

Meg looked up at him. "What about them?"

"Didn't you ever wonder about them? Weren't you curious? Did you want to find them? Don't you think they wanted to find you?"

Meg shrugged. "Maybe they did." Her voice was soft.

"What do you mean?"

Meg traced the lip of the cup with one long, delicate finger. "I was always happy with my family—my adoptive family. And I was never really desperate to know more than they could tell me. But I did have a fantasy—" She stopped speaking as the door opened and one of the technicians came in, plunked his money into the vending machine, extracted a sandwich, gave her long legs a leer, then left again.

"And that was?" Owain prompted.

"That they would find me," Meg said simply. "That my natural parents would care enough to see that I was all right, that I was happy. It's what I would do," she told him, then corrected herself. "It's what I *will* do."

"Adoption records are sealed."

"I'd find a way," Meg had said, confidence unshaken. "I wouldn't disrupt its life, just as I wouldn't have wanted anyone to disrupt mine. But I will want to know."

Owain was skeptical, but Meg was certain.

And someday, he thought now as he parked the car and walked slowly back to his dark motel room, she would probably have done it.

But she had died first.

So he had done it for her.

At least that was the original notion. When he had got the news of her death, when the child whose adoption release form he had signed without even letting himself stop and think beyond knowing that what he was doing was right for the child, himself and Meg at the time, had suddenly become real in the two-by-three black-and-white photos he had held in his hand, he had remembered Meg's vow to be sure the child was happy.

Well, Hugh and Bronwen Williams were happy. There was no doubt about that.

"Mission accomplished," he said aloud as he let himself into the room and flung himself down on the hard foam mattress with its brown velour spread.

He ought to be feeling pleased with himself. He had won out, had succeeded against overwhelming odds. Thank heavens Meg had opted for a private adoption in the Midwestern state of her birth rather than staying in California and placing the children through an agency. He doubted he ever would have found them if she had.

He reached for the two small pictures, worn now from al'
his handling, plucking them off the nightstand by the bed
and staring at them. He wondered which was Bronwen and
which was Hugh, and why he had never guessed that the
presence of two pictures might mean twins.

Probably because nobody had said anything about twins
anywhere along the line. But then, no one person had parted
with very much information either. He had pieced things
together himself as he had gone along. And lots of pieces
had still been missing when he had finally learned that his
child's adoptive parents, Cara and Martin Williams, had
moved to this small Wisconsin town five years ago.

He hadn't waited for further news. He had taken the next
flight out of L.A., stopping in Madison only long enough
to buy a state map and to rent a car.

He had driven straight to the town, found Martin Williams's address in the local phone book, asked at the gas
station where he could find that particular street and, once
locating the house, lurked in the park watching the children play.

He sighed and shut his eyes, remembering the moment he
had first looked down into eyes exactly like his mother's. He
had been mesmerized. At that moment the ephemeral child
he had been seeking became a real person to him.

And when, minutes later, he had discovered that she apparently even shared his mother's name, he hadn't been able
to let things rest.

And now?

Now he felt as if he had been flattened by a truck. Not
just one truck—a whole convoy of them.

He had been prepared to see the child, Bronwen, again.
He had braced himself for the effect she would have on him.
But he had not been prepared at all for Hugh.

Twins. Even now he could scarcely believe it. But, lying
there with his hands locked behind his head, replaying the
scene over and over again, examining the images in his

mind, he supposed he could see a bit of Meg in the tall, blond boy. There was, perhaps, even a bit of himself in Hugh's eyes.

He had tried not to study either child too closely. Bronwen had already seemed sensitive to his gazes. And he hadn't wanted to come on too strong. He had, in fact, been trying to keep a bit of perspective about the whole incident. He wanted to have the memory, of course, but that was it. He wanted to feel good about where they were now. He wanted to feel that he had made the right decision about giving them up in the first place.

And he did.

So he ought to go away satisfied.

And that was his intention—or at least that had been his intention until he got his final shock of the afternoon—the discovery that Cara Williams was a widow.

Now he had some thinking to do.

"I KNOW WHAT I SAID, Dougal," Owain shouted into the phone, as if raising his voice would somehow improve the faint, fuzzy, transatlantic connection that had just jolted him out of bed.

He hadn't been sleeping—he had scarcely slept all night—but he didn't feel exactly coherent either. It was only, he discovered by consulting his watch, just gone seven in the morning, and how on earth Dougal McNab had tracked him down was a mystery indeed.

Only Sam Travers, their agent, knew more or less where Owain was. Obviously Sam had shared the news.

Owain rubbed his eyes and tried to make sense of what Dougal was squawking about. It wasn't hard to grasp the subject. Dougal almost never got passionate about anything except his music. And right now it seemed that the lack of material for his new album had him close to frantic. It was material that he was expecting Owain to provide.

"Calm down," Owain tried. "I'm sorry. I haven't ha
time. I thought I would and that I would have it for you b
the time you left London, but I don't. In fact," he added
"I'm not even sure I'll be back in L.A. for a while."

Even as he said the words, he recognized in them the trut'
he had been wrestling with all night long. It had take
Dougal's call to crystallize his thinking, however.

Faced with the prospect of an immediate return to L.A.
of writing the music for Dougal's new album, and trying t
force himself to concentrate on the finishing up of his doc
toral dissertation, he knew instinctively what he intended t
do instead.

He was going to stay put.

"What!" Dougal's outrage was evident even across si
thousand miles of transoceanic transmission. Owain coul
imagine perfectly the flared nostrils and bobbing Adam'
apple as Dougal grappled with this new information.

"But I need you! I need your songs! For chrissakes
man," Dougal shouted, "where's your sense of responsi
bility?"

Owain's eyes flickered over to where the pictures of th
infants, Bronwen and Hugh, lay on the nightstand. "My
sense of responsibility?" he echoed. Good question. "I'm
thinking about that."

Dougal spluttered incoherently for a moment, then askec
suspiciously, "Are you high, Owain?"

As a kite, Owain thought. But, "No, I'm not," he saic
firmly. He had never had much use for drugs. They wen
with the territory when he was performing, but they were
one vice he had never had any interest in. And he couldn'
imagine them giving him anything close to the kick in th
head he had had yesterday.

"Listen, Dougal, I gotta go. I'll call you."

"When?" Dougal pressed him. "I'm supposed to be
working out the material for this album in November. We

cut it before Christmas, you know. I'll be back in L.A. next week. Will you be there then?''

"Maybe. I'll call when I know.''

"You'd better,'' Dougal said darkly. "I can understand your not wanting to perform anymore. Lord knows that gets old fast. And I didn't fight you when you wanted to quit, did I?''

"Not really.''

"Right. But I need you to write my songs, man. You got things in you that want singing, Owain. I know you do! And, damn it all, I need to sing 'em!''

"Yeah.'' But Owain was agreeing more with Dougal's assessment of his own needs than with his estimate of Owain's. He hadn't had anything in him in months that was worth singing about. He had felt hollow and aimless for quite a while, musically speaking at least. All the driving energy that had made him work so hard to make a success of Cardiff Connection in the first place seemed to have deserted him. Or maybe he was just finding out that success had its limitations.

He had thought that his doctoral work would fill the void, and it went a long way. But that, too, fell short. Lately he couldn't even work on it without staring off into space mindlessly. The only thing that had given him a sense of purpose lately was searching for his child.

When he had opened the mail and had found those pictures, they had given him a goal, a focus.

And now that he had found the twins—and their mother—he didn't want to leave.

"What the hell are you doing in Wisconsin anyway?'' Dougal demanded. "Looking for inspiration?''

"Something like that.''

"Well, I hope to God you find it.''

"So do I,'' Owain said with a fervency that surprised him.

"And then you'll write me some good stuff,'' Dougal went on. "Stuff like you wrote for *Tangle of Roots*,'' he added, mentioning the extremely successful album that Cardiff Connection had cut four years earlier. It had been Owain's last as a guitarist, and it was, he felt, a fitting conclusion to his active performing career. A blend of songs with their roots in his family's Welsh traditions on the one hand, and the harder-driving British rock of the mid-seventies to which he owed some inspiration on the other, it summed up what Owain had tried to accomplish in his career.

The cover had been a collage of pictures: of himself, Dougal and Mike, of their families—parents, children, grandparents and great-grandparents—along with silhouetted images of some of the groups that had given him his rock music roots. But it was not the past that interested Owain now. It was the present—and the future.

"I'll give it a try," he told Dougal without much conviction. "But you ought to be looking around to see if you can find someone else whose stuff you like as well. Or better."

"There isn't any—"

"I mean it, Dougal. Give my love to Karin and Annie," Owain said firmly and hung up.

Then he reached for his jacket where it lay on the floor and groped in the pocket for a packet of cigarettes. He didn't often smoke these days. But then he didn't often discover that he was the father of twins either. Or that the mere sight of their mother sent his senses spinning out of control.

He guessed, for once, he was entitled.

Dragging them out, he lit one with shaking fingers, then settled back against the headboard and tried to decide what to do next.

Ever since he had begun his search, whenever he had run into a dead end or had encountered a particularly large stumbling block, he had stopped and asked himself, "What would Meg do?"

Somehow just evoking her name had helped him overcome the obstacles. But asking what Meg would do wasn't going to help him any longer.

He knew the answer without asking. Meg would have assured herself that the children were fine. She might have shed a few tears, but then she would have turned around and gone back to L.A. and stayed out of their lives.

But then, Owain thought as he stubbed out his cigarette in the heavy glass ashtray, Meg would never have been attracted to their mother.

And that, in a nutshell, was his problem.

After six years of touring all over the Western world with Cardiff Connection, Owain knew women. He could recognize brittle sophistication at five hundred yards. He could also spot immaturity, starstruck awe and zombielike devotion whenever he saw them.

He hadn't seen any of those things in Cara Williams.

She exuded a warmth and a sincerity that drew him immediately. He liked the soft, mellow sound of her voice, the way her green-gold eyes flashed when she laughed or when she watched the children. He liked the no-nonsense way she had of managing her honey-colored mane of hair.

It was the same matter-of-fact, no-nonsense way she had handled Hugh's bloody nose. It was wholesome, warm, maternal and, somehow, exactly right.

He was enchanted.

She was, he decided, exactly the sort of woman he would have chosen to be the mother of his children if he had been thinking of the consequences of his actions seven years ago with Meg.

He found himself thinking of those consequences now, and wondering how hard things were for Cara, as a widow, with two young children. It couldn't be easy.

He would like to be able to help her somehow. Maybe, if he put his mind to it, he could.

He hoisted himself up off the bed and crossed the room to stare out the window. It had snowed again during the night. Yesterday's Indian summer breezes, which had been perfect for kites, might as well have been a dream. His bare feet were cold on the thin carpet, and though the heat cut on as he stood there, he still shivered as he looked outside. He hurried to get dressed.

He wasn't equipped with the right sort of clothes for staying here. The few he had brought with him were no more than he would need to get through a Southern California winter. But he could buy more suitable ones, he decided, while he got settled.

His first job was going to be to find himself a place to live. And that meant hunting up last night's newspaper or—and the more he considered this possibility the better he liked it—he could simply go door to door in Cara's neighborhood until he found a room to rent.

In a college town, it shouldn't be that hard. Rooming houses ought to abound, even though they would be a far cry from the more opulent living quarters he had become used to.

Stuffing his feet into his loafers, he shivered again at the thought of subjecting them to another walk through freshly fallen snow. The first item of the day was going to be buying a pair of suitable hiking boots.

"A ROOM?" The old lady looked at him as if his questionable morals were written in indelible ink on his forehead. "Well, I might have. And then again, I might not."

Owain shifted from one foot to the other and wondered what would make the decision for her. He tried to look honest and upstanding and God-fearing, and not as desperate as he was beginning to feel.

Mrs. Garrity's rooming house would be perfect. It sat directly across the park from Cara Williams's house, and it was, he discovered, the only rooming house on the street.

Most of the ones he had looked at so far had been on the other side of campus. Mrs. Garrity, it turned out, didn't advertise, you had to be recommended. A rather disreputable man in one of the seedier places he had looked at had "recommended" her to him, but he wasn't sure if that counted. He hoped so, but from the looks of her, he thought his hopes were slim.

Mrs. Garrity resembled nothing more than an apple doll sculpture. But if the outside appeared soft, Owain suspected that the inner core was pure steel. She had been running her boarding house for more than thirty years, she told him. "And I run a *clean* house," she added, thwacking his feet with her broom as if illustrating her point. He was glad he had bought the new boots first. He doubted his loafers would have passed inspection. "Meals are provided, except for Sunday night. No smoking in the rooms." She fixed him with a narrow gaze. "You smoke?"

"No." Owain deliberately forgot the one cigarette he had had earlier. "I used to. I quit."

"Humph." She gave a brisk little nod that he hoped denoted approval. "How long would you want the room for? All year? All semester?"

"How about by the month?"

Mrs. Garrity scowled and went back to fussing with the hand mixer that she had been using when he came in. It started and stopped, then started again. Finally she set it down with a thump and glared at him. "Don't sound like a student to me. By the month?" she muttered doubtfully.

"I'm writing my dissertation. I don't know when I'll finish."

"Humph," she said again, and this time it didn't sound like approval at all. She looked him up and down, probing for defects, as if he were a used car being sold by a not quite trustworthy dealer. He felt a tremendous urge to tell her he could buy and sell her house twenty times over. But he had the feeling that money wouldn't impress Mrs. Garrity, and he rather liked that. So he tried to appear virtuous instead.

"Come have a look," she invited him finally and headed briskly up the back staircase, obviously expecting him to follow. "I have one room in the attic available. Only came up empty last week. Fellow got mono-nu-cleosis." She said every syllable very carefully, making sure Owain felt the full weight of the word. "Kissing disease," she confided. "Glad he's gone, actually. Don't hold with that here."

"Kissing?" Owain asked, unable to stifle a grin.

"Not in *my* rooms," she said in a voice as starched as her curtains.

"No, of course not," Owain murmured, rolling his eyes heavenward. He thought of his years on the road and wondered what Mrs. Garrity would make of them.

He didn't have to wonder. He knew. And he knew if she found out, he wouldn't have a prayer of getting her attic room.

Mrs. Garrity came to a halt at last, three flights up, and opened a narrow white door. Stepping into the room, she motioned Owain to follow her.

"Not big," she told him. "But clean."

Neither was an understatement. Ducking his head, Owain entered the room. It was, perhaps, big enough to swing a cat in—provided the cat had very short legs. It was also spotless.

The narrow iron bedstead that nestled under the sloping ceiling was made up with pristine white sheets and a white spread, creased with military precision. A multicolored rag rug that looked as if it had been washed within a thread of holding together sat in the middle of highly polished wooden floorboards. A three-drawer oak dresser with a horseshoe mirror gleamed against the inside wall. It only lacked a bowl and pitcher, Owain thought, feeling as if he had stepped into a time warp. He wondered if there was a chamber pot under the bed.

"The bathroom is one flight down," Mrs. Garrity told him, scotching that notion. "Everyone has an assigned time in the morning. You get from 7:10 to 7:25. Rest of the day is up to you. So, what do you think?" She fixed him with a steely stare that dared him to find fault.

Owain had no intention of doing so. In fact, oddly enough, he liked it. He didn't need anything fancy. And it appealed to him in the same no-nonsense way that Cara Williams had.

"I like it."

Mrs. Garrity beamed. "One month's rent in advance. You can move in tomorrow. I'll clean first."

Owain wondered where she would find dirt to clean up between then and now. But even as he thought it, she ran her finger along the windowsill and tsked loudly.

He grinned. "About noon. I'll fix your mixer," he said.

HE WAS READY far before noon. He had never been able to contain his enthusiasm for anything new. He had always been, to his parents' dismay, the first one up on Christmas morning, the first one ready to go on vacation, the first one to try to do anything different. Moving into Mrs. Garrity's was just the same. His impatience was hard to contain. He had had the very devil of a time not letting himself lurk around Cara Williams's house at all that day. But discretion was of paramount importance, he decided.

It was nice that discretion was rewarded. The next morning when he checked out of his hotel at nine and had three hours to kill before he could move into Mrs. Garrity's, he decided to spend it getting some more suitable clothes. And in doing so he discovered a heretofore unrealized perk of small-town living—he saw Cara Williams three times in the course of the morning.

The first time he was just parking his car and she was emerging from the dry cleaners down the street. She saw him, waved and gave him a smile that made his heart tap-dance against his ribs. But before he could get out and cross the street to speak to her, she had got in her own car and had driven away.

An hour later he saw her again just as she was going into the supermarket. From the length of the list she was consulting, he figured she would be in there quite a while. Still, all the time he was next door buying himself new heavy corduroy jeans, wool shirts and socks, and a sheepskin-lined jacket that was guaranteed to keep out the worst of the winter winds, he kept an eye on the supermarket door.

His timing was perfect. He had just stowed his purchases in the trunk of his car when he saw her coming toward the door of the supermarket with her cart laden with groceries. And he had just enough time to be leaning nonchalantly against the lamppost in front of the automatic doors when she came through them.

"Hi."

Cara looked up and blinked. "Oh. Mr. O'Neill. Hello."

Owain fell into step beside her. "Call me Owain," he said. "Please."

Cara gave him a quick glance, as if she were assessing him for potential trouble, rather in the same way that Mrs. Garrity had the day before. Then, apparently satisfied, she smiled. "Owain," she said in her quiet, mellow voice. The simple sound of her saying his name sent a shiver right through him.

Owain swallowed hard, stuck his hands into the pockets of his new jacket, which seemed unaccountably warm all of a sudden, and almost forgot what he had been going to say.

In fact he had helped her load all her groceries into the back of her old blue Volvo before he remembered to say, "About that typing . . ."

She opened the door to the driver's side of her car. "Yes?"

"I'm staying. I'd like you to do it if you will."

Cara looked slightly surprised. Then she nodded, as if she had readjusted her perceptions somehow. "All right. If you're not in a hurry. I have other clients, too."

"No. That's fine."

She slid into the car. "Bring it by then. You know where I live."

"Yes."

She was about to shut the door. He spoke up quickly. "How about a cup of coffee with me?"

She shook her head regretfully. "Sorry, I can't. I have a dentist's appointment in fifteen minutes."

"How about after?"

"I'm expecting the kids home for lunch today."

"And when they go back to school?" Owain was surprised at how desperately he wanted to keep her talking.

She smiled. "Then I'm working."

"Typing?" he asked hopefully.

"Not today. Today it's bookkeeping. For the five-and-ten."

Owain frowned, stymied. "You do a heck of a lot of stuff," he grumbled.

"I told you I did. I am the official bookkeeper/accountant for Miller's Drugs, the Ben Franklin, Breck's Shoe Repair and Video Store, and Trevorrow's Feeds. I am also the typist for seven of the college faculty members and countless students, the sender of overdue notices at the library, the custodian of records for the county's genealogical society and historical society and the landlady of the town's matchmaking service!"

"The *what*?"

Cara rolled her eyes and laughed. "Don't ask. You wouldn't need it anyway. It's Suzy's—you know, the girl you met. My baby-sitter. In exchange for baby-sitting, she gets access to my computer. When I'm not using it," she added, "which is seldom."

"Sounds like it," Owain said dryly. "Don't you get any time off?"

"Not much. But I don't really care. It keeps me home with the kids, which is where I want to be. Time off isn't important."

"But being a good parent and being independent is?" he guessed.

"Yes. Very."

For a moment neither of them said anything. The silence seemed charged with electricity.

Owain wanted to ask her how he could help her at the same time that he realized she wouldn't want his help. He looked at his toes, then back at her, and couldn't tear his eyes away.

"Well," she said, suddenly flustered, "I'm going to be late to the dentist. You just bring that typing by any day. I'm always available."

She drove away, and Owain, watching her, was sure she didn't mean that in quite the same way that he wished she had.

He wanted her. It had been all he could do not to reach out and touch her when they had stood there those few minutes staring at each other. Even now he felt a tug on his heart, almost as if it were aching to follow her.

She worked hard, he thought. Too damned hard. She ought to lighten up, enjoy life a bit. She ought to stop and have a few cups of coffee along the way.

It was up to him, he decided, to see that she did.

Chapter Three

It turned out to be even easier than he thought.

A sheaf of rough-draft copy, two onion bagels and a half a pound of Colombian coffee beans later, and Owain had successfully infiltrated Cara Williams's life.

He had brightened it up a bit, too.

At least he told himself he had.

Cara had looked tired and a bit hassled when he had knocked on her door the next afternoon. It wasn't her work, though, she explained after she let him in. It was because she was trying to get a pill into a very stubborn cat.

"This one?" Owain nodded at the very large, very ornery-looking marmalade cat that she was hugging against her breasts.

"This one," Cara agreed grimly. "He has a skin infection."

Owain grinned. "Acne?"

"I wouldn't be surprised. Sometimes Nestor is a very adolescent cat." As she spoke the cat wriggled in her arms and she dropped him unceremoniously to the floor. He shot out the door between Owain's boots and vanished around the side of the house.

Owain turned to stare after him.

"Don't worry about him," Cara said. "And I won't ask you to chase him either. Supper always brings him home."

"Speaking of food..." Owain said and proffered the white bakery bag he was holding.

Cara regarded it dubiously.

"If you won't come out for coffee," he told her, "the coffee is coming in to you." And with that he stepped past her and set the sack on the counter, then set the brown one containing the coffee beans alongside it.

"I *am* working," Cara protested. But Owain knew halfhearted when he heard it.

"So work already," he told her briskly. "I can make a pot of coffee as well as the next guy. Go on." He chivvied her out of the kitchen, pointing her in the direction of the computer, which he could see set up on a work table at the far side of the family room.

"If you insist." But she didn't go at once. Instead she lingered on the other side of the counter and watched Owain make the coffee.

He had taken a chance on buying the beans. He had no idea if she had a grinder or not. But he thought she was the sort of woman who would. She seemed to like doing things from scratch. Not an "instant" sort of lady. Thank heavens he had been right.

Now as he dumped the beans into the grinder he shot her a quick grin. "See. I'm doing fine."

She gave him a bemused smile. "I guess you are at that. Well, make yourself at home."

"Thanks. I will."

She had no idea how appealing the idea was. For a man who had been priding himself on his "rolling stone" existence for the better part of the past ten years, he was astonished to find that Cara's kitchen brought out some latent desire to curl up by the hearth fire and settle down. He'd have traded places with Nestor any day.

It was, he told himself, just that it looked and smelled so much like what he always thought "homes" should look and smell like. A hint of cinnamon and freshly baked bread till lingered in it. A bowl of apples sat on the counter, and a shelf of well-thumbed cookbooks perched behind the breakfast nook. It reminded him of the kitchen he had grown up in.

His mother would have been as comfortable here as he was. He turned again to look at Cara, now seated at her computer, squinting at the screen, tapping things incomprehensible to him onto the keyboard, and he sent her a silent thank-you for giving Hugh and Bronwen the same warm childhood memories that he had had.

While she typed and the coffee brewed, Owain looked around. The two rooms he could see reflected the same solid homey virtues that Cara did. The furniture was well-worn but attractive, suitable for a family raising growing children. The family room was just that, a room for all members of the family. He could see toys that belonged to the children as well as the computer where their mother made her living. It even, he noted, had a fireplace and a raised hearth just right for curling up on.

Smiling wryly he moved on, looking around the kitchen. Beside the refrigerator he found a bulletin board that arrested his attention at once. For on it he discovered a chronicle of his children's lives.

At the very top, tacked right next to a small wedding snapshot of a very young Cara and a tall, lean bespectacled man—Martin, no doubt—were the same pictures that Meg had sent him! Cara and Martin must have been given copies of the twins' newborn pictures, too.

Beneath them were several less formal snapshots. A chubby Bronwen, all dimples and curls, was balancing on a tiny Tyke Bike and giggling at whoever was taking the picture. A very intent, almost bald Hugh was looking cross-eyed at the single candle on a birthday cake. Cara was holding the two of them as toddlers on her lap in front of a huge Christmas tree. Hugh was perched on Martin's shoulders, his fists clenched in Martin's hair. Both children were sitting on twin tricycles, each holding up four fingers of one hand. And at the bottom they both stared out from recent school pictures—semitoothless grinning imps. Owain felt his throat constrict as his eyes flickered from top to bottom.

Had he really thought it would hurt less to know his children in the flesh? Had he ever really considered what it would be like to be confronted with all he had missed?

In a word, no.

But nothing in him wanted to walk away. He was here now. He was involved. And if it hurt, well, so be it.

He suddenly realized that Cara had stopped typing, and when he looked up he discovered that she was standing just inches behind him, looking at the pictures he was looking at, then looking at him.

"You look homesick," she told him with a gentle smile. "Are you married? Are you missing your children?"

"No," he managed after a moment. "I'm not married. And as far as children go—" he gave her a wry smile "—I'm just envying you yours."

Cara brightened. "Well, I think they're rather special, I'll admit. Especially since they're all I have now."

Owain took the two coffee mugs she handed him and poured them each a cup of coffee. Then, lifting his, he leaned against the counter and cradled the mug in his palms. "How long have you been a widow?"

"A little over three years."

He nodded at the picture on the bulletin board. "Is that him?"

Cara nodded, her eyes bright. "Martin."

"He looks older than you."

"Some. I met him in college. We dated for four years. Then we got engaged. A year later we got married."

"That's *five* years!" Owain spluttered. He couldn't imagine anyone waiting five months to marry a woman like Cara Williams.

"We thought we ought to know each other well, be sure of things. You know. Besides," she added quietly, "we found out that Martin couldn't have children."

"Oh." He tried for more indifference than he felt.

"So we adopted some." She looked at him carefully as if trying to gauge what his reaction would be.

"Good idea."

Cara smiled then. "Thanks for saying so. You have no idea how many people just clucked sympathetically and told me how sorry they were for me that Martin and I couldn't have our own. And then," she added with a bitter twist of her mouth, "when Martin died, they considered me 'saddled' with the twins. They always say how generous it was for Martin and me to take them in, poor little dears, but surely now that I'm alone I can't mean to keep them!"

"Not keep them?"

"That's what *they* think," Cara said irritably. "All those sententious people who always think they know what is best for everyone. They all told me I would be better off without Bronny and Hugh. Well, that's a joke if I ever heard one! I don't know what I would have done without the kids after Martin died."

"The luck works both ways then?" Owain asked.

"Exactly." Cara sighed and brushed her hair back from her face. Owain wished he dared reach out and touch it. "I needed—no, I *need*—those children desperately. And they need me. Families are made, not born. And we are a family! No one could love those kids more than I do. No one at all!" She glared at Owain, her startling eyes fierce and angry. Her voice shook with the intensity of her words.

Owain didn't doubt the truth of it for a minute.

She blushed, red staining her cheekbones. "Sorry," she mumbled, burying her face in her mug. "I was on my soapbox again."

"No, I understand."

"Thank you. It just annoys me sometimes how people can think that just because something might be hard, you shouldn't bother to do it."

"No one is likely to try to take the kids away from you, are they?" he probed.

"They'd better not."

If he had even briefly considered telling her that he was their natural father, now, he knew, was not the time to do it. Cara would see him as a threat, even if he told her he had no intention of trying to get the children away from her. After all, she could well say, he had come looking for them, hadn't he?

And he didn't want to add to her worries; he only wanted to help her, to make things a bit easier in her life.

"You've done a great job with them," he told her softly. "Nobody could have done it better."

Cara bowed her head. "I think to be fair you should say *we* have done a great job."

"We?"

"Hugh, Bronny and I. They've done just as much for me as I've done for them. We've all helped each other cope. That's what's made the family survive." She cleared her throat self-consciously. "Anyway, I don't want to bore you with my problems. Tell me about yourself, Owain O'Neill. And tell me about this dissertation that you've brought for me to type."

Owain latched onto the second question far more readily than the first. He spoke at length about the research he had been doing, about the recent first-generation immigrants, mostly from Mexico and Vietnam, that he had interviewed over the past two years.

"And now I'm back here looking for first-generation immigrants who came over at the beginning of the century. The people who settled around here. I'm doing a comparison of the experiences of both generations."

It wasn't what he had set out to do originally. When he had begun he had decided to chronicle the experiences of people like himself—uprooted individuals—people who had recently left one culture and had to learn to cope with another, people caught between cultures, between ways of life. People who were seeking a dream and who had dared to abandon their old life in order to find it.

He hadn't thought of extending his research until recently. Then his director had mentioned that he thought it would be interesting to see if the generations had different experiences, and if so, what they were. But it wasn't really necessary, he went on. It was only food for thought.

Owain hadn't thought much of it until he had arrived here. Actually not until he had mentioned it on the spur of the moment to Cara the time Suzy put him on the spot. But since he had been here he'd had a sense of something that was rooted in his own experience and yet had gone beyond it. It was, he thought, because so many of these people were immigrants, too.

He was glad he had decided to include the older generation of immigrants in the study. It was a great way of legitimating his stay here, too.

"You mentioned a grandmother?" he ventured.

"Yes. She's from England." Cara pointed to a thin, smiling older lady in one of the Christmas photos on the bulletin board. "I'll introduce you if you like."

"I'd like."

"Wonderful. And she'll be thrilled if anything she tells you ends up in your book. Speaking of which—" she turned and picked up the dog-eared manuscript pages off the counter "—I had better get back to work."

She dumped the dregs of her coffee in the sink and polished off the last of the bagel. "It was wonderful," she said around the last bite. "Thank you, I think."

"You think?"

"Well, you are corrupting me, you know."

Owain grinned. "I'd like to corrupt you a lot more."

Cara's cheeks went crimson. The electrical charge that had seemed to arc between them yesterday sizzled again, and Owain admitted to himself that there was far more to his coffee and bagels than simply cheering Cara up.

The desire that kept nagging at him wouldn't go away. In fact, it got worse by the minute.

He thought he ought to feel like a heel for wanting her the way he did. She was, after all, the mother of his children. But he couldn't squelch the feeling. Neither could he ignore it.

But he wasn't sure what to do about it, either. That would require more thought. He cleared his throat, wondered what to do with his hands and generally felt more inept than he could remember since he was about fifteen.

Finally stuffing his hands into the back pockets of his cords, he rocked back on his heels and said, "If you, uh, want to look over the typing I've brought to see if you have any questions..."

"I'll do that." She sounded suddenly businesslike. "Thank you for bringing it."

"You're welcome."

They stared at each other again, trapped by the charge of awareness they shared. Then the phone began to ring and Nestor started clawing at the back door.

"I have to go," Cara said, not moving.

"Yes."

The phone rang again.

"I ... I'll let you know if I have any questions."

"Okay."

Cara glanced at the phone as it rang again. "I ..."

"Go answer it," Owain said. "I'll let myself out. But Cara..." He caught her hand as she moved toward the telephone.

"Yes?"

"Let's do this again."

THEY DID—the following afternoon. This time he brought date bear claws to go with the coffee. And though Cara protested that they would go directly from her mouth to her hips, she ate one.

She also sat down with him this time while they drank their coffee. She had read his dissertation—all the interviews he had done with the Californian immigrants and the conclusions he had drawn about the similarities of their experiences.

"It was fascinating," she told him. "Most of the stuff I type for these professors here is mind-dulling stuff. Things like 'Wordsworth's use of floral imagery in his later poetry' or 'Precambrian geological formations in the western United States.'" She stifled a yawn even as she said the titles. Then she grinned. "Yours was much more interesting." She picked up the title page off the table between them. "'Dream Chasers.'"

Owain shook his head. "You didn't read the subtitle." He took the page from her hand and read in his best droning, professorial voice, "A Comparative Study of Immigration Experiences, 1900-1920 and 1965-1975."

"Well, it still was more exciting than it sounded. But all I found were the more contemporary immigrants. Where are the 1900-1920 ones?"

"That's what I'm doing here—looking for people to interview. Like your grandmother, perhaps?"

"You were serious?"

"Absolutely. Have you asked her?"

"No, but I will. I didn't want to get her hopes up if you weren't really interested."

"I want to meet her." And not just because she would make a good resource either—at least not just about her immigration experiences. He wanted to meet her because she was Cara Williams's grandmother. He wanted to meet her because the more he knew about Cara, the more he wanted to know. He had spent all last evening thinking about her.

He had, of course, spared a few thoughts for Hugh and Bronwen. But they weren't the focus of his thoughts anymore.

His main interest now was their mother.

It was insane, he reminded himself frequently. She was not the sort of woman who would have an affair with him, then let him walk right out of her life. And how could he ever think of staying, given who he was?

"Does she live around here?"

"In the next town. About ten miles away."

"Were you raised around here, then?"

"No. My mother was. Then when she married my father, they moved to Michigan. I was born there." She went on to tell him about growing up in Michigan, about the summers on the lake with her parents and her sister. She told him about climbing trees and fording creeks, about catching butterflies and picking cherries. Then she asked him about his own childhood.

Fortunately he didn't have to lie. As long as he talked about things in the past—before he had gone on to fame with Cardiff Connection—there was nothing he couldn't tell her.

They talked the whole afternoon.

The more he knew about Cara Williams, the more he found that he wanted to know.

And the more he wanted to know, the more he asked.

The more he asked, the more she told him.

The more she told him, the more he cared.

And the more he cared, the guiltier he felt.

She was sharing her life with him frankly and openly. He was hiding something from her.

But, damn it, what was he supposed to say? *Oh, by the way, I just thought you ought to know something.... I'm Bronwen and Hugh's natural father.*

Sure.

But it wasn't getting any easier, the longer they talked.

When he came back at the end of the week she gave him some of the typing she had finished, then offered him some cookies she had baked. "My treat this time," she had said, smiling.

Then she had proceeded to ask him more about his own family and his own immigration experiences.

He hadn't had to lie, really. Just evade a lot.

He had spoken fondly of his mother and her penchant for baking and for mothering anyone who had the slightest need of it. She had practically raised Dougal McNab when his own parents had split up. But he didn't mention Dougal's name.

He had told her about his father, an electrician who had indeed been another of the "dream chasers." Tom O'Neill had come to America eighteen years before with little more than the shirt on his back and a head full of hopes. He had retired last year, selling off his electronics supply business for several hundred thousand dollars.

He told her that his parents were planning to return to Wales to retire very near the homes they had grown up in. And he told her about his younger brother, Evan, who had taken up with electronics where his father left off, and who was now doing something very lucrative and entirely incomprehensible with computers.

"You know all that talk about America being a land of opportunity?" he asked her.

"Mm-hm."

"Well, in my family it was true."

"For you, too, Owain?"

For him more than anyone else. His own career had flourished here. But he didn't say that to Cara. For most of his adult life he had been saddled with the trappings of success. People had always wanted to know him because of who he was. Cara, on the other hand, had no idea who he was. She simply enjoyed him for himself.

So what difference did it make?

"I did fine, too," he told her vaguely.

"But you didn't go into the family business?"

"No. I did my bit in the summers sometimes. But it isn't what I want to do for the rest of my life."

"You've always been the scholar?"

"I suppose." He traced a line on the Formica table with his thumbnail.

"You must have been going to school for a long time."

He heard the question in her voice and grinned. "Is that a polite way of asking if I'm a perennial student?"

Cara reddened. "Well, some people are, you know. We see a lot of them around here."

"I imagine you would. But I'm not one of them. I did my fair share of work over the past ten years. It's only in the past couple that I've gone back to school full-time. Before that I did a lot of different things . . . moved around a lot."

He found that he really didn't want to look like a layabout in her eyes either. But it was hard not to when he had eight years to account for and nothing to tell her. The longer he was around her, the harder it was to lie.

But the truth was dangerous, too.

The truth would change things. And Owain didn't want things changed. He liked them the way they were. For the first time in he couldn't think how long, he felt more or less at peace. He liked what he was doing and with whom. He was no longer chasing the dream. He had it.

Or he had a part of it, anyway.

What had started out as simply a way of learning more about his children had, quickly and irrevocably, changed into something else.

It had become a way of getting to know Cara.

It was dangerously close to courting Cara.

And that, he knew, was absurd.

However much he might think he wanted to stay here, he couldn't. His time here was an interlude. He and Cara were like people passing in the night. Just that and nothing more.

But Owain knew, late at night in rare moments of total honesty, that he was beginning to want it to be very much more indeed.

But he also knew he couldn't have it.

But, he told himself, it didn't hurt to pretend now and then. And it didn't hurt to enjoy. And pretending and enjoying were all he was really doing.

He was still there enjoying Cara's company that afternoon when Hugh and Bronwen came home from school.

"Are you coming to pick pumpkins with us, too?" Bronwen asked hopefully. "Is he, Mom?"

Cara looked at Owain dubiously.

"Pick pumpkins?" Owain asked.

"You don't have to," she assured him.

"But you can if you want to," Hugh said magnanimously.

"I'd love to."

"And he could stay for dinner, too," Bronwen said.

"I—"

"Bron!" Cara scowled at her daughter. "I'm sure Owain has plenty of other things to do."

Bronwen stared up at him, unblinking. "Do you?"

"No."

She shot a triumphant look at her mother. "See."

"It could be a date," Hugh suggested.

Cara looked as if she would like to strangle both of them.

"I could take you all out to dinner," Owain offered.

"Hey, wow! Neat-o!" came from both the children.

"No!" And there was no arguing with Cara when she used that tone of voice. She faced both the children, her hands on her hips. "Enough is enough. If Owain wants to come with us, fine. But that's as far as it goes. Until you're cooking dinner, you don't make dinner invitations. Not without checking with me first."

The kids squirmed uncomfortably under her glare. Hugh kicked at the chair leg.

"We were only bein' polite," he objected.

"You ask me first. Otherwise it's my decision whether to offer a dinner invitation or not." She looked up at Owain, who had been watching the entire exchange with interest. "Sorry about this."

He shrugged. "No problem."

"You don't really have to come unless you want to. I won't have them railroading you into things. No more than I'll let them ramrod me."

"I'd like to," he assured her sincerely.

She nodded. "Good. Then would you like to stay to dinner with us as well?"

"But—"

"*I* am offering the invitation." Her green eyes were smiling at him.

"Then, thank you, yes, I would."

"Hooray!" cheered the twins, undaunted.

"Let me get my jacket then." Cara fetched a heavy, lined corduroy jacket from the closet, then blinked in surprise when Owain lifted it from her hands and held it so she could slip it on. "I can do that," she told him, obviously flustered.

"I wanted to. A date, after all, is a date." He grinned. "Even if it has been arranged by a third party and is only going to the pumpkin patch."

Cara laughed, chivvying the children out the door ahead of her, then tossing the cat back inside when he tried to sneak out past her. "We can take my car if you don't mind."

"I'm liberated," Owain assured her with a grin.

Cara stopped halfway across the yard and stared at him. A child hung from each of his arms. He was smiling at her. "I think," she said with a shake of her head, "that you might just be too good to be true."

Owain's eyes slid guiltily away.

But the phrase flickered in and out of his consciousness for the rest of the afternoon. Everything that was happening between them was too good to be true. It wouldn't last. Couldn't last.

But when it was over, at least they would have the memories.

"Do you pick pumpkins every year?" he asked the kids as Cara headed the Volvo out into the countryside.

"Every year," Bronwen told him. "We get to carve them, too. Mom lets us use the knives as long as we have a grown-up to help. You could come and help, couldn't you?" she asked, then clapped her hand over her mouth. "Wasn't I supposed to ask him that either?" she asked her mother.

Cara sighed. "I suppose it's all right. As long as he knows he can refuse."

"He won't refuse. He likes us."

Cara groaned.

"Don't you?" Hugh asked Owain.

"I like you. I don't know how much help I'd be though," Owain admitted with a rueful smile. "I've never carved a pumpkin before."

"Never?" Hugh was aghast.

"Never. Halloween wasn't a big deal where I grew up. But we had other things. Guy Fawkes Day, for instance. November fifth."

"What did you do for Guy Fawkes Day?" Bronwen leaned forward, her eyes sparkling with interest.

"Built huge bonfires. Some of them were fifteen or twenty feet high. And we made a 'guy' to burn on it."

"A guy?" The twins' eyes were like dinner plates.

"An effigy. Kind of like a scarecrow. We stuffed a pair of my dad's old pants and a shirt, then we made a gunnysack face."

"And you burned it?" Hugh was amazed.

Cara made a face. "Grisly, weren't you?"

"Very. We burned it after my brother made money off it."

"Made money?" Bronwen was all ears now. "How'd he do that?"

"Took it round the neighborhood chanting, 'Penny for the guy.' Lots of kids did that. They bought fireworks with the money."

"Fireworks?" Both children were leaning forward now.

"We set them off at the bonfire. It was a bit like the Fourth of July, too."

"Could we make a guy?" Hugh wanted to know. "Would you show us how?"

"Hugh!" Cara protested as she turned the car off onto a gravel road.

"I'll make a deal with you," Owain said. "You teach me to carve a pumpkin, and I'll teach you to make a guy."

"All-ll right!" Hugh cheered. He and Bronwen began chattering together, making plans in the back seat.

Owain glanced over at Cara. "Do you mind?"

"Not if you don't," she said, resigned, as she pulled into a farmyard where a pick-your-own-pumpkin patch was advertised. "And if you're sure it's no imposition."

"It's no imposition." And that was the gospel truth, he thought. He was happy to do it. He *wanted* to do it. It would be giving the kids a true taste of their cultural heritage, he told himself. The broader implications of the commitment he chose to ignore.

The car stopped, the back doors flew open and Hugh and Bronwen bolted out.

"Let's go pick a pumpkin," Owain said.

Cara nodded. "Let's."

Owain had been on more dates—*real* dates—than he could remember. But none of them—not the one with the Academy Award-winning actress, not the one with the Playboy bunny or the Miss America runner-up—came close to being as memorable as just picking pumpkins with Cara Williams.

The afternoon was crisp and bright, the scents of fall in the air. Owain tipped his head back and took a deep breath, pulling in the tang of wood smoke, the aroma of apple cider fresh from the press and—when Cara was close—the heady scents of cinnamon and spice that were so much a part of her.

Bronwen and Hugh shot ahead into the field where frost-browned pumpkin vines were withering, and their bright orange fruits lay just waiting to be picked. The kids danced from one to the other, exclaiming over each one, calling for Cara and Owain to come and look.

But Cara and Owain were in no hurry. They took their time, picking their way through the uneven fields. Cara tripped over a vine and Owain moved quickly, taking advantage of the change to catch hold of her arm and prevent her from falling.

"Steady on," he muttered, pulling her up close to him. His arm slipped around her, his hand coming to rest just beneath her breast. And he thought suddenly that it was his own heart he was speaking to, not Cara.

"Are you okay?" he asked her, feeling oddly breathless himself.

"Y-yes." Cara pulled away, and Owain let his arm drop, but he couldn't relinquish the contact completely. It was the first time he had really touched her. And he didn't want to end it. Of its own accord his hand simply slid down her arm and wrapped itself around her fingers, warm and secure.

Cara looked down at their entwined fingers, then up to meet his eyes again. A tremulous smile flickered on her lips.

Owain licked his. "Come on," he said gruffly. "We'd better catch up with the kids."

They moved on, their fingers still wrapped together. And they stayed that way until three pumpkins had been rounded up and declared satisfactory. Then Owain had to let go in order to stuff them into the trunk of the Volvo. He felt almost bereft as he did so.

"We really need four," Hugh said as they were paying the farmer.

"Why?" Cara asked. "These three are about the biggest pumpkins I've ever seen."

"Yeah. But we always get one for each of us," Hugh reminded her. "And this year we've got Owain."

"Three's enough," Owain said quickly. "You can share yours with me."

"I'll share mine," Bronwen offered.

"No, I will," came from Hugh.

"You both can," Cara said. She turned to Owain. "With pumpkins this big they're going to need all the help they can get. So just you remember that you volunteered."

"No fear." Owain followed her around the car and opened the door for her, then stopped her with a hand on her arm for just a second before she got in. His hand slid up her arm, brushing her shoulder, then came to rest against the back of her neck. She looked at him, wide-eyed, startled and totally kissable.

Owain wanted to kiss her more than he had ever wanted to kiss a woman in his life. His jaw tightened, his whole body seemed to ache and, when her eyes dropped to look at his mouth, he almost gave in to the temptation when the look in Cara's eyes seemed to say she wanted it as much as he did.

Then Hugh's "What're we waitin' for?" broke the spell, and Owain dropped his hand.

"No fear," he repeated and waited until Cara got into the car.

"Would you like to stop and meet my grandmother? She only lives about three miles from here."

"Sounds fine."

Cara's grandmother, he discovered, was every bit as welcoming as her granddaughter. She gave him a curious, assessing look when he arrived and was introduced as "a friend and a man I'm typing for." Then, when no further amplification was made, she shook his hand genially and told him she was delighted to meet him. She was also enthusiastic when Cara mentioned that Owain would like to interview her about her experiences as an immigrant.

"I'd love to," she assured him, "whenever you have the time."

"Monday?" Owain suggested.

"Not now?" She sounded disappointed.

"I need to bring along my tape recorder. I'm not really prepared today."

"Besides, Gram," Cara said, "I've got to get home and do some work myself. I have a whole stack of overdue notices from the library to type and run off."

Mrs. Nute patted her granddaughter's arm. "Whatever you say, dear." She turned to Owain. "I'll be ready whenever you are. I'd be interested in hearing your experiences, too."

"I'm sure they aren't nearly as interesting as yours," Owain said.

Mrs. Nute shook her head. "I wouldn't be too sure about that," she said enigmatically. "Sure you don't want to stay for dinner, Cara?"

Her granddaughter shook her head. "Not on this short notice, Gram. But thanks anyway."

"I like your grandmother," Owain told her when they were driving back to the house. "I think I'm going to enjoy talking with her."

"No more than she'll enjoy talking to you."

The kids went outside to play on the swings in the park when they got back, and Owain followed Cara into the house. She set one of the pumpkins on the counter and he put the other two beside it.

She turned and scowled briefly at the stack of material from the library that was sitting beside her computer. Then she opened the refrigerator and stood staring into it.

"Want me to fix dinner?"

She turned, startled. "What?"

"I saw the way you looked at the library stuff. I thought maybe you'd like to get right on it. I can cook."

"But—"

"Really."

"*I* invited *you*."

"Sure. But that doesn't mean I can't cook, does it?"

"I was going to make homemade pizza."

He shrugged. "I think I could manage that. With a little help from Hugh and Bron. And you can get your work done. What do you say?" He gave her an encouraging grin.

"Are you sure?" Cara sounded somewhere between suspicious and astonished. "Can you really cook?"

"Lady," Owain assured her, "I can do anything I put my mind to."

"I think I believe that," Cara said quietly. "All right—" she waved her hand in the direction of the stove "—be my guest. Or should I say, my host."

"Compatriots," Owain decided. "I think we're in this thing together."

And the smile Cara gave him made him wish that he meant far more than just for dinner.

Owain had never made pizza before. But Cara provided him with a recipe that she said she followed "more or less." Owain decided to follow it "more." And with some encouragement from Hugh and Bronwen, who came in just in time to roll out the dough, he turned out two quite passable pizzas, a lettuce and tomato salad and, after a quick jog to the grocery store down the road, some garlic bread.

"I'm impressed," Cara told him as she finished her second piece of pizza. "This is delicious."

"I enjoyed it," Owain said. He had never spoken truer words.

He lingered after dinner, volunteering to wash the dishes while Cara got the children into the bathtub, then ready for bed. From the way she acted—the way she practically said goodbye before she even took the twins upstairs—Owain knew she expected him to finish the dishes while she was upstairs and be gone when she came back down again.

But he couldn't seem to make himself go. Instead, he built a fire in the fireplace, picked out a moodily romantic George Shearing album from her collection of old records—two of his own among the pile gave him a start, and he shuffled them into the middle of the stack—and then he settled down on the couch to wait for her to come back.

When she did, she paused halfway down the stairs, raised her eyebrows and gave him a wondering, teasing look. "George Shearing?"

He grinned lazily. "It's your album."

"I had it in college. I used to play it on lonely Saturday nights when everyone had a date but me." She gave him a slightly wistful smile, and he tried to imagine a night that Cara wouldn't have had a date. It wasn't easy.

He wanted her terribly, had wanted her all day. But now, with the slow, seductive rhythms from the stereo feeding his desire, it was worse than ever.

"Come here," he said thickly.

For a moment Cara hovered unmoving. Then, apparently pulled by similar needs, she gave in, coming down the stairs and crossing the room, letting him pull her down onto the sofa next to him.

"That's better," he murmured as he cradled her against the solid wall of his chest. Her head rested against his shoulder and he could smell the cinnamon and flowers of her shampoo, and touch, at last, the warm silk of her hair.

She leaned against him, and he wrapped his arms tightly around her. The feel of her body, soft and yielding against the hardness of his own, was undoing all his good intentions, making him aware first and foremost of how much he wanted her.

It was playing with fire and he knew it. It was temptation personified and he was flirting with it. Cara was lying halfway across his body now. And wherever they touched, he felt a heat so intense that it almost destroyed his reason.

He half expected that she would resist. Half hoped she would! For if she didn't, how was he going to be able to control the feelings that were threatening to swamp him? How was he going to be able to walk away from her like this?

Nothing in him wanted to walk away. His feet stayed flat on the floor. His hands stroked down her back, the soft angora sweater hinting at the softness he knew lurked beneath. It drove him mad.

Cara's fingers kneaded his sweater. His breathing quickened. He lifted one of his hands to her hair, tugging on it gently, tipping her head back so that he could read the expression on her face. Her eyes were slumberous, a dark jade-green with golden highlights picked out by the reflection of the fire. They looked back at Owain with a desire that echoed his own.

He drew a sharp breath.

"Owain?" She breathed his name. For a moment he thought he would hear her tell him to stop, to move back, to pull away. But he didn't. He only heard his name on her lips again, and then her hands moved around his back, slid down and lodged against his belt.

He ought to stop. The memories he was after were getting out of hand. They were going beyond anything he had let himself dream about. They were becoming real. All too real. And the hurt after would be real, too.

He felt her squirm against him, and he groaned, twisting away, breathing as if he had just run up the side of the Grand Canyon.

"Owain?" Cara pulled back and looked at him, concerned. Her hand rested on his heaving chest.

"It's the effect you have on me," he said raggedly. "Feel?"

He expected to shock her by pressing his hips hard against hers, letting her feel the hard evidence of his desire. But she didn't seem embarrassed in the least.

She smiled—an angel's smile, a witch's smile—and leaned forward to touch her lips to his.

"I feel," she whispered.

It nearly undid him. As it was the hunger it released was awesome. The butterfly's touch of her lips on his sent his heart galloping, his body throbbing. And the aching need inside him would not be assuaged until he had kissed her back, drinking her in, taking his fill.

All rational thought fled. Who she was—who *he* was—ceased to matter at all. The only thing that mattered was his teasing exploration of her mouth, the silken feel of her skin against his palms as he slid them up under her sweater, the dance of her fingers down the length of his spine.

His fingers found her bra strap and undid the clasp. Then he shifted so that Cara lay on the couch and he bent over her, his breathing shallow and raspy as he pushed her sweater up and stroked her breasts.

"God, Cara, you're beautiful!" The words were wrung out of him, and he dropped his head, resting it against her, pressing it lightly into the valley between her breasts. He felt her fingers thread through his hair, the soft wind of her breath blew it, feathering it lightly, and she touched her lips to it again and again.

"Oh, Owain." Her voice was whisper-soft.

He lifted his head to look at her again.

She smiled at him, a dreamy, beckoning smile. Then her lips parted slightly and she whispered, "Ah, love."

Owain froze.

Cara blinked, confusion on her face.

In slow motion, Owain pulled back, sucked in a deep breath and expelled it harshly. A tremor ran through him. Love.

One word. One simple word.

Cara yanked down her sweater, flustered. "Owain? What is it? What's wrong?"

He shook his head, not daring to look at her, furious with himself for letting things get out of hand. Furious with himself for wanting what he had no business wanting.

"Nothing. Nothing's wrong. It…it's just not the…right time for that sort of thing, Cara."

"You mean I'm not the right woman?" she asked him bluntly. He could tell she thought he was rejecting her. He could see her begin to close in on herself, and he hurried to correct her first impression.

"I mean it isn't right! You're special. Too special." He couldn't make sense without telling her the truth. And the truth right now would devastate her.

Cara gave him an odd look. "Too special?"

Owain shrugged awkwardly. "Too special to take advantage of." He got to his feet and stuffed in the tails of his shirt, then pulled down his sweater and adjusted his jeans. He felt like a heel.

Cara sat up and pulled her knees up against her chest, wrapping her arms around them. Tilting her head to one side, she considered him carefully. Owain shifted awkwardly under her scrutiny.

"You know, there aren't many men who would have stopped, Owain." She was looking happier now, touched by his sensitivity.

He ducked his head. She wasn't going to make him out to be a saint now, was she?

She unwrapped her arms and got to her feet. "You're very special, too, Owain O'Neill," she told him. And she leaned forward then and gave him a quick soft kiss on the lips. "Thank you."

You wouldn't thank me if you knew, Owain thought despairingly.

He grabbed his jacket and pulled it on, hastily zipping it up. Then he glanced around the room one last time, almost as if he were taking inventory, storing it up for one of his blasted memories that were all he was going to have from now on.

Because he knew—even if Cara didn't—that things had gone far enough.

Chapter Four

Scruples.

Owain hadn't known for certain that he had any.

He wasn't sure it was such a great relief to discover that he did.

It certainly didn't make him sleep any better at night. And lying there in his little garret room, staring out the window at the night sky and, across the park, at Cara's house, he found very little comfort in the fact that a bedroom light—Cara's?—was on over there for a long while, too.

And the longer he lay awake in his narrow bed, the less he knew what he ought to do.

No, scratch that. He knew exactly what he *ought* to do.

He *ought* to pack his gear and get the hell out of Cara's life. Because there was no way he could kid himself anymore.

There was no way he could simply tell himself that what he was really interested in was a brief acquaintance with his children and their mother. There was no way now that he could pretend that all he wanted were the memories.

He knew damned well what he wanted. He wanted Cara.

His mind tormented him relentlessly, playing over every event of the day, from the easy conversation and the soft smiles right down to the enticingly yielding warmth of Cara pressed against him.

He could still taste her heated lips where he had kissed her, he could still smell the spicy fragrance of her shampoo. And—God help him—he could still feel the tight ache in his loins that had scarcely subsided even now.

He couldn't ever remember having stopped himself before—not when he was that close to losing control. And his body still protested strongly that he shouldn't have done it this time. Cara was willing, O'Neill, it reminded him sharply.

How well he knew it! He knew he could have had her, knew he could have made love to her, could have made her climb the heights of ecstasy with him. She had wanted him too!

God! He rubbed a hand over his face, wiping away a thin sheen of perspiration.

But if he had made love to her, what would have happened then?

Would he have been able to blithely turn and walk away?

Did he even want to?

And if he didn't, then what?

He groaned and rolled onto his side, trying to blot out everything in his mind. He needed self-discipline, he told himself. He needed backbone.

Well, his body complained, he had shown a little backbone tonight. He'd had a sure thing, and he had walked away.

If he were smart, he told himself, he would keep right on walking.

IT WASN'T as easy as that.

Ties bind. And Owain discovered just how quickly the following afternoon when he was sitting in Mrs. Garrity's kitchen repairing her toaster.

"God love you, Owain, it was a blessing the day you moved in," she bubbled at him from where she was scrubbing the lunch dishes in the sink.

He gave her ample back a wry grin. Mrs. Garrity, he had discovered, had a bark far worse than her bite. And when she had discovered that he could put together almost anything that had gone ailing in her gadget-filled house, she hadn't even so much as barked at him again. And she had been aghast when he mentioned going back to California.

"You wouldn't!" She gave him a look that accused him of the direst betrayal. "Have we done you wrong?"

"No," he assured her quickly. "I...have obligations out there."

"Do you?" She dried her hands on the terry towel. "More obligations than you have here, then?"

"What obligations has Owain got here?" Suzy, Cara's friend, wanted to know.

Owain looked up from the toaster warily. He had discovered that Suzy also lived in Mrs. Garrity's rooming house almost the first day he had arrived. And since then he had made it a point to avoid her. Suzy, he thought, had a sixth sense when it came to ferreting out news. It was the same sense that helped her match people up. She said she did it with the computer. But he happened to know that she spent very little time at Cara's on the computer. Mostly she just mulled over the people she had to match up, and then matched them. It made him nervous.

Suzy made him nervous, if the truth were known. She had been the recipient of his first foray into Cara's life, and she had been giving him the occasional odd and somewhat suspicious glance ever since. Not without reason, he had to admit.

It had seemed the better part of discretion to avoid her ever since. But now, with the toaster disemboweled on the table in front of him, no quick getaway presented itself.

"Obligations? My toaster, for one," said Mrs. Garrity. "But then he says he's going back to California."

Suzy gave him another of her measured gazes. "Oh? When?"

"Soon," Owain muttered.

"That's too bad." Suzy perched on the counter so she could watch him work. He felt as if a hawk had settled on the branch above his head and was considering him for lunch. "You've been good for Cara," she added.

Owain controlled his wince as best he could. Whether he had been good for Cara or not was distinctly debatable. "Thanks," he mumbled and bent his head, concentrating again on the toaster. He hoped if he ignored Suzy, she would leave.

Unfortunately she did no such thing. Instead she told Mrs. Garrity all about her term paper for political science, which had something to do with totalitarian governments. Then she started talking about her matchmaking service.

Mrs. Garrity clicked her tongue in disgust.

"It's a great way to meet men," Suzy assured her. "You ought to sign up."

"Harumph! I'm a widow, not some floozy," Mrs. Garrity scoffed, straightening the tea towel and hanging it on the rack.

"I have widows registered," Suzy countered. "Widows, divorcées, bachelors. Everyone!"

"Cara?" Owain asked before he could stop himself.

"Cara? Don't I wish! I could have a list of men five yards long who'd want to date Cara. But she doesn't date much. And she likes to do her own picking."

"She does date though?" The idea didn't please him much.

Suzy grinned. "Worried about the competition?"

Owain scowled and began to reassemble the toaster. "Just curious."

"Cara Williams is a wonderful lady," Mrs. Garrity stuck in. "Raisin' them two children all by herself."

Owain grunted, knowing what Cara would say about that. He was relieved when Mrs. Garrity went to answer the telephone. Now, if Suzy would just leave, too.

"It's for you," Mrs. Garrity told him, handing him the phone.

"Me?" *Let it not be Dougal,* he prayed. He hadn't sent Sam a new phone number. A post office box was good enough, he had decided. But Dougal was resourceful, and Owain didn't doubt his friend could track anyone down if he had a mind to. So he steeled himself to hear Dougal's clipped British tones.

"Owain?" The voice was tiny. A child's.

"Yes?"

"It's me. Hugh."

"Hugh!" His stomach did a flip-flop.

"I . . . I was wonderin' . . . um, I wanted to ask you . . . and I can," he added, " 'cause it's *my* dinner. Would you come with me?"

Baffled, Owain asked, "Dinner? What dinner?"

"My swimming banquet," Hugh explained. "It's at the Y. It's supposed to be a . . . a father-son thing. But it's okay for me to take my mom, on account of me not having a dad anymore. But I always take her and . . . and I wondered . . . would you come instead?"

Common sense told him to say no.

"Yes," he said.

"Great!"

"When is it?" he asked, avoiding Suzy's interested gaze and Mrs. Garrity's smug smile.

"Monday night. At six. We gotta take a salad. But my ma will make that. Is that all right?"

Owain heard Cara in the background saying, "Don't nag, Hugh."

"It's fine," he assured his son. "I'll pick you up about twenty minutes to six."

"Awwwright! Thanks," Hugh added a second later when Cara had muttered something else to him.

"Thank *you*," Owain said softly. But Hugh had already hung up.

"Hugh," Suzy said.

"Yes."

"His swimming awards ceremony?"

"Yes."

"You're going?"

"Yeah."

"Good. He could use a father figure."

"Mmm." Owain concentrated on the toaster again.

Suzy smiled and swung herself off the counter, then clapped him on the shoulder. "You'll have a great time. More power to you, Dad." And with no idea of the effect her words had on Owain, she sauntered blithely out of the room.

Mrs. Garrity wasn't so unobservant. She took one look at Owain's stricken expression and put her own interpretation on it. "Fatherhood scare you?" she asked him.

Owain sighed and stared down at the toaster whose complexities he completely understood. "Not fatherhood," he said softly, and went back to his work.

HE STAYED AWAY FROM CARA'S until Monday. It was better that way. Less temptation.

But less temptation meant more time alone to stew about things. He got to work.

That meant seeing Cara's grandmother, Mrs. Nute. After his encounter with Cara on Friday night, he had been going to call her grandmother and beg off. Now he couldn't decide if he ought to or not.

It would be torture to do it. Talking to her would be like talking to Cara. It would be another reminder of what he couldn't have. Maybe it would be good for him. A lesson in coping with adversity or some damned thing.

It wasn't easy.

He found that he liked Mrs. Nute immensely. She was a perceptive old lady who probably saw far more than other people realized that she did.

Owain realized it right off because he had far more that he needed to keep hidden. In other circumstances he would have cultivated her friendship. She reminded him a great deal of his own grandmother, who had died several years earlier. He had been close to her and had missed her a lot. She had understood him well. He suspected that Mrs. Nute would, too. That was the problem.

So he cut short his visit to her, excusing himself when he had just the barest bones of her story. It fascinated him, and he would have loved to pursue it. But he didn't dare. So he thanked her for her time and prepared to leave.

"We'll talk again another time," she told him. "I've enjoyed this."

"I have, too," he said honestly. "But I'm not sure when I'll be able to get back."

"Then I'll see you when I see you," was all she said.

He got back to Mrs. Garrity's in time to shower and clean up. Then he fixed a broken window sash for her. She was delighted and promised him lasagna for dinner.

"I'm not stopping," he reminded her. "It's the swimming banquet tonight."

"Ah." She looked as pleased as if he had said he would clean out her gutters. "Lovely family, the Williamses. Especially that Cara." She gave him a significant look over the tops of her wire-rimmed glasses.

"Mmm."

"Deserves a good man," she offered as she dropped spoonfuls of dough on the cookie sheet.

"Mmm." Owain feigned great interest in the crows that were settling into the tree just across the garden.

"Like you," Mrs. Garrity added firmly when it became obvious that subtlety wasn't gaining the desired results.

Owain sighed heavily. "I'm only taking her boy out tonight, Mrs. G."

"Well, it's a start," she said, meaning to be comforting, he was sure.

The trouble was, he didn't feel comforted in the least. He felt instead how very much he was missing. Cara, Hugh and Bronwen were exactly what she had said they were—"a lovely family"—one a man would be proud to claim. And Cara was, indeed, something special. No one had to tell him that.

No one had to tell him, either, that she deserved a good man. But beyond that he would not let himself think. He knew that he wasn't destined to be the man. And the best thing he could do for her would be to get out of her life.

"See you later," he said and, shrugging on his jacket, he let himself out into the night.

He arrived on Cara's doorstep at a quarter to six. Cutting it close, he knew. But arriving earlier would have been worse. He might have been invited in. He might have had to make small talk with Cara, sound normal, behave sanely. And the chances of his doing that weren't good enough that he wanted to risk it.

No, better that he just snatch Hugh away for the evening. Then, when he brought the boy home, he could make up some excuse about having to go back to L.A. in the morning and hope she would understand.

Hugh opened the door the second Owain's foot hit the first step. "I thought you weren't coming," Hugh accused. He was already wearing his winter jacket, and Cara tugged a hat down over his ears as he went out the door.

"Sorry. I was helping Mrs. Garrity," Owain said. He lifted his eyes to Cara's, about to promise that he would have Hugh back early. But the words died on his lips.

She was standing right behind the boy in the doorway. Her long hair was pulled up again into a knot on the back of her head. A few tendrils escaped, taunting him, reminding him of the last time he had seen her. He felt an urge to take all the pins out and run his hands through it the way he had that evening. He felt a primitive ache spring to life deep inside his gut.

"C'mon," Hugh urged, handing him the salad bowl. "We're gonna be late."

Owain nodded jerkily. "We'd better get going." His voice was almost a croak, as if it wanted to betray the adolescence of his feelings.

"You know the way?" Cara asked. She sounded strained, almost unsure of herself, too. It was the first time he had heard her sound that way.

"I can show him, Mom." Hugh grabbed Owain's hand and almost dragged him off the porch. "C'mon!"

Owain went.

But his son's hand tucked snugly inside his felt almost less real than the memory of Cara's expression, which lingered inside his head.

The two of them walked side by side through the darkness, Hugh chattering nonstop all the way. And gradually Cara's image receded, and Owain concentrated on the moment, storing up more of those memories that were suddenly seeming so inadequate.

The YMCA building was modern, as at odds with the rest of the town as a Picasso would be in an exhibit of Renoirs. But Owain found its incongruity rather charming. And in any case, he didn't care what it looked like as long as it succeeded in taking his mind off the major problems in his life.

It did. And then again, it didn't.

While a banquet of sixty boys and their parents provided more than enough in the way of noise and distraction, it also gave new direction to his thoughts. He stood leaning against one of the brick walls of the gymnasium, breathing in the smells of varnish, old sweat and spaghetti sauce, and watching his son race around with three other little boys his age. One of them darted under the table for a quick word with his own father, got a grin and a slap on the back, then took off again. Owain looked at the man—bespectacled and semibald—and felt a surge of envy so sharp it almost left him breathless.

No one else there would have to turn around at the end of the evening and walk out of his son's life.

He was relieved when the meal got under way at last. Fathers and sons were seated together at long, cafeteria-style tables, their plates heaped high with institutional spaghetti, a variety of homemade salads, garlic bread and thick slabs of chocolate cake that were in danger of being flooded by vividly orange French dressing. Hugh dug in at once. Halfway through the meal he glanced over at Owain.

"Aren'tcha hungry?"

"Not very." Owain wound some spaghetti around his fork.

"It's not as good as Mom's," Hugh said loyally, even as he polished off his helping.

"I'll bet it isn't."

"You'll have to have some of hers," Hugh went on.

Owain nodded, then turned to answer a question from the father sitting on the other side of him. It was just as well he was leaving, he thought. With every sentence he was getting himself in deeper.

The dinner was cleared away quickly, all the boys anxious for the awards presentations to start. And the closer they got to announcing Hugh's class, all of whom had passed and were going to be receiving their Polliwog patches, the more tense the boy got.

Owain watched him, his fingers gripping the chair, his small knuckles white as they curved around the metal seat. And when, at last, the coach called, "Hugh Williams," the boy launched himself out of his chair like an arrow from a bow.

Owain grinned as the boy wove his way to the platform, but his throat felt tight and there was a mysterious aching behind his eyes. It wasn't all that much, he told himself. Just an elementary swimming patch. And, intellectually, he knew that was true.

But intellect had never ruled Owain O'Neill. All he could respond to was what he felt at sharing this moment with his son, knowing that he wouldn't be sharing the future ones. He swallowed hard—pride, pain and pleasure mingling in the smile he gave Hugh as his son came back to him.

"See!" Hugh thrust the patch at Owain, his blue eyes bright with pride at his accomplishment. "Mom can sew it on my trunks. Then when I get to be a Minnow, she can put that one on, too. And then..."

He proceeded to give Owain a rundown of all the patches he was expecting to receive as his swimming ability grew. His gestures grew more expansive, his whispers louder.

It was like watching himself in miniature, Owain thought. He remembered that feeling, too—that same sense of endless possibility, of limitless horizons. Of dreams. His eyes stung. He wondered if it was from the fluorescent lights.

Reaching for Hugh instinctively, he gathered him in his arms and settled the boy in his lap. "Shh, now," he said in his son's ear. "They're giving out the next batch of awards. Let's just be polite."

And Hugh was, settling back and leaning against him, though Owain could still feel the energy emanating from his small body by the way Hugh shifted on his knees, by his bouncing excitement when a boy he knew who was just a year older got an advanced swimmer's award.

"I'll get a Shark, too," Hugh vowed. "I know I will."

The awards ceremony was just ending then, and Hugh's swimming instructor, overhearing the boy's prediction, ruffled Hugh's hair and said to Owain, "He will, too."

"Will what?"

"Hugh will get a Shark patch. He's a go-er, your boy." He patted Hugh on the head. "He's got a tremendous amount of drive. If he wants a Shark, he'll get it. That's for sure."

Owain returned the man's smile as best he could. "Yes," he said above the shouts of milling children. "I reckon he will."

The coach turned to speak to someone else then, and Owain leaned a hand on the chair, feeling suddenly old and tired. His eyes followed Hugh's blond head as his son bobbed in and out of the throng. He wished he could think of a way to change things, a way to begin again.

He couldn't think of a single one.

They were among the last to leave. Owain knew he ought to have hustled the boy out earlier. It was, after all, a school night, and he knew Cara liked the children in bed by eight-thirty. But it was already after nine when they left the gym.

"It was super! Super, super, super!" Hugh chanted as he danced down the sidewalk toward home. "Wasn't it super, Owain? Aren'tcha glad you came?"

Owain let his hand slide out of his pocket and brush against the silvery blondness of Hugh's head. "I'm glad," he said.

Hugh reached up and laced his fingers through his father's. They were small and warm. Trusting. Owain's throat ached. They walked along silently, each lost in his own thoughts. Every once in a while Hugh would give a little hop or skip. And every once in a while Owain's step faltered.

Cara had left the porch light on, soft and warm in the frosty night. Its golden glow reminded him of the way the light in the window had beckoned him on that first afternoon when he had found Bronwen and had believed she was his daughter.

Full circle.

But the satisfaction he had expected to feel had left him days ago. Now he only felt lonely. Bereft.

"Can you come in?" Hugh asked.

Owain shook his head. "It's late. You have school tomorrow. And it's time you were in bed, old man?"

Hugh giggled. "Me, old?" Then he shrugged. "Awright. Anyway, tomorrow we carve the pumpkins. I'll see you then."

"I don't think so."

Hugh stopped on the doorstep and turned around. "Why not?" His childish voice was sharp. "You promised."

"I have to go back to L.A.," Owain told him, coming as close to the truth as he dared. "It's urgent."

"But—"

"Hugh, if I could stay, I would. Believe me." He was firm, adamant.

Apparently Hugh sensed his sincerity. But it was obvious that he didn't think he had to like it. He sagged against the porch railing, then sighed audibly. He took a deep breath, and Owain saw him square his shoulders inside his bulky winter jacket. It looked as if he'd had more than a little experience confronting disappointments and broken expectations in his young life. Owain felt guilty at handing him one more.

"Okay," Hugh said softly. He put his hand on the doorknob.

"I'm sorry."

Hugh dredged up a tremulous smile. "It's okay, I guess." He paused. "Anyhow, thanks for bein' my dad tonight."

The pain was so fierce Owain might have had a knife slipped between his ribs. "You're welcome," he said hoarsely. "Good night."

He had almost reached the sidewalk again, walking quickly, his head down, his eyes stinging, when light spilled once more across the brown grass and Cara called his name.

He stopped and turned slowly, his reluctance obvious.

"Owain?" she ventured. "I need to talk to you."

Not now, he thought. *Dear God, not now.* He couldn't talk to her tonight.

He wanted the clear stark light of day to make him do the things he had to do. He wanted distance and impersonal behavior. He wanted a businesslike relationship. Because that was the only way he was going to be able to make the break.

But he couldn't walk away from her now. Not when she was standing there in the cold, her slender figure outlined by the bright kitchen lights. He tucked his hands into his pockets and walked slowly back toward the porch.

"What is it?"

She looked flustered. "Could you stop for a cup of coffee? Just for a minute. I—I have something to say. But I want to get Hugh to bed first."

There was no way out. "All right."

She gave him a tight smile. "Thank you." Turning, she went back into the kitchen. He followed her, trying to maintain the distance he knew he would need.

He poured himself the coffee, then paced the family room, running his fingers along the smooth grain of the stereo cabinet, then along the worn bricks of the hearth. The Shearing album was still sitting on the top of her record collection. He picked it up, balancing it between his fingertips. Then he slid it out of sight among the other records. There was no place for Shearing tonight.

The time for pretending was over.

He picked up his coffee mug and walked another lap around the family room, cradling the mug in his palms. Soft going-to-bed sounds filtered down from upstairs. He heard the water running, the patter of Hugh's feet along the hall floor, the soft shush of his mother, then the creak of the stairs as Cara came down.

Owain took another quick sip of coffee. He wished for something stronger. False courage. He wondered, not for the first time, what she wanted. She had looked nervous when she had asked him to come back. Apprehensive.

She hadn't found out, had she?

No, of course, she hadn't.

All the same he felt a fist of fear sock his stomach when she reappeared. She looked as wary as he felt. Her own hands were shoved into the back pockets of her jeans. "You could sit down," she suggested.

Owain shrugged. Standing seemed safer, somehow.

Cara stood, too, rocking back on her heels, staring first at the floor, then, at last, lifting her face to meet his eyes.

"I want to apologize," she said.

Owain blinked.

"I...I don't want you to think that...that...what I did with...you...I don't want you to think that I do that...with...with...every...man." The words seemed to be strangling her slowly. Then the rest poured out all at once, the dam breaking. "I mean, I haven't! Not once. Not ever. Not...not since Martin!" She bowed her head. "God, it was so...so...forward! I mean, I don't blame you for not coming back, for thinking that I'm some oversexed widow or—"

"Hey!" Owain cut in at last. "Hey, I never thought that! Not ever!"

He set down the cup on the coffee table and went to her, taking her in his arms, forgetting every resolution he had made. "Cara, hey, I wanted..."

And now *he* was strangling.

"Ah, hell, Cara..."

He couldn't let go of her. He needed her too badly. Needed her touch, her warmth. And to think she had been thinking *she* had been at fault. She thought *she* had driven him away? *My God!* His arms tightened. He buried his face in her hair, breathing in, trembling. And apparently his touch unleashed something in Cara as well, for it felt all of a sudden as if something snapped. As if the tight rein on which she had been holding herself broke, and her arms came around him, holding him tightly as she pressed her cheek into his shoulder.

He had a mouthful of golden hair and a mind full of broken resolutions. "Cara, really, no," he murmured. "It wasn't like that."

"You'd been coming every day," she choked. "And then, all of a sudden, you didn't come anymore. And after what happened that night . . . after what I did . . ."

"Not you, Cara," he said urgently. "Us. I . . . I just needed to think . . . to get a little perspective. I . . ."

Oh, hell, more lies.

He rested his forehead against hers, taking deep breaths. "I wanted you." And God knew, that was the truth. "I just needed to . . . to step back and decide what wanting you meant." And that was the truth, too.

Cara didn't move. He could feel her heart thrumming like a hummingbird's wings, caught against the solid wall of his chest.

"I needed to think about what getting involved—I mean, *really* involved—would mean," he went on slowly, carefully, feeling his way. "If I made love to you," he told her gently, "it wouldn't be easy to walk away."

More truth.

"And you had to decide if you wanted to walk away?" Her voice was soft with understanding. And it hurt him worse than Hugh's had.

He nodded his head against her hair. His arms tightened around her. Outside he heard an owl hoot. Inside the aquarium filter bubbled away. He heard the shallow intake of Cara's breath and the shuddering inhalation of his own.

"What did you decide?"

He closed his eyes and prayed for more divine understanding than he knew he had a right to. "I decided I'm not going anywhere."

Chapter Five

It was Cara's honesty that undid him.

He couldn't walk away, leaving her to think that it was her own brazen behavior that had driven him off. Not when the opposite was true—Cara Williams attracted him like no other woman he could ever remember. And knowing she wanted him, too, was almost more than he could bear, especially when his own dishonesty was the real reason he had been going to leave.

And now?

Now he had come to a different decision.

Standing there, his arms locked around Cara, feeling hers locked around him, he realized something else. He realized that the truth about whose father he was or wasn't didn't matter a bit compared to a far deeper truth—he was in love with Cara Williams.

The part of him that had never found joy in his musical success, the part of him that still searched and yearned after some elusive dream, even now that he was close to finishing his Ph.D.—that part of him had found what it sought with Cara.

She brought him a warmth, a peace, a contentment that had eluded him everywhere else. He wanted to spend the rest of his life with her. He didn't care whose natural children Hugh and Bronwen were. They came with their mother.

And he knew he would love them just as much and just as easily had they been Martin's and not his own.

That wasn't important. That didn't matter. Loving them mattered. Loving Cara did.

He hadn't been able to do more than promise her that he wasn't leaving that night. He had held her in his arms and kissed her with a tenderness that only hinted at the way he was beginning to cherish her. And then, he had pulled away.

"Owain?"

"There will be time," he promised. "Plenty of time, my love."

And he'd forced himself to leave her and go out into the night.

Now, at four-thirty in the morning he was still sleepless. He had tossed and turned, wishing he hadn't left her, yet knowing that it was right. But sleep wouldn't come. And at last he reached for his guitar. He kept it close as a matter of habit. He hadn't played it in ages.

Now, though, it seemed right.

His fingers curved round the neck, finding the frets. His other hand played lightly over the strings. He stopped, tuned, plucked a bit more. Tuned again. Then he leaned his head back against the headboard and let the soft chords ripple forth.

Words of love, of promise, of dreams sought and found, floated through his head. He murmured them softly. Images of Cara wove in and out of the words and the melody. Love.

Owain had written songs about love before. A dozen of them. Maybe two dozen. Or more. Million-sellers, most of them. But what had he ever really known about love until now? Besides the platitudes and cheap clichés?

What did he know about it now? he asked himself. Save that he couldn't seem to let Cara out of his life. When he had seen her pain and embarrassment earlier in the eve-

ning, he couldn't let her endure it. He had had to take it for
his own.

It wasn't her fault, he had assured her.

Now he had to reassure himself.

He *was* doing the right thing, staying. He loved her. She
loved him. And as far as being Hugh and Bronwen's natural father went, he would simply never mention it. No one
else was going to tell her. No one knew, save himself.

He would simply be the man who loved their mother. The
man who was going to—he tasted the word—*marry* their
mother. And maybe someday he could adopt them. Stranger
things had happened, after all. Neither Cara nor anyone else
need find out why he had come here in the first place.

And as far as the other went—his conveniently unmen-
tioned career as a singer-songwriter—of course he would tell
her about that. But in that case he had a perfectly reasonable excuse for not having told her at once who he was.

Once people knew he was a member of Cardiff Connection, they stopped remembering that he was a human being.
He was simply a "success" with a capital *S*. And he hated
that.

Cara would understand. She, with her homey warmth and
gentle directness, would sympathize with a man who felt he
was always being judged as if he were on a stage. She had
accepted him as a man first. Had, he hoped, *loved* him as a
man.

She would understand that he had feared being loved for
what he had and not who he was. Too many people in the
music business never found a love like that. He felt grateful
it hadn't been like that for Cara and himself.

The words of his song came more quickly now. He played
a lilting tune as he wove the words together. The refrain, a
simple poignant verse about love lost and found, echoed in
his head. He closed his eyes and let it wash over him.

Then he stopped and wrote it all down—words and music—before he put out the light.

IN THE MORNING his heart was still singing. He came downstairs, swung Mrs. Garrity around, twirling her through the kitchen and leaving her breathless and wondering when he gave her a smacking kiss on the cheek.

"Is that because you're leaving?" she asked him suspiciously.

He grinned widely. "It's because I'm not!"

Her mouth opened and closed. "Not?"

"Not." He reached out and gently tipped her chin up. "I'm digging in." He dug into his pocket and pulled out his billfold, peeling off several bills. "Here. Next month's rent in advance."

"Oh, my," said Mrs. Garrity. "Oh, my." She beamed at him. "You're not! Sit down. Sit down. I'll just make you a nice batch of French toast."

Mrs. Garrity's way to celebrate anything was to cook for it. Owain felt too keyed up to eat. Nevertheless, he ate. Then he grabbed his briefcase with his notes in it and headed out.

"Off to the library?" Mrs. Garrity asked him.

"Yes."

He had intended to get his files in order and to map out the interviews he would be doing here in earnest. Instead he spent the morning daydreaming about Cara. By ten o'clock when he knew he wasn't going to get anything done, he decided to go see her.

Chances were she was working. Chances were she wouldn't want to be disturbed. But, he thought with a smile as he loped through the park and leaped easily over her split-rail fence, chances were even better that she was just as distracted as he was.

He asked.

She was.

"Let's get out of here, then!"

She cocked her head and stared at him as if he had suggested eloping to Las Vegas. "Go out?" she asked cautiously.

He nodded.

"Where?"

"Exploring."

"Exploring?" She gave him a wary look. He grinned engagingly and held out his hand.

She took it. "Exploring," she said.

They took his car, driving south along one of the two-lane highways, aimlessly at first, then when Cara spotted a roadside advertisement for House on the Rock, she touched Owain's arm.

"Let's go there."

He lifted his eyebrows. "What's there?"

She smiled. "You'll see."

He did. It boggled his mind. Expecting a house built onto a rock—being literal-minded, basically—he was wholly unprepared for what he found. Oh, there was a house—a house such as he, even with his Hollywood connections, had never seen before. A house to dream about, to fantasize in. And a million more things besides. Every sort of mechanical contraption known to man. A whole orchestra that played mechanically. No musicians, just instruments. A whole elaborate diorama of mechanical people doing *The Mikado*, complete with fierce expressions and eyes that actually moved. Owain was enthralled.

"Fantastic, isn't it?" Cara asked.

"Unreal."

"You haven't seen anything yet."

He didn't believe her until they had gone clear through the Streets of Yesteryear section that had followed the house tour. And just when he thought his eyes had seen everything they could possibly imagine and plenty of things they never had, he came face to face with the merry-go-round.

Lit with red and white lights, swirling in time with the lilt of a magical tune, it was, without a doubt, the most astonishing thing he had ever seen. Rows of mythical animals rode up and down, dazzlingly painted, reminding Owain of some of the more psychedelic art he had seen. Owain hadn't been able to imagine it existed in real life. He could now. The House on the Rock was beyond anything he had ever dreamed.

"Holy cow," he murmured.

"What'd I tell you?" Cara grinned.

Owain shook his head. "Wow," was all he could muster. He looped his arm around her shoulders and hugged her close. She wrapped her arm around his waist and left it there as they walked toward the garden area to get something to eat.

"So, what do you think?" Cara asked him when they were sitting on one of the benches sharing Cokes and a bag of chips.

"I think that if you hadn't shown it to me, I wouldn't have believed it was true."

She nodded. "I know what you mean." She nibbled on a chip reflectively. "Sort of like the way I feel about you."

Time seemed to stop.

Owain swallowed. "What's that supposed to mean?" he asked gruffly.

"Nothing bad," she assured him quickly. "It's just that the past couple of weeks have been like something special— something like the House on the Rock, I suppose. And—" she shrugged "—I don't know. I guess maybe I wanted to come here to prove to myself that the house was real, too."

"It is," Owain said firmly. "And so is the way I feel about you."

Cara dipped her head for a moment, then lifted it and leaned forward to brush her lips across his. "Thank you."

"Anytime, ma'am." He finished off his Coke and threw away the cup. "Come on. Just sitting here staring at you is driving me wild." He pulled her to her feet and started walking her toward some of the smaller displays that were activated with a coin.

Cara fell in step with him. "I need to distract you, do I?"

Owain shook his head. "You already distract me," he admitted. "Far too much."

"Good."

They had to hurry to get back before the twins got home from school. In fact, they were pulling up in front of the house when Bronwen and Hugh came running across the park.

"Hey, great, you're still here!" Hugh shouted.

"I didn't have to go to California after all," Owain told him, tossing him into the air as he came running up.

"You were going to California?" Cara asked him quietly.

He met her eyes. "Until I straightened out my priorities." He saw her visibly relax, the wary, worried look disappearing from her eyes.

"Can you stay now?" Hugh asked him.

"Are we carving pumpkins now?" Bronwen wanted to know.

"Tonight," Cara said. "After supper. Will you share it with us?" she asked Owain when Hugh turned a silent beseeching gaze on her.

He shook his head. "Can't. I promised Mrs. Garrity I would clean out her gutters. And she's making me meat loaf as a reward."

"I'll make you meat loaf if you'll clean mine," Cara offered, grinning.

"Lady, I'll clean your gutters for nothing." And right there in front of her children, he kissed her full on the lips.

"Oh-ho," Bronwen said in a small wondering voice.

"Told you so," chanted her brother.

She hit him with her book bag. "You did not!"

"Did so!" And he darted off toward the back door, Bronwen hot on his heels.

"Lovely children." Cara looked after them with a mother's tolerant disgust.

"Terrific," Owain agreed.

"I'm surprised they haven't driven you away."

He reached up and brushed a loose tendril of hair out of her eyes. "No fear of that." He tilted her chin up and kissed her again. The kiss lasted longer this time. It heated his blood and made him want to forget his recently discovered scruples. It made him want to make love to her right there in front of her house. "I'll be back tonight."

"Are you really going to clean out Mrs. Garrity's gutters?"

"I really am."

She gave him an impish grin. "And what about mine?"

"I'll do yours."

"Tonight? After the pumpkin carving?"

He shook his head, slowly and deliberately. "I've got far better things to do tonight."

"I THOUGHT you were going to fall and break your fool neck." Mrs. Garrity thumped a plate of meat loaf, potatoes and acorn squash in front of Owain and glared down at him before she went around and sat at the head of the table.

"Me?" Owain gave her an innocent stare as he cut his meat loaf with his fork. "Perish the thought."

He dug into his dinner, smiling inwardly, his thoughts on Cara. He wouldn't have dared fall off that roof. Life was too wonderful at the moment.

"I heard you playing the guitar last night," Suzy said offhandedly as she buttered her mashed potatoes.

Owain stiffened. "Oh? I . . . hope I didn't keep you awake."

"No. I was studying for midterms anyway. Besides, you're really good."

"Thanks." He bent his head over his meal, concentrating on his meat loaf.

"You want a job playing?" Suzy went on.

"What?"

"Just thought you might like to do a stint at the Pizza Shack. My friend Terry hires instrumentalists on the weekends. And grad students usually need the money."

Except in this case, Owain thought grimly. "I can't," he said carefully.

"Can't?"

"Statute of limitations."

Suzy wrinkled her nose. "Playing the guitar some kind of crime these days?"

"Not that kind of limitation. For my dissertation. I have to have it finished before spring so I need to concentrate on it full-time. Besides," he added, "I have a bit saved up. But thanks."

He hoped she was convinced. Actually his statute of limitations lasted for three more years. But he wanted it done far sooner than that. And he certainly didn't want to play guitar at the Pizza Shack. The chances of someone recognizing him with a guitar in his hand were far too high.

"Well, let me know if you change your mind."

"Thanks. I will." He turned his attention once again to the meat loaf, and was relieved to see Suzy push back her chair and get to her feet, evidently finished with dinner.

"I'll see you tonight," she called as she carried her plate back into the kitchen.

"Huh?"

"I'm carving pumpkins, too."

"Oh?" He felt a stab of disappointment that it wasn't going to be just Cara, the twins and himself.

"And Greg," Suzy added before the door swung shut.

"Who's Greg?"

"My rocks prof. He was a colleague of Martin's."

"Oh?" Maybe he was a very old family friend, Owain thought. *Old* being the operative word.

"He's sweet on Cara."

"We'll see about that," Owain said, his tone ominous.

Suzy grinned and rubbed her hands together gleefully. "Like that, is it?"

"Like that."

AND GROWING MORE LIKE THAT with every passing minute.

Owain hurried through dinner, the goad of knowing that some Greg person was going to be at Cara's making him hurry even faster than he might have been hurrying otherwise.

When he knocked on the door, he decided his hurrying had been justified. Greg Whoever looked like potential trouble. He was tall—taller than Owain—with blond, graying hair and a pleasant smile. The sort of person one would expect to be a "rocks prof"—solid, responsible, dependable. And another time Owain might have enjoyed meeting him. Now all he could think was that this man was interested in Cara.

"Yes?" It was clear that the man wasn't expecting him.

"I'm Owain O'Neill. I've come for the carving." A good offense seemed like the best idea, and he had never felt more proprietorial in his life.

"O'Neill? Uh, come in, won't you," the other man said belatedly for Owain was already hitching his hip onto the corner of the kitchen table. "Cara is . . . is still upstairs. I'm Greg Christopher."

Owain nodded dismissively. "Suzy mentioned you."

Greg Christopher seemed to brighten. "Ah, you're Suzy's friend, then."

"No. Cara's."

That stopped that particular avenue of conversation.

Greg Christopher made a production out of clearing his throat and scratching his jaw in a puzzled manner. Then, apparently deciding that he should at least act like a good host, he offered Owain a glass of apple cider.

Owain shook his head. "I'll wait for Cara."

The silence between them reminded Owain of the kind you heard in bars just before the fight broke out. It lasted until Cara came down the stairs a few minutes later and said, "Oh! You're here!" to him. She glanced at each of them in turn, and she looked suddenly very nervous.

"You've introduced yourselves?" she asked, her voice falsely bright.

"More or less," Greg said. It was evident that he had plenty more questions in those three words. And Owain knew that Cara was aware of them.

"Did he tell you that I'm typing his dissertation?" she asked Greg.

"No." But his tone said that that was still no reason for Owain's being there.

It was fortunate for Cara that at that moment Suzy came bustling in the door with Bronwen, bearing another gallon jug of apple cider and a big bag of doughnuts. At the same time Hugh came hurtling downstairs.

In the resultant chaos the tension between Greg and himself seemed momentarily masked. Until the question of who was going to help whom carve a pumpkin arose.

"Owain's helpin' me carve," Hugh announced, spreading out a thick layer of newspaper on the floor under the direction of his mother.

"No, he isn't!" Bronwen objected. "He gets to help me! He went to *your* swimming thingy!" She gave him a hard shove.

"Bron!" Cara grabbed her daughter. "Stop it!"

Greg gave Owain a hard stare, as if it were all his fault. Then he bent down and said sternly to them both, "Stop this now or you'll have to go to your rooms."

Hugh's jaw set stubbornly and Bronwen gave Greg a mutinous look.

"I have an idea," Owain said quickly. "I think I need help more than either one of you. Remember, I've never done this before. So why don't you have Suzy and Greg work with you, and your mother can teach me?" He tilted his head and grinned teasingly at Cara, delighted when he saw a faint flush creep into her cheeks.

"How about it?" he asked her.

Greg scowled, then snorted in disbelief. "Never carved a pumpkin?"

"Never."

"Harumph." But it was obvious he knew when to back down, even if he did it with less than graciousness.

"That sounds like the only real solution," Cara was saying. She didn't sound overly enthusiastic, but the look she gave Owain was enough to make the desire he had been banking all day flare to life again inside him.

"I guess we'll just have to bow to the inevitable," Suzy said to Greg with a grin.

He gave her a glum look. "I guess."

As the evening wore on, the inevitable was that Owain and Cara were a couple. Whatever Greg Christopher had been to her before, it wasn't what Owain was now. And thank God for that, Owain thought.

They made a good team, he discovered as they carved their pumpkin together. Their ideas seemed to mesh, to balance one another. Owain was the artist, Cara the more practical executioner of what he dreamed up. They bickered and they argued amiably. But the end result was superb.

Hugh and Bronwen griped and groaned when their mother's pumpkin turned out to have an obvious piratical personality while their own were nice, run-of-the-mill jack-o'-lanterns, cute but not memorable.

"It isn't fair," Hugh moaned.

Owain ruffled his hair. "Life isn't fair, sport."

"I guess not." Hugh set his pumpkin next to Owain and Cara's on the hearth and stared at them for a long time. Then he shrugged. "Well, now you know how. So next year you can help me with mine."

"I'd be delighted."

"He probably won't be here next year," Greg put in deftly.

Owain gave him a level look. "I wouldn't bet on that."

Greg subsided, for the moment at least, into silence.

It didn't last. Once the children were in bed and the grown-ups sat down to share a cup of coffee and to polish off the last of the doughnuts, Greg started in again.

Twice he brought up Martin's name. Dragging out the big guns, Owain thought. Trying to make Cara feel guilty. And he glanced at Cara several times to see what effect Greg's words were having.

They were making her mad, it was clear.

And by the time Suzy gathered up her things and hinted to Greg that she wouldn't mind an escort across the park, Cara's lips were pressed into a tight line.

"Good night, Greg," she said firmly as she saw them both to the door.

Owain was still leaning against the kitchen counter, cradling a cup of lukewarm coffee in his hands, with no intention of going anywhere. He smiled at them. Greg noticed.

"What about him?" he asked Cara abruptly. "Isn't he going?"

"In a little while. I have something to do here," Owain said easily before Cara could speak.

"What?" Greg demanded.

"Earlier Cara taught me how to carve a pumpkin," he said, moving to her side and slipping an arm around her shoulders. "Now I'm going to teach her something."

Cara swallowed audibly. Her cheeks flamed.

"Teach her what?" Greg's voice was sharp, almost drowning out Suzy's snort of laughter.

"Welsh." Then he left Cara's side and went to the door, nodded a polite good-night to both Greg and Suzy and shut the door on Greg's tight-lipped face.

"Owain!" Cara was laughing.

He turned and wrapped her in his arms. "I am," he muttered against her lips, just before he claimed them with his own. "Tonight I'm learning you, and you're learning me. I don't know what you are, but at least half of me is Welsh." He grinned and kissed her hard.

"Which half?" Cara surveyed him from the top of his dark hair to his run-down shoes. Her eyes paused briefly at his lips, then skated lower over his forest-green sweater and his new cord jeans, lingering for a moment at a spot just below his belt. He felt the heat rise in him again and reached for her, drawing her with him into the family room, stopping just long enough to turn off the kitchen light.

"I'll be only too happy to show you, my dear," he whispered in her ear as he drew her body into the welcome circle of his arms.

The three jack-o'-lanterns glowed eerily, smiling their wide vacant smiles. A soft orange glow diffused over the room, like the glow of warmth that Owain felt inside him. He bent his head and very gently he tasted Cara's mouth. This kiss was wholly different from the one he had given her moments before. That one, in reaction to Greg's attitude all evening, had claimed the right to kiss her; this one asked for the privilege.

And Cara willingly granted it to him.

Her lips parted easily under the touch of his mouth. She let him draw his tongue along the full line of her lower lip, learning its contour. And then she welcomed him when he pressed his lips once more to hers and slipped his tongue between them, exploring her teeth, touching her tongue, teasing it. Tormenting himself. Wanting more. Much more. All the frustration that had been building in him since he had scrupulously left her that night culminated at last. The kiss became desperate.

Cara's need matched his. Her tongue met his, dueling with it, savoring him the same way he savored her. He felt her heart quicken against his ribs and felt his own hammer in unison with it. The ache that was building in him low-ered now and centered.

He pulled away, breathing raggedly. "Cara?" He knew what he was asking with that one word. And so did she.

Her hands locked around him, squeezing tightly as she lifted her eyes to meet his. "Yes," was all she said.

He nodded, licking his lips, then waiting silently while she turned out the rest of the lights. She opened the back door and let the cat in. He blew out the candles in the pumpkins. Then he felt her take his hand in the dark and lead him to-ward the staircase. Her hand was warm and moist as it held his.

She halted at the door of what he supposed was her bed-room, and Owain felt her hesitate. Was she thinking of Greg? Of Martin? Having second thoughts? Another woman he might have hurried through the door without letting her question what they were about. Not Cara.

"Are you sure?"

She lifted her face and he saw her smile slightly in the dim glow of the night-light down the hall. "I'm sure," she whispered.

Pushing open the door, she led him into her room.

It reflected Cara, Owain thought, even though he could see it only in shadows. The furniture was Spartan but warm, somehow. Old and lovingly refinished. The bed was brass and covered with a patchwork quilt. There was a sheaf of computer printout on top of it. He smiled. Patchwork and computers. Yes, definitely Cara. Practical and no-nonsense, but warm.

He looked around for a photograph, expecting to see Martin smiling at him from the top of the dresser. But it was almost bare. Just a brush and comb, a tube of lipstick, which was all the makeup she ever wore, a paperback novel and a small bottle of cologne. He couldn't remember her ever wearing any. The smells he associated with Cara were cinnamon, apples, flowers, and wood smoke.

Cara stood by quietly, watching him look around. She looked slightly nervous, as if he might judge her. He wondered if she had even let another man up here besides Martin. He doubted if Greg had made it.

It made him feel humble. Her openness taunted him. He wished he could bring the same to her. He wished he could bring her the same purity he suspected she was bringing to him. The thought surprised him. Purity had never been high on his priority list. But Cara seemed to require it.

At last, apparently deciding he had looked around enough, Cara drew him down onto the bed with her. Then she lay back and opened her arms.

Owain accepted the invitation. Lying beside her in the darkness, he skimmed his hands under the soft blue sweater she wore, caressing the silky softness of her skin. It was as soft as Bronwen's, like a child's. But her body was all woman. His fingers trembled as they slid around to her back and fumbled for the hook of her bra. He felt her gasp slightly and go rigid under his touch.

"What is it?"

But her split second's hesitation vanished. She shook her head mutely. Her fingers set about undoing the buttons of his shirt, then they dragged lightly down his chest, splayed across his ribs, then slid inward and settled against his belt. Owain sucked in his breath, as rigid now as she had been before.

"Owain?" Now it was Cara asking him.

"Are *we* sure?" he asked in a gravelly voice that mocked them both.

"I am." And Cara moved her hips beneath him in such a way that, if he had any doubts, he would have doubted no longer.

"Me, too." He lifted her up so he could tug her sweater over her head.

The only light in the room came from the street lamp across the way and the night-light down the hall. But it was enough for him to marvel at Cara's beauty.

He had seen her running in the park, typing at her computer, mixing up a batch of cookies, mothering a child. And he had found her enchanting however he had seen her. But her sheer physical beauty had never struck him fully until this moment. He knelt back against his heels and unzipped her jeans, drawing them slowly down her long legs, leaving only a scrap of cotton covering her feminine mysteries.

He smiled. Cotton. Sensible, serviceable and seductive for all that. Ah, Cara! He grinned.

"What are you laughing at?"

He traced the waistband of her panties. "Just thinking how practical you are."

She scowled at him. "Now?"

"Why not now?" He was still grinning as his fingers slipped inside the elastic and tugged the last barrier away. "Makes my life so much easier."

"And you like easy?" Her eyebrows arched indignantly.

"I like you." He bent forward swiftly and kissed the tip of her nose. "I want to love you."

The indignation vanished. "Oh, Owain, do," she whispered and, reaching for his sweater, she lifted it over his head, pulling his already unbuttoned shirt with it. He stripped off his own jeans quickly. But before he could shed his briefs, Cara's "My heavens" stopped him.

"What is it?"

She was smiling now. "They're not white."

It was his turn to scowl. "So?" In the dim light she wouldn't be able to tell what color they were, which was just as well. He moved to peel them down over his hips.

"I've never made love with anyone who didn't wear white underpants before." She blew in his ear softly. He squirmed.

"What color are they?" she asked him.

"What difference does it make?" He was burning for her touch. Her finger traced a teasing line at the top of his briefs. He arched his hips. But still she didn't touch him.

"What color?" Her breath blew softly against the fine line of hair that arrowed down from his navel to the top of his underpants. He bit his lip. She giggled, but didn't venture any closer toward relieving his growing frustration.

He sighed and grimaced. "Red."

"You're joking!"

"Why would I joke?" he said sourly.

"Red? Really? Can I see?"

"Not now! Now we're doing this!" And he bore her back on the bed, kissing her hard, his fingers tangling in her hair, his leg insinuating itself between hers, his manhood pressing firmly into the cradle of her hips. In moments Cara was kissing him back, the color of his underpants forgotten in her haste to remove them.

"Come to me," she whispered when they were both naked. "Now, Owain. Come to me now." And she drew him down between her legs, sheathing his silken heat within her.

He thought he might die. He thought he might explode before he had a chance to really love her. He shuddered and went completely still, holding himself rigid, waiting for a slight easing of the tension within him. "God," he muttered. "Oh, Cara. Oh, God." Nothing had ever felt like this.

Cara held his face in both her hands and raised her head to kiss him. Her tongue slipped easily inside his mouth, then withdrew, teasing him, then entered again.

Owain shuddered, then began to move.

Cara moved with him, drawn into the primordial dance of love. Her fingers dug into his back, her legs wrapped him tightly. His mind reeled under the onslaught of the sensations she was building within him. She possessed him totally, driving out all other thoughts, all other needs. She made him hers in a way that no other woman ever had.

He stiffened, trembled, then could hold back no longer. The splintering climax shook him, making him groan her name. And he could have wept when he felt her shudders of completion coincide with his own.

He had never loved before. Not like this. There had never been this sense of wonder, of joy, of completion and contentment in any other woman's arms. He kissed her cheek. It was damp. He nudged it with his nose. Then he lifted his face higher and kissed her eyelids. They were wet.

Tears.

Panic stabbed him.

"Cara?" His voice shook.

Her hands reached up languidly to stroke his back as if to soothe him. "It's all right, Owain. It's fine. *I'm* fine." Her voice trembled though. It sounded breathless, reedy.

"Really?" He wasn't convinced.

She kissed him again. And again. His lips, his nose, his jawline, his chin. "Truly."

"You're crying. Those are tears."

"Of joy."

The lump in his throat suddenly choked him. He wanted to say, "You, too?" but he didn't.

He simply lifted himself off her, levering himself up on one elbow while he smiled tenderly down into her face. "Cara," he murmured. "My Cara."

The wondrousness of it was almost beyond him. He was close to tears himself.

"What about you?"

"Me?"

"Any regrets?"

He looked at her for a long moment, wondering how she could even ask that. "No, *cariad*," he assured her, using the Welsh term of endearment that his parents so often used with each other. "No regrets at all."

He lay back on the bed and stared up at the ceiling, one arm folded under his head, the other wrapped around Cara, holding her close to him. She rested her head on his perspiration-slick chest. Her chin touched his breastbone, one of her hands stroked his hip.

He considered asking her to marry him tonight.

But he knew at once it was too soon. There were women who could be swept off their feet, women whom you could rush to a Las Vegas chapel just days after you had met them. But Cara Williams wasn't one of them, and Owain knew it.

Their love was beautiful, and it was right. But if he wanted to end where he wanted it to end—in a new beginning for them both—he would have to handle it right.

Loving was enough for tonight. It was a part of the foundation on which their relationship would be built. But it wasn't going to be built overnight. And he couldn't ask her to marry him until she knew what he really did for a living. He knew now she loved him for himself—the same way he loved her.

He thought about telling her now. But explanations would be necessary. They would have to sit up and talk. He would have to explain. She would have questions. He would want to answer them. No, not tonight.

Cara turned and Owain curved his body around hers, holding her against him. She hugged his hand against her breasts. They slept.

He didn't wake again until it was almost light. Then he pulled on his jeans and his shirt and sweater quietly, trying not to wake her. But he made a noise when he was scuffling for his shoes and she turned, sitting halfway up in bed.

"Owain?" Her voice was sleepy and warm.

On his knees on the floor, he straightened up almost next to where she lay. "Shh," he whispered. "Go back to sleep. I'm just going before the kids get up."

She smiled muzzily at him. "Good idea." She shut her eyes again and drifted back to sleep. Owain leaned over and kissed her lightly on the lips. She smiled.

He stuffed his feet into his shoes and tiptoed out the door. All at once the bed creaked and he turned to see her sitting bolt upright.

"You are coming back, aren't you?"

He came back right then and touched her cheek with his hand. "You'd better believe I am."

Chapter Six

"A sorcerer! I'm gonna be a sorcerer!" Hugh looked up from the black tagboard cone he was stapling into the shape of a hat, and beamed at Owain who had just come in the door. "And Bron is gonna be a toad!" He stifled a giggle with his hand.

"Am not!" Bronwen retorted hotly. "I'm going to be a princess." And Owain could hear royal strains in her haughty tone.

"But first you gotta be a toad," Hugh insisted.

Owain squatted down next to them, holding the tagboard for Hugh so he could put in the last staple. "I think it's the prince who has to be the toad first, Hugh," he said gravely.

"Oh." Hugh was momentarily crestfallen. Then he brightened. "Well, just so long as it isn't the sorcerer."

"I wish you were a sorcerer," Cara said darkly, looking around the room. "Then you could just wave your magic wand and clean up this mess. Honestly, Hugh, I don't know if there's more glue on you or on your costume."

Hugh considered the state of the room. "On the floor, I think. But it washes, Ma."

"And so, thank heavens, do you." She shook her head at Hugh, but her expression was tender. And when she looked away from her son to the man hunkered down beside him, her expression softened even further.

Thank God, Owain thought. He had been afraid she might have had some second thoughts. But she didn't look as if she were regretting what had happened at all. She seemed, perhaps, a tiny bit awkward, even shy. But that was understandable enough. She wasn't the sort of woman who went around having affairs. She hadn't had to tell him he was the first man to arouse her this way since Martin had died. He could tell every time she looked at him, every time she spoke in a certain tone of voice. And he had been able to tell with absolute certainty last night when they had made love.

She smiled at him now and he felt the shiver of awareness that always crackled between them whenever they were together. He wished he had come over earlier when the children were still in school. They could have made love again.

But he wasn't giving in to his impulses at the moment. He was trying to act responsibly. And acting responsibly meant that he had spent hours interviewing Mrs. Garrity's oldest boarder, Norbert Hill.

Mr. Hill, it turned out, was an immigrant like himself. A perfect source for material he needed. An extremely verbose one. Mr. Hill went on about his experiences for ages while Owain's mind wandered over to Cara's time and time again. He wondered what she was doing, if she was thinking of him, missing him. Wanting him. He wanted her terribly.

But he had tried not to think about it, instead forcing himself to take copious notes. But after about three hours Mr. Hill decided that he had talked enough for one day.

"You've got better things to do than listen to an old codger like me," he had told Owain. "And I need a little nap."

Like a schoolboy who had his eye on the clock, Owain shut his notebook and fled. He got to Cara's about half an hour after the children did.

"Do you want milk and cookies, too?" Cara asked him.

"Sounds wonderful." He stood up and followed her into the kitchen. "I might let you adopt me, too."

She turned and lifted her eyebrows. "You want me to be your mother, do you?"

A grin twisted his mouth. "Well, now that you mention it, that wasn't quite the relationship I had in mind."

She handed him a mug of milk. "I should hope not. And when you're finished eating, I'm putting you to work."

"Work? Lady, you don't know how tired I am today. I had a very strenuous night last night!"

Cara blushed and poked him in the chest. "Don't be smart. It's just peeling apples."

Owain took a bite of cookie. "That I think I can handle."

While Cara sat at her sewing machine and hemmed up the full skirt of Bronwen's princess costume, Owain peeled apples. It was about all he was good for, his concentration being otherwise totally shot. He kept glancing up, unable to tear his gaze away from Cara for longer than a few minutes. He loved looking at the burnished gold of her hair. He liked to watch the muscles of her back play under the soft cotton of her shirt as she bent over the sewing machine, moving the skirt as she sewed. He was enthralled with the way she would stop occasionally and shove an errant strand of hair back behind her left ear.

"Ow! Damn!" He popped his finger into his mouth.

"What is it?"

"Cut my finger," he mumbled.

Cara abandoned the sewing machine. Hugh and Bronwen scrambled up off the floor. He felt like an idiot.

"It's all right," he said, his voice gruff.

"Let me see."

"It's all right." The warm metallic taste of blood was filling his mouth.

"Owain." Cara glared at him sternly. Reaching for his hand, she pulled his finger out of his mouth. Blood dripped onto the counter.

"Oh, yuck," Bronwen said and hurried back to her spot on the rug.

Cara dragged Owain by the hand off the stool where he was sitting and shoved his hand under the cold water tap. Then, with the blood washed away, she looked at it more closely.

"Quite a slice," she murmured.

"Is he gonna need stitches?" Hugh obviously had all the liking for gore that his sister did not.

Owain frowned at him. "Don't sound so eager."

"Shall we take him to the 'mergency room?" Bronwen asked from the other side of the room.

Cara examined the finger again. "No. We'll just slap on a Band-Aid, I think." She shook her head, then reached for the knife that Owain still held in his other hand. "Give me that. Don't you know better than to cut toward yourself?"

"I was daydreaming."

She rolled her eyes in exasperation. "About what?"

"You." He winked at her. "About last night. About—"

"Hugh, get me a Band-Aid," she cut in. "And, Bronwen, find the antiseptic. Upstairs. Now!"

The twins scampered off.

"...and about the way you looked in the moonlight," Owain went on, undaunted, teasing her even as his own blood quickened at the memory.

"Owain O'Neill!"

"Well, you wanted an explanation."

She picked up a bar of soap from beside the sink and began to scrub his hand briskly. "I want you to hush."

"But—"

"Now. Or I will use this soap on your mouth as well."

Owain tugged on her braid. "Try it." He leaned close and whispered in her ear, "I dare you."

But she didn't, because at that moment Hugh and Bronwen came hurtling back down the stairs with the Band-Aid and the antiseptic, and Owain didn't say anything else. He did grin at her though, and he did drop a surreptitious kiss on her neck when she was bending over his hand to put the bandage on. She didn't react, except for the high color in her cheeks. But, Owain decided, that was reaction enough.

When she had finished bandaging his hand, she picked up the knife and pointed at a chair across the room. "I will finish the apples. You go sit over there, out of harm's way."

"I can't help anymore?" He gave her a hurt look.

"You can finish hemming Bron's skirt if you want." Her own grin was cheeky.

Owain shrugged. "Sure."

She stared, nonplussed. "You sew?"

"Why not? I can probably even keep my fingers out of the way of the needle, too."

Cara pointed him in the direction of the sewing machine. "Be my guest."

"I don't want to be a guest."

The words hung between them, a hint of what he hadn't yet brought himself to say. They looked at each other for a long time, Owain afraid of pushing too hard, and Cara—the way Cara looked made him hope that it wouldn't be long before he was as much a part of the family as she and the twins were.

By the end of the evening he felt he was well on his way. At Cara's invitation he had stayed to supper. And then he had shepherded the twins on their trick-or-treating route through the neighborhood.

"Don't you want to?" he had asked Cara.

"I don't mind. I've done it all the other years. Besides, this time I won't have to rush back to open the door to the rest of the neighborhood's goblins. I can just stay here with a good book and answer the bell when it rings. In fact," she added, "I'm a bit grateful not to have to be a single parent tonight."

The moment she said it, she seemed to feel as if she had gone too far. Her face flamed and she backed off at once. "I don't mean to rope you into—"

"I'm delighted," Owain assured her.

He enjoyed every minute of it. And he enjoyed reading the kids a bedtime story later, after the costumes were hung up and the makeup washed off. But he enjoyed most the time after they were tucked soundly in bed and he had their mother to himself.

He stayed with her again that night and the next, loving her for all she was worth. And he knew from the light in her eyes and the warmth in her smile that was exactly the way she was loving him.

It was time to broach the subject of his former career, he decided on his way back to Mrs. Garrity's in the still-dark of the second morning. He thought he was ready to spring the question at last. He thought she would say yes. But he had to tell her that first, not because it mattered much to him anymore, but because it would matter to her. It made demands on his time even now. It might, someday, mean that he wouldn't always live in a small Wisconsin town.

He frowned when he saw the light on in Mrs. Garrity's kitchen. And when he opened the door, she frowned, too, and slapped the bread dough she was kneading down hard on the counter.

"Out early, were you? Or is it in late?"

He could feel her disapproval. Her eyes punched him with the same ferocity that she was hammering the dough with.

He rubbed a hand around the back of his neck to ease an already loose shirt collar. "I'm an adult."

"Then act like one."

He shut the door with unaccustomed firmness. "What the hell does that mean?"

"It means that adults behave responsibly."

Owain scowled, waiting for her to continue.

"And pussyfooting around at all hours of the night and coming in at the crack of dawn when you've been over at Cara Williams's is not responsible!"

"How the hell do you know where I've been?"

"This isn't Los Angeles. It's a small town, in case you've forgotten. And I'm sure I'm not the only one who knows you were with Cara Williams all last night." And others, she might as well have added.

"Gossip." Owain snorted angrily.

"Could be." Mrs. Garrity flipped the dough down again and smacked it. "But gossip is no worse than them that make it possible."

Owain sucked in a sharp breath.

"You love her?" Mrs. Garrity demanded.

He nodded. There was no playing games with Mrs. Garrity.

"Then marry her."

"I want to, damn it. Give me a chance to propose!"

"So what are you waiting for?"

"We've only known each other about two weeks."

"How long does it take?"

"There are things to discuss, for heaven's sake!"

"Then discuss 'em," Mrs. Garrity said implacably. "But until you have, stay away from her house overnight. Cara's got kids and a reputation to protect."

Owain tucked his hands into his pockets. "Yeah. You're probably right." He moved to go past her up the stairs. Mrs. Garrity reached out and patted his shoulder as he went by.

"Talk fast," she advised.

He would. Tonight.

"DINNER?" Cara said when he called her on the phone. "Go *out* to dinner? Tonight?"

"I know it's short notice," he said. "But—"

She sighed. "I can't."

He felt a tension begin to work between his shoulders. "Can't?"

"I have to spend the evening with Mr. Trevorrow going over his books. We set it up weeks ago. I'm sorry." He could hear real regret in her voice. The tension vanished.

"Tomorrow then?"

"I'd love to."

"Good."

A pause hung in the air then, neither of them willing to hang up, neither able to think of anything further to say. At last Owain managed something. "I'm going to go interview your grandmother this afternoon. Then, if it's okay, I thought I'd come by and get the kids. We need to get started on the guy."

"You don't *have* to do that, you know," Cara told him quickly. "They won't mind."

"I want to. Besides, it's part of their heritage."

"What?"

"They...they told me, when we were discussing names, that they're part Welsh. That makes them British. And Guy Fawkes Day is a British celebration."

"If you say so."

"I'll be over about three-thirty."

He would have preferred talking to her tonight. Typically, when he finally decided to do something, he didn't like waiting around. But obviously he had no choice.

Still, he wished he could have done it sooner, for not only had Mrs. Garrity given him hard looks that morning, but Cara's grandmother gave him a few in the course of the afternoon.

It was an odd afternoon. They seemed to hit it off beautifully most of the time. She warmed to him immediately when it came to telling him about her experiences. She was a born storyteller, and Owain enjoyed listening. But when things ventured into a more contemporary set of topics after they had closed the formal interview, she seemed to become a bit more distant.

"You certainly have become a big part of my granddaughter's life recently," she remarked over a pot of tea and a plate of homemade raisin cookies.

Owain nodded. "I'd like to become an even bigger part," he told her honestly.

"Is this serious, then?"

"I'm serious."

"Why?"

He was momentarily taken aback. Then he said firmly, "Because I've fallen in love with her."

Mrs. Nute looked at him steadily. He felt as if she were seeing clear to the depths of his soul. Everything in him wanted to squirm away out of her sight. But he held fast, meeting her gaze, letting her look into his heart.

At last he saw a hint of a smile and a look of satisfaction cross her face. He didn't know what sort of gauntlet he had just run. But whatever the test, he seemed to have passed.

"I'm so glad," was the only thing she said.

The conversation drifted then with her asking him about the other people he had interviewed, with him asking her as much as he dared about Cara and the kids. It was nearly three-thirty when he finally recollected the time and made his excuses.

"I'll be back in a week or so, if that's all right?"

"I'll be looking forward to it," she told him as she walked him to the door. "If I come across my father's diaries, I'll have them ready for you. Or if I see Cara sooner, I'll send them along."

He took her hand. "That would be great. Having his recollections of his own experiences will be a real plus. Thanks." He pressed her hand between his.

"Not good enough," she said and reached up, pulling down his head and giving him a papery-soft kiss on the cheek.

He blushed.

She smiled. "Go on with you now. Don't keep my great-grandchildren waiting."

He went, smiling, his fingers stroking the spot on his cheek where she had kissed him. It was as if she had given him her blessing.

Hugh and Bronwen appeared quite ready to give him their blessing as well.

Shortly after he arrived to choruses of "You're awful late!" and "We thought you weren't comin' at all!" they confided to him that they had seen the way he had kissed their mother when he thought they weren't looking.

"We wanted you to know we don't mind," Bronwen told him gravely.

"We think it's a good idea, really," Hugh added.

"What are you three whispering about?" Cara asked from the other side of the room where she was scowling at her computer screen.

"Owain kissing you," said Bronwen frankly.

Cara spun around in her office chair, her eyes wide with consternation.

"We were saying we didn't mind." Hugh gave his mother a benevolent smile.

"Hugh!" She looked as if she might like to strangle him. "That's not polite."

"But it's the truth."

"Anyway," Owain put in easily, coming to her rescue, "it isn't as if I hadn't had the same idea myself."

Their eyes locked, both of them remembering the kisses they had shared when no prying eyes had seen them. Owain felt the warmth begin to build within him. He looked away. "Let's get busy here, troops. Creating a guy is a serious job."

The guy consisted of one of his flannel shirts, a pair of Cara's old jeans, a gunnysack face, and Cara's old gardening gloves. They stuffed him with rags and newspapers until he was positively fat and propped him on the couch.

Nestor hissed at him. Cara turned away from her computer long enough to say he was lovely and to remark that now she knew why people celebrated Guy Fawkes Day.

"Why?" Owain asked.

"To get rid of all their old rags and papers, of course."

He tossed a wad of torn-up sheeting at her. "Where's your sense of history, woman?"

She shook her head, smiling. "A pragmatic computer operator like me? I don't have one."

"I suppose I'll have to have enough for both of us then," he said, getting up from where he sat on the floor.

Cara didn't reply for a moment. Then she said, "I suppose you will."

Then it was Cara who looked away, turning back to the computer and typing something in very fast, then closing her program and standing up. "Well, I've got to get going if I'm going to see Mr. Trevorrow. Suzy will be along to fix dinner, guys," she said to the kids.

"Why can't Owain do it?" Hugh asked.

"We're not imposing on Owain for everything," his mother said briskly. She turned and headed up the stairs.

Owain followed her to the bottom of them. "Yet."

The one word stopped her midflight. She turned and looked down at him, questions and hopes mingled in her eyes.

He gave her a smile. "Tomorrow night. I'll pick you up at seven."

SHE ANSWERED THE DOOR wearing a full-length navy velvet skirt. The rich fabric draped her hips beautifully, and the skirt's dark simplicity contrasted with the Victorian frills of the high-necked, full-sleeved blouse she wore. The multitude of tiny pearl buttons that climbed the front ended in a cameo brooch at her throat. Owain wondered if the pulse that beat beneath it was racing anywhere near as fast as his own.

He had never seen her looking like this. But his imagination couldn't have done it better. It was totally Cara—proper but tempting, demure and yet alluring. And it definitely put the lie to the notion that she had no sense of history. She looked like history incarnate. The sort of history he wanted to know more and more about.

Owain wondered if he would have the patience to undo all those buttons. He grimaced wryly, tossing a backward glance at Mrs. Garrity's across the park. He didn't even need to worry about it. Until they were married, he wouldn't have a chance to test his self-control!

Her hair wasn't pulled back or knotted on top of her head for once. Instead it cascaded down her back, pulled just behind her ears with a navy velvet ribbon. He longed to untie the ribbon and run his hands through the long golden waves.

"Wow," he muttered.

Cara smiled. Suzy giggled.

"I could say the same myself," Cara told him, her eyes raking him with the same thoroughness that his had traversed her.

"Me, too," Suzy breathed. "You have all the luck," she told her friend. "Look, he even blushes."

He ought to be used to it, Owain knew. Women had considered him a sex object often enough in his performing days. But that had rarely bothered him. *This* was different. *This* was Cara. And the way her eyes lingered as they took in his dark suit, pale blue shirt and burgundy-and-navy rep tie made him swallow hard. He knew he had done precisely the same thing, but it didn't make him less self-conscious.

"The kids are to be in bed at eight-thirty," Cara was telling Suzy. "Did you hear that?" she asked the twins.

"Yes, Mom," they chorused. They were lying on the floor watching something on television, but they turned and gave her angelic smiles. She gave them a worried look in return. Her eyes flickered up to Owain's, as if to ask, "What are they up to?" He shrugged, then gave them a conspiratorial wink.

Hugh giggled.

"Mind Suzy," Owain said sternly.

"You sound like a father," Bronwen told him. Then, "Ouch," she squeaked as Hugh kicked her.

"Go on." Suzy urged them out the door. "I'll handle these two. Just have a good time. Don't hurry."

"No," Owain promised as he held the door for Cara. "We won't."

A full moon hung just above the treetops, lighting everything with a silvery sheen softened by the occasional drifting cloud. The night reminded Owain of porcelain, beautiful and fragile. He hoped he had the grace to handle it without breaking it. He knew marriages to rock stars—even former rock stars—weren't easy. Dougal was on his second wife. The first one, Marilyn, hadn't lasted a year. Karin, so far, had lasted eight. But it had been a struggle for them. Mike had been divorced twice. Owain thought he was past the rough spots since he was out of performing. But he still wrote. And periodically the pressure came to go back on the road again. Every time Dougal came up with a new idea, you could almost count on the word "tour" being mentioned. Owain had resisted. But who knew how another person—how a whole family—would handle such pressure?

He sighed.

Cara smiled up at him. "You sound like I feel. I can't believe I'm going out tonight."

"We should have done it before." He helped her into the car and shut the door after her, then went around and got in on the driver's side.

She was still smiling at him in the darkness. "I guess. But I'm glad we waited."

"Why?"

"It's sort of like Christmas, I guess. Worth waiting for."

He leaned over and kissed her lightly on the lips. The passion that always lingered just beneath the surface when he was around her flared to life and he groaned.

"What's the matter?" Her voice was tender.

"You're saying all the wrong things."

Her eyes widened. "I am?"

"If you want dinner, that is."

She straightened up in the seat and folded her hands demurely in her lap. "Lead on, kind sir," she said.

He laughed and put the car in gear, then reached over and folded his fingers around hers.

"Where are we going?" Cara asked him moments later when he drove past the last restaurant in town and headed out onto the highway.

"You'll see."

He had asked Suzy and Mrs. Garrity, soliciting suggestions for the best possible place.

"The most romantic, you mean?" Mrs. Garrity had asked hopefully.

"The most romantic, he means," Suzy said.

They agreed that meant The King's Men. It was a supper club nestled in the rolling western Wisconsin hills about seven miles outside of town. The waiters and waitresses wore Elizabethan costumes, torches in wall sconces provided most of the light, Suzy told him. And the menu, though limited, was reputed to be excellent.

"If you want to go all out, that's it," Suzy said.

Owain did.

"Cara will love it," Mrs. Garrity predicted and walked out of the room humming the "Wedding March."

And it was obvious from Cara's shining eyes and stunned smile when Owain pulled into the parking lot, that Cara did.

"But, Owain," she protested when he urged her out of the car and up the walk toward the heavy oak door. "It's so expensive!"

"It's all right."

"But grad students can't afford—"

"I can," he said firmly and opened the door onto the stone-flagged anteroom. Cara preceded him, looking around her as if she were trying to absorb all sensations at once. Soft lute music enveloped them. The smell of roasting beef and heady wine mingled with pungent spices. A tall woman in a long brocade gown welcomed them and led them to a table, handing them menus written in early English script.

Cara laughed. "You're trying to develop my sense of history."

"You mean, if it isn't a computer program, you can't read it?"

"Something like that." She closed the menu and looked across the table at him. "Anyway, I'll put myself in your hands tonight. Whatever you choose."

"I hope you mean that."

He ordered for them both, then sat back looking at her, simply enjoying her enjoyment. He wanted to do this more often. He wished, despite what she had said and how happy her words had made him, that they had done this before. It was the sort of thing that was missing from her life. She did all the basics, and she did them well. Superlatively well, he admitted to himself. But she needed occasionally to be surprised by joy. A touch of unexpected pleasure never hurt anyone.

The waiter brought him a bottle of burgundy to try. He nodded and poured them each a glass, then handed Cara hers around the flickering candle. Lifting his own, he touched it to hers gently.

"To us."

Cara swallowed audibly. The candle flames sparkled in her eyes. They seemed unusually bright. Were those tears? Owain wondered.

"To us." Her voice cracked. Then, to cover her embarrassment, she took a long swallow, choked and started to cough.

"Oh, heavens," she mumbled, obviously mortified. She was laughing and fumbling with her napkin. "I ought not to be let out in public!"

Owain shook his head. "No. I think you just need more practice. We'll have to do this more often."

"We can't afford to do *this* more often," Cara said flatly, her eyes taking in the expensive ambience.

"That's something we have to talk about."

Cara's brows lifted.

The waiter came with the meal then—thick slices of roast beef medium rare, served with thick crusty homemade bread and fresh carrots cooked just until they were tender. In the background a recorder joined the lute in songs that ranged from sprightly to soulful as they wove their spell.

The waiter left again and before Cara picked up her fork, she looked at him levelly. "What do we have to talk about?"

Owain took a deep breath and wished he'd had more time. "Money. And me. I . . . I'm not just a grad student, Cara."

"Oh?" There was a wealth of curiosity in the one word.

"I—" Oh hell, now he was going to sound like a pompous ass. "I'm a grad student now, but that wasn't what I always was. You know how you were wondering whether I was working for my dad in his electronics firm?"

She nodded, waiting for him to go on.

"Well, I wasn't. It never interested me. Poetry interested me. And music. And...and history..." *Cripes, man, get to the point,* he badgered himself.

She smiled brightly, still waiting.

"You know the rock group, Cardiff Connection?" he asked finally, desperately.

"Of course."

"I was one of them."

She stared at him as if she had never seen him before. Then she asked cautiously, "You were a member of Cardiff Connection?"

"Yeah." He ducked his head, watching his own fingers drum lightly on the tabletop.

For a long moment she didn't say anything. Then she ventured, "You must have a great deal of money then."

"Uh-huh." He still didn't look at her.

"Goodness."

He glanced up to see her take a long swallow of her wine. "I couldn't let you go on thinking that the only thing I was—or ever had been—was some history student." He swirled his own wine around his glass, watching the flickering of the candlelight in the burgundy liquid. "Because my life is more complicated than that."

"I'll bet it is." Cara's tone was matter-of-fact. He couldn't tell if she was pleased or displeased. She seemed simply to accept it. "You're not performing anymore though, are you?" she went on. "I mean, Martin and I had a couple of your records. But I don't recall seeing any new ones lately."

Owain shook his head. "Not for the past four years. Now I just write material for them. But sometimes Dougal—he's one of the guys in the group—wants more. Dougal still works as a single. And he's not immune to pressures to get the group together again."

"Do you think you will?"

"No. I pretty much go my own way these days. But I'm not as anonymous as I'd like to be."

"You seem to be around here," Cara said dryly.

"Thank God. I prefer it. If people know who I am, they..." He shrugged. "They..."

"They love you for your money and your fame and not yourself?"

He met her eyes. "Yes."

She took another sip of her wine.

"You didn't," he said softly.

"No."

"I was just Owain O'Neill, grad student, for you."

"Um-hmm. And I was just Cara Williams, small-town woman, to you," Cara said with a self-deprecating smile.

"You are the most important person in my life. I need to know how you feel about me now," he said carefully. "Now that you know . . ."

"Know your deep dark secret?" she teased.

He made a face. "In some places it's hardly deep, and there was a time I couldn't walk down the street without someone knowing who I was."

"Must be tough." She grinned at him, then sobered. "I shouldn't tease you about it. I suspect it could be . . . very rough. At least I know when people like me they like me for myself."

"I love you," Owain told her softly.

The recorder broke into a jaunty folk tune just behind them. Cara didn't even blink. Owain held his breath.

"I love you, too," she said.

"All of me?"

"All of you."

When he asked her to marry him, she said yes.

ALL THE NEXT DAY he walked around hugging the secret to himself. In typical Owain O'Neill fashion, he had wanted to go home, wake the kids and tell them the news. Cara, more practical, had said no.

"They won't go back to sleep," she told him.

"So? I'm not planning on sleeping much either."

"But you'll be at Mrs. Garrity's, remember?" He had told her about Mrs. Garrity's demand that he preserve her reputation. Cara had smiled, then had agreed that it wasn't a bad idea, considering.

Owain gave her a glum look in response, then shrugged. "Okay. But when? After we get you a ring?"

Cara considered that. "Not a bad idea. Hugh and Bronwen would probably believe a ring."

"You don't think they'll believe it otherwise?"

"I think six-year-olds are literal-minded. If they don't have a ring to believe in, they'll probably insist that you drag me off to Las Vegas tonight."

"I would," Owain offered.

"We can wait," Cara said.

"Like Christmas again?" he said sourly.

"Not that long. When can we get a ring?"

"Tomorrow."

"I have to go into Madison tomorrow," she said. "With Mr. Trevorrow, to talk to a tax man."

Owain grimaced. "The man is a menace. All right, then, I'll get it myself. Tell me your size."

When she told him, he jotted it on a scrap of paper and stuck it in his wallet. Then he said, "We can tell them at the bonfire on Guy Fawkes Day. With a celebration and everything."

"Perfect," Cara agreed. The kiss she gave him as they stood on the doorstep made him inwardly curse small-town gossips. Even harder was having to walk Suzy home through the park.

But he managed, and he managed to hold his tongue too. And the following morning while Cara was in Madison with Mr. Trevorrow and the kids were in school, he bought a ring.

The speculative glances he got at Penhallow's jewelry store assured him that the gossips would have plenty to talk about tonight whether he spent it at Cara's or not.

"You're looking smug," Mrs. Garrity said to him when he got back.

"I am?" Owain gave her an innocent smile.

"Ah." He heard satisfaction in her sigh. Then she tossed him a glance over her shoulder. "Seeing as everything is right with the world these days, could you do me a favor in the morning?"

Feeling magnanimous, he grinned at her. "Sure. What?"

"Mr. Hill keeps telling me his reading light is shorting out. I think it's his ancient old lamp he insists on using, but he thinks it's the wiring. Could you check it out?"

"You bet."

IT TURNED OUT that Mr. Hill was right. It was the outlet and it needed replacing. Tucking the ring in his pocket, Owain went to the hardware store to get a new one. He drove past Cara's, giving the house a longing glance. Her car wasn't there either. He wondered if he would have to wait all day.

When he got back, Mrs. Garrity beamed at him. "You're a jewel, Owain," she told him as he went through the kitchen on his way up to Mr. Hill's room. "Oh, by the way. Cara came over. Said she had some diaries for you—from her grandmother. They're in your room."

And he had missed her. Damn. Oh, well. "When did she come by?"

"About forty-five minutes ago."

"Did you say I'd be right back?"

"She didn't seem inclined to want to wait. Actually when she came down, she seemed in a hurry to get home."

Owain stopped on the stairway. "Came down?"

"I told her to take them on up."

"Oh, God." He could feel the blood drain from his face. He turned and bolted up the stairs three at a time.

The diaries were on his bed. Three thin, leather-bound volumes. But he scarcely looked at them. His eyes went right to the nightstand beside his bed. Right to the scattered pile of sheet music and, on top of them, the now worn photos of Hugh and Bronwen.

"God, no," he murmured. He walked over to the nightstand and stood staring down at it. The pictures hadn't been moved. Nothing had changed.

He hoped.

He turned and, checking in his pocket for the ring box, as if it might work as a lucky rabbit's foot somehow, he hurtled back down the stairs.

"Hey, where's my outlet?" Mr. Hill called after him in a querulous voice.

"Later. I'll put it in later," he called over his shoulder.

He shot through the kitchen, leaving Mrs. Garrity staring after him, her jaw sagging, and he took off at a dead run across the park.

He hammered on Cara's door, his heart in his throat, praying every prayer of supplication he could ever remember. She took forever answering.

"Cara!"

Nestor hopped up on the porch and wove between Owain's legs, purring.

He pounded again. "Cara!"

At last the door opened. Bare inches.

Cara stood gripping the side of it, knuckles white, her eyes wide and wounded, her mouth tight.

"Cara?"

He really didn't have to ask if she knew.

She did.

Chapter Seven

"You're their father."

The words hit him like stones in the gut.

"Listen, Cara, I can explain."

A tiny muscle in her jaw twitched. Otherwise she moved not at all. "What's to explain?" Her voice was wooden, flat.

A chain saw ripped through the stillness half a block away.

"I want to come in."

For a moment he thought she would shut the door in his face. Then she simply gave an indifferent shrug, turned on her heel and walked back into the house, leaving him to follow if he would.

He shut the door behind him carefully, as if a loud noise would somehow make things worse. It was irrational. Nothing could make things worse, and he knew it.

"Cara . . ."

"You *are* their father." Her voice was hard now, cutting.

Their eyes met. Hers challenged, daring him to deny it, begging him to. He wished he could. His head dipped. His own knuckles were as white as hers. He felt sick, bile scorching his throat. He gulped, then looked up again to meet her accusing stare.

"Yes."

"Why?" Anguished.

"Why what?"

"Why didn't you just come right out and tell me? Why did you have to—" her voice broke, she spun away "—have to *lie*?"

"I didn't lie. I . . . I just—" He floundered, drowning, wondering how he had possibly ever thought he could explain. Why me? he wanted to ask. Why now? For God's sake, why *now*?

She had taken refuge behind one of the overstuffed chairs in the family room as if there whatever he said to her couldn't hurt her anymore.

"You wanted to get them."

"No! I only wanted to see them. Just to know . . . to know they were all right."

Cara stared at him, disbelieving.

"That's why I came. Why I was in the park."

"Lurking."

He made a wry face. "Yeah, that's what it seemed like to me too."

"Because that's exactly what you were doing! Sly, underhanded . . ." Her voice rose, rage making it quiver.

Owain's fingers clenched on the tabletop. "Would you rather that I'd just walked up to them and said, 'Hi, I'm your old man'?"

"I'd rather you'd never come at all!"

He jerked away from the table and walked toward her. "You don't mean that."

"I mean every word."

"Cara, I love you."

She snorted.

"*You* love *me*!"

"Shut up." She turned her head, hiding her face behind the cloud of golden hair that hung over her shoulders.

"Cara, be reasonable!" He reached for her, flinching himself when she jerked away from him. "You wouldn't have wanted me to just walk into your life and announce who I was.''

"You think I'd rather have you sneak in on false pretenses? Worm your way in and pretend to fall in love with me so that—"

"I *do* love you. I'm *not* pretending!"

"Says you." She gave him a scornful look.

"Cara!"

"Damn you! You come waltzing into my life, acting like the greatest thing since sliced bread. Mr. Oh-so-sincere. Mr. I-just-love-your-kids-lady." She slammed her fist against the mantel, rattling the knickknacks, making the barometer jump. "You liar! How dare you come around the other night just to set things straight? Set things straight! There's a laugh. You tell me you were afraid to let me know who you were because everyone wanted something from you. Who the hell are you to talk?"

"Cara, damn it, I don't want the kids from you."

"No, you just want to weasel in here and share them for the moment. God knows what you'd have wanted if I'd married you!"

"You are going to marry me. You said so."

"Well, sweetheart," she drawled, "I changed my mind."

"Cara, I don't care whose kids they are. It isn't important. I love them, sure. But I'd have loved them if they'd been Martin's or anybody else's."

She gave him a hard glare. "Pardon me if I don't believe you. You wouldn't have been here in the first place, would you, if it hadn't been for the kids? All that garbage about the dissertation was just that, wasn't it? Garbage!"

"No, it wasn't." He strode across the room and grabbed her arm, hauling her down on the sofa next to him, holding her though she struggled against him. "Listen to me."

Cara's jaw set in a mutinous hard line; her body went rigid, radiating hostility.

"Listen." He tried to sound calmer than he felt.

HARLEQUIN

❤ PRESENTS ❤

A Real Sweetheart of a Deal!

7 FREE GIFTS

PEEL BACK THIS CARD AND SEE WHAT YOU CAN GET! THEN...

Complete the Hand Inside ➤

It's easy! To play your cards right, just match this card with the cards inside.

Turn over for more details . . .

Incredible isn't it? Deal yourself in <u>right now</u> and get 7 fabulous gifts.
ABSOLUTELY FREE.

1. 4 BRAND NEW HARLEQUIN AMERICAN ROMANCE NOVELS – FREE!
Sit back and enjoy the excitement, romance and thrills of four fantastic novels. You'll receive them as part of this winning streak!

2. A BEAUTIFUL AND PRACTICAL PEN AND WATCH – FREE!
This watch with its leather strap and digital read-out certainly looks elegant – but it is also extremely practical. Its quartz crystal movement keeps precision time! And the pen with its slim good looks will make writing a pleasure.

3. AN EXCITING MYSTERY BONUS – FREE!
And still your luck holds! You'll also receive a special mystery bonus. You'll be thrilled with this surprise gift. It will be the source of many compliments as well as a useful and attractive addition to your home.

PLUS

THERE'S MORE. THE DECK IS STACKED IN YOUR FAVOR. HERE ARE THREE MORE WINNING POINTS. YOU'LL ALSO RECEIVE:

4. A MONTHLY NEWSLETTER – FREE!
It's "Heart to Heart" – the insider's privileged look at our most popular writers, upcoming books and even recipes from your favorite authors.

5. CONVENIENT HOME DELIVERY
Imagine how you'll enjoy having the chance to preview the romantic adventures of our Harlequin heroines in the convenience of your own home at less than retail prices! Here's how it works. Every month we'll deliver 4 new books right to your door. There's no obligation and if you decide to keep them, they'll be yours for only $2.49! That's 26¢ less per book than what you pay in stores. And there's no extra charge for shipping and handling.

6. MORE GIFTS FROM TIME TO TIME – FREE!
It's easy to see why you have the winning hand. In addition to all the other special deals available only to our home subscribers, you can look forward to additional free gifts throughout the year.

SO DEAL YOURSELF IN – YOU CAN'T HELP BUT WIN!

You'll Fall In Love With This Sweetheart Deal From Harlequin!

HARLEQUIN READER SERVICE
FREE OFFER CARD

PLACE YOUR WINNING CARD HERE!

4 FREE BOOKS • DIGITAL WATCH AND MATCHING PEN • FREE MYSTERY BONUS • INSIDER'S NEWSLETTER • HOME DELIVERY • MORE SURPRISE GIFTS

☐ *Yes! Deal me in. Please send me four free Harlequin American Romance novels, the pen and watch and my* **free mystery gift** *as explained on the opposite page.*

154 CIA NA8B

First Name		Last Name
PLEASE PRINT		
Address		Apt.
City	State	
Zip Code		

Offer limited to one per household and not valid for present subscribers. Prices subject to change.

HARLEQUIN NO RISK GUARANTEE
- There is no obligation to buy – the free books and gifts remain yours to keep.
- You pay the lowest price possible – and receive books before they're available in stores
- You may end your subscription at any time – just let us know.

Remember! To win this hand, all you have to do is place your sticker inside and DETACH AND MAIL THE CARD BELOW. You'll get four free books, a free pen and watch and an exciting mystery bonus.

BUT DON'T DELAY! MAIL US YOUR LUCKY CARD TODAY!

If card has been removed write to: Harlequin Reader Service, 901 Fuhrmann Blvd., P.O. Box 1394, Buffalo, N.Y. 14240-1394

She turned her head away from him. He held her wrists in his hands and he tugged on them gently.

"Cara?"

"I'm listening." The words came through clenched teeth.

"I came because I got the kids' pictures in the mail about six months ago. Their natural mother died, and among her effects was an envelope with my name on it. One of her relatives sent it on." He leaned toward her, holding her hands a fraction more loosely now. "And that was what started it."

He told her everything—all about Meg, about her background, about how at the time he hadn't been grown-up enough to take the responsibility for anyone save himself. He told her that both he and Meg had wanted the best for the kids. And he told her about Meg being adopted, about her fantasy of having her own natural parents find her, about wanting to be sure herself later on that her own child was happy.

He didn't know if he was getting through to her at all. She sat in stony silence, listening. At least he hoped she listened, while he spilled his guts.

"Anyway, it wasn't for them," he concluded at last, "that I stayed. It was for you. When I first saw you, something in me twisted up—"

"Your conscience maybe?" she said sarcastically.

He gave her a hard stare. She subsided, but if sarcasm was all the reaction he was going to get, things didn't look good.

"It was you, Cara. Not them. You. The rest of it... Hell, I don't know.... It wasn't important."

"It was important enough for you to have spent six months of your life looking for them."

"It was something I had to do."

She snorted. "You could have left once you saw I didn't beat them."

"I intended to. I wanted to," he confessed. "At least a part of me did. But another part of me didn't. Couldn't. I don't know whether it was because I wanted to know them better or because I had met you,'' he said honestly.

"Don't blame this on me."

"I'm not. I'm only saying how it was for me. I was envying Martin. I thought he had it all."

"And when you found out he was dead, you thought you'd just step in and take over."

Put that baldly it sounded a hell of a lot more crass than it felt. Owain released her hands and pressed his own against his eyes. He leaned his elbows on his knees. There was nothing much else he could say.

Cara didn't say anything either.

At last he sighed heavily and looked up at her. "It wasn't premeditated, Cara. You have to know that. I don't do things that way."

She chewed her lower lip as she stared across the room, refusing to look at him. Her eyes were bright with unshed tears. He saw her throat work convulsively. Suddenly she jumped to her feet and fled into the kitchen, burying her emotions in the clatter of doing the breakfast dishes. Her stiff spine and shaking shoulders said the words she would never say.

Owain heaved himself to his feet and stood helplessly, wanting to go up behind her and put his arms around her, wanting to comfort her, and knowing it was impossible. He wanted to tell her it didn't matter. But to her it did.

"Cara?" He ventured as far as the counter that separated the kitchen from the family room.

She thumped a frying pan into the dish drainer.

He drummed his fingers on the counter, then ran a hand through his hair. His other hand slipped into his pocket, clenching around the velvet ring box.

"So what are we going to do?" he asked.

She didn't turn around. "I stay. You go."

"Go?"

"Go. Away. For good. Forever. And—" she turned now and met his gaze fiercely "—*don't come back*! Bronwen and Hugh are my children now. They're mine and Martin's. Not yours! You had no right. You *have* no right!" She glared at him through red-rimmed eyes, then swiped at them ineffectually with the dish towel. "Just go away, Owain O'Neill." She spat his name. "Get out of my life!"

She tossed the towel onto the counter and brushed past him, heading for the stairs.

For a moment he just stood, dumbstruck, and watched her go. Then, frantic, grasping at whatever straw he could, he called after her. "Cara?"

She stopped with her hand on the newel post, but she didn't turn.

"What about tonight?"

"What *about* tonight?"

"It's Guy Fawkes Day. We're supposed to burn the guy."

"*We* will burn him." As opposed to "you," he heard in her tone.

"The kids are expecting me."

"They can take the disappointment," Cara said flatly.

"No."

"What do you mean, no?" The tonelessness disappeared from her voice. It was ragged again, angry. Owain didn't know which was worse.

"I mean I won't disappoint them. I said I'd be here."

"And you're always so responsible."

He winced at her words. "I won't disappoint them," he repeated.

"Tell me again how it wasn't the kids you were interested in then?" Cara baited him.

"I—"

"Don't bother." She turned away again and gave a negligent shrug. "Come if you must."

She disappeared up the stairs. He heard the door to her bedroom close. He stood rooted to the spot. Finally the brush of the cat's tail against his ankles roused him. Nestor walked to the door and stood looking at Owain expectantly.

"You want me to leave, too, huh?" he muttered. Reaching over absently, he opened the door and let the cat out.

Half a minute later Cara reappeared at the top of the stairs. "Oh," she said, her displeasure obvious when she saw him still standing there. "I thought you'd left."

"I let the cat out."

"But you're going."

He wished it had contained the slightest hint of question. It didn't. He took a last look around the room, his eyes lingering on Bronwen's hair ribbons scattered on the sewing table, on Hugh's soccer shoes, on the kite he had given them now stuck behind the chair.

"I'm going," he said heavily.

He went.

THE NIGHT WAS like dark crystal, clear and delicate, its stillness shattered by Hugh's shouts and the slam of the storm door behind him as he came running out of the house. He raced ahead of Owain, who carried the guy into the yard.

Cara stayed in the house.

"Don'tcha want to come, Ma?" Hugh had asked her moments before.

Cara had shaken her head. "I'm getting a cold," she had said. And her bloodshot eyes and blotchy nose made it sound like the truth.

The truth, Owain knew, was that she would have nothing more to do with him. If he had hoped she might have had a change of heart over the afternoon, he had hoped in vain. She hadn't even come down the stairs when he had arrived to help the kids get the pile of trash ready to burn.

"Mom's upstairs," Bronny had told him. "She isn't feeling good."

"Maybe you should go up and see her," Hugh suggested.

But Owain hadn't dared. "Let her rest," he had said quietly. "Maybe she'll come down in a while."

She had, but only long enough to tug a cap down over Bronny's ears and to admonish Hugh about staying back from the blaze. She hadn't even greeted Owain. The kids had looked from one to the other of them, their expectant faces turning slowly grim. And then they had all gone out. All but Cara, that is.

Owain felt a sort of helpless rage. But the person who made him angriest was the last person he could rail against. Instead he set to work, hauling wood for the bonfire, kicking the branches into a heap, wiping his filthy hands on the sides of his jeans. Several of Hugh and Bronwen's school friends came over, and the children lent their hands, dragging more wood, old cardboard boxes and heaps of dry leaves to the mound. At last, when it was nearly as tall as he was, Owain put the guy on top.

"Now?" Hugh demanded, hopping from one foot to the other. "Can we light 'im now?"

"In a minute. Go get your mother."

But Bronwen had already gone. "Come on," he heard her urging Cara, and he saw her tugging her mother by the hand down the steps. "Just for a few minutes, Mom?"

Cara didn't want to, and Owain knew it. But she knew about not disappointing children, too. She let her daughter haul her down the steps.

"Can I light it?" Hugh asked.

Owain looked at Cara. "Can he?"

"Why ask me?"

"You're his mother."

Cara stared at him. He willed her to say the words he knew she would never say. *You're his father.* She let her breath out slowly, leaving in the air a lingering cloud of frost. "He can light it."

Owain helped Hugh with the match, cupping his hands around it as Hugh struck it and then touched it to the newspaper clumped at the base of the bonfire.

It caught quickly, a bright orange swoosh shooting upward. The paper crackled and snapped. Owain snatched Hugh back and lifted him high onto his shoulders, stepping back to join Cara and Bronwen. The other children clustered around, silent now as they watched the flames lick higher and higher.

Dark shadows of bare trees loomed overhead, forked against the sky. A silver cast of moonlight couldn't even compete with the searing red of the flames. How different it was from last night, when moonlight had seemed to say it all.

He glanced at Cara. She stood motionless with Bronwen in front of her, her hands resting on her daughter's shoulders, kneading them softly as a cat might. Owain remembered their touch and felt the pain rip through him. But he couldn't bring himself to look away.

"There he goes!" Hugh yelled. "It's gettin' his feet. Look!"

The tattered old bedroom slippers they had stuck on the guy had disappeared into the flames. Seconds later the hems of Cara's old worn-out jeans were engulfed. Beside him Cara tensed.

"It's pagan," she muttered.

"Historical," he corrected.

"I don't have much use for history," she said.

"There's a rhyme, isn't there?" a tiny blond boy called Matthew interrupted before Owain could comment. "My mom says she heard one once."

"There is," Owain agreed.

"D'you know it?"

Owain nodded.

"Say it! Say it!" Bronwen urged, her eyes shining. Looking into them Owain remembered other nights—nights like this one when he was a child, eyes like hers, only his mother's eyes. Memories flooded him as the words echoed in his head.

"Remember, remember the fifth of November,
Gunpowder, treason and plot.
I see no reason why gunpowder treason
Should ever be forgot."

He said the words slowly, quietly, so that the children had to strain to hear him over the crackle of the flames. His voice cracked on the last word and he took a deep shuddering breath, smoke catching in his lungs.

He looked at Cara. She was looking at him.

Treason, her eyes accused. Treason.

"What's treason?" the blond boy asked.

"Betrayal," Cara said. "Letting someone down." Her eyes never left Owain's. And he knew that, like Guy Fawkes, he was going to go a long time before his own betrayal was forgotten.

The smoke stung his eyes. He chewed on his lip, unable to meet Cara's eyes any longer. A branch snapped and the guy crumpled to the earth, consumed by the flames.

Then, while they stood there, the fire died down, the flames diminished, flickering, then gradually burning out. In less than half an hour all that remained were a few glowing embers and a pile of ashes.

Like their relationship.

"Damn," Owain said under his breath.

"So fast," Bronwen mourned. She leaned back against her mother, then nuzzled her cheek against her mother's arm.

"Let's make another," Hugh suggested.

"One is enough," said Cara.

Hugh made a face, but seeing the firm refusal on his mother's face, he turned and picked up a stick to poke at the embers with instead.

"Be careful," Cara said sharply. "It's hot."

"Not for long, Mrs. Williams," Matthew said. "It'll be stone cold by morning."

Owain walked away, the taste of ashes in his mouth.

"Well," he heard Cara say, her tone brighter now. Probably because he had crossed the yard, he thought grimly. "That's it, folks. Scoot on home. I'll watch you until you're safe inside, Matthew, Jeremy and Sarah. See you tomorrow. And you two—" she directed these words at Hugh and Bronwen "—it's time for baths and bed."

The neighbor trio dashed across the park. Owain watched them disappear without a backward glance. But he saw Cara keep an eye on them until they were safely indoors. Then she took the stick away from Hugh and scattered the ashes herself. She never even glanced at Owain.

"Can we have some cocoa, Ma?" Hugh begged. "Please? I'm thirsty."

Cara shook her head. "It's late, Hugh. After nine. And you have school tomorrow. Enough is enough."

"Aw." Hugh's lower lip went out. He turned on the porch and glowered at her.

"Hugh!" Owain said sharply. "Mind your mother."

Cara whipped around and glared at him. "I can handle this myself, thank you very much."

Owain tucked his hands into his pockets. "Yes, I know," he said quietly.

Their gazes locked for a long moment. It seemed like forever, and yet it still wasn't long enough for everything their eyes had to say.

"Night, Owain," Hugh said hesitantly.

Owain reluctantly shifted his gaze away from Cara to the small boy with his arm hooked around the porch support who was looking at him. He remembered when he was eleven and had seen his own father off to America. He hadn't really realized then how long those two years would be until he saw his father again. It had seemed a lifetime.

But it was nothing, he knew now, compared to the eternity that his life would be if he never saw Cara or Hugh or Bronwen again. Damn it, why was she doing this to them? His throat tightened. He swallowed trying to ease it. He tried to smile.

"Good night, Hugh," he managed, his voice steadier than his emotions.

Bronwen, who had been hovering in the doorway, took a quick glance at her disapproving mother, who was looking at her watch, and darted off the porch to fling her arms around Owain and squeeze him hard.

"It was super! Super-duper! Thanks! I'll see you tomorrow." And before either he or Cara could say a word, she had darted back up the steps and into the house. Hugh followed her, his "See you tomorrow," echoing in the night as the door closed.

"You didn't tell them," Owain said, watching her carefully.

"That you were their father?" she said with false sweetness. "You're damned right I didn't."

"No, you didn't tell them anything."

"What would you have me tell them?"

"That you're going to marry me."

"Don't be absurd."

He fished in his pocket for the ring box, hauled it out and held it out to her. He might as well have offered her a snake. She shrank from him.

"Cara." He opened it. The diamond winked in the moonlight, hinting of promises, of joy, of a life to be shared.

"Go away." She turned her back on him.

"I love you."

"I don't believe that."

"You're a fool."

"Yes," she said bitterly, "I certainly think you could say that." She climbed the stairs.

He followed her, touched her arm. "Cara, take it."

"I won't marry you!"

"Don't say that."

"Reality too hard for you to take?"

"No. Reality is me loving you."

"Reality is me not believing it. How can I, damn you?" Her voice throbbed with pain.

"How can I prove it to you?"

She looked at him levelly over her shoulder. "Go away."

He stared, nonplussed.

"Loving someone is wanting what's best for them," she said. "The absolutely best thing in the world for me would be you going away."

"Cara!"

"I mean it. I meant it this morning, I mean it now. Go!"

There was no point in talking. Cara wasn't listening. He grabbed her hand and tried to press the ring box into it. She yanked her arm away.

"I said no, Owain."

"At least keep the ring."

"No!"

"I'm leaving it here, Cara."

"You're the fool then." She opened the door to the kitchen and went in. But she looked back at him over her shoulder.

He held out the box to her.

She shook her head.

Impasse.

He walked over to the porch railing and set it there, then turned to look at her.

"Goodbye Owain."

He couldn't say it, and his eyes blurred as he walked into the darkness of the park.

Chapter Eight

It was an entirely new feeling—helplessness. Owain hated it.

But he felt it nonetheless. He told himself it would stop. Either Cara would come to her senses and call him back to her or he would eventually start missing her less.

That was the theory at least. Unfortunately, it had little in common with the reality of his everyday life.

He ought to have been glad to get back to Los Angeles. It was certainly more hospitable in November than Wisconsin was. Warmer. Greener. But it didn't feel that way. The cold that permeated Owain's being didn't come from the outside. The icy whiteness that made him shiver lay within him, and balmy ocean breezes and temperate days didn't touch the coldness that had settled in his heart.

He went through the days like a zombie, his mind two thousand miles away. He holed up in his house writing gritty depressing song lyrics that reflected his state of mind, or he sat in the recording studio and let Dougal's bitching and griping wash over him without comment. It was as if he had stopped existing as a whole human being the minute he had been banished from Cara's life.

For three days after the Guy Fawkes Day disaster, he had sat waiting in his garret, hoping for the miracle that never came. Every time the phone rang downstairs, he had waited for Mrs. Garrity to call him down to talk to Cara. And every time the doorbell rang, he waited for someone to tell him that Cara was there to see him.

But he waited in vain.

And the longer he waited, the more certain he became that she wasn't going to call; she wasn't going to come.

And the less he blamed her.

He knew how badly he had hurt her. He knew how deeply she felt his betrayal. And he didn't know what to do about it. If he had loved her less, he might have hung on, waited longer or pressed harder. But he loved her more than he loved himself. And he couldn't cause her any more pain.

So he decided to do what she asked. He decided to leave.

It was the hardest thing he had ever done.

And Mrs. Garrity and Suzy didn't make it any easier.

"You're leaving?" his landlady had demanded, open-mouthed with astonishment when he had come downstairs at last and made his announcement.

"Yeah." He avoided looking at her, not wanting to face her shrewd, assessing gaze.

"When are you coming back?"

He shrugged. He supposed he should have been honest and said that he wasn't. But it seemed too final, too irrevocable. He couldn't even face the idea yet himself. He needed some sort of hope, even if it was a vain one.

"I haven't decided. I've got things to do in L.A.," was all he told her, and then he retreated up the stairs before she could ask more.

Suzy, coming in an hour later and having been told, followed him up and cornered him in his room, bearding him like a lion tamer come to the den.

"What's going on?" she demanded. "Mrs. G. says you're leaving."

He tossed a couple of shirts into his suitcase. "Uh-huh."

"I thought you guys were getting married."

He grunted.

"Did you ask her?"

He grunted again.

"Yes or no?" Suzy prodded.

"Yes," he muttered through clenched teeth. Cripes, didn't she ever leave well enough alone?

"And she said no?" Suzy sounded equal parts horrified and disbelieving.

"She said no." He threw the underwear on top of the shirts.

"I don't believe it." Suzy sat down on the bed and stared.

Owain didn't reply. There was nothing he could say.

"She isn't going to marry Greg then, is she?" Suzy wanted to know.

He knew what she was asking. Suzy liked Greg far more than Cara did—at least romantically. Owain hadn't had any trouble figuring that out. But Greg didn't seem to notice much. But perhaps that was because he was used to thinking of Suzy only as a student. Owain wished he could reassure her. But who knew what sort of frame of mind Cara was in at the moment.

He shrugged. "Who knows?" She might very well marry Greg right now just to spite him, he thought. Then, *Over my dead body,* immediately followed it. He slammed the suitcase shut and snapped the lock.

"Explain," Suzy demanded.

But Owain couldn't. It was all he could do to carry his suitcase downstairs, sling his guitar case under his arm and say goodbye to Mrs. Garrity, Mr. Hill and Suzy. Then, with a lingering backward glance at the white-shingled house that had felt as close to being a home to him as he could ever remember, he left.

It would get better, he told himself when he got off the plane in L.A., feeling like the shell-shocked victim of an emotional war. In time it would get better.

But it had been almost two weeks now and he was beginning to lose hope.

The nights were just as long and sleepless as they had been, the daydreams just as vividly painful, the feeling of being half alive just as strong.

He felt physically ill—and was beginning to look it. His dark haunted eyes and gaunt features were becoming more and more noticeable to Dougal and everyone else.

"You look like hell," Dougal told him that afternoon at the studio in his house where they were working out some arrangements of songs Owain had written. He set a cup of coffee on the table and turned the chair around so he could straddle it, resting his arms on the back while he stared into Owain's pale, hollow-eyed face.

"Thank you very much," Owain said dryly.

"Have you been drinking?" Dougal's voice was soft, concerned.

Owain stiffened. "No. Of course not."

Dougal frowned, unconvinced. "Are you sure?"

"I haven't been drinking!"

"Well, it's never been women before, but—" Dougal gave him an assessing look "—I guess there's always a first time."

"There's always a first time," Owain agreed heavily.

"Ah." Pleased to have hit on it at last, Dougal gave his friend a sympathetic smile. "Anything I can do?"

"No."

"The Wisconsin woman?"

"How'd you know that?"

Dougal grinned. "Well, it wasn't intuition. It could have had something to do with you disappearing up there into the back of the beyond and refusing to come back, and then reappearing all of a sudden looking like someone who'd been hit by a train."

"That noticeable?"

Dougal nodded. "And getting more so by the minute. Besides, you were writing me 'Everything's coming up roses' and now it's all gloom-and-doom stuff. Not bad though,'' he added quickly. "At least you're working.''

Owain grunted and rubbed his hands through his hair.

Dougal clapped him on the shoulder. "Another month or so and we ought to have everything all wrapped up. We should be able to cut this thing before Christmas.''

Another month? It sounded like an eternity to Owain. The past two weeks had felt longer than a year. He sighed and took a long swallow of coffee. It was so bitter he couldn't even think of it as the same beverage he had shared so often with Cara. But it made him think of her just the same.

Everything made him think of Cara—the blond receptionist who wore her hair up the way Cara did, the woman next door who had a flannel shirt that reminded him of Cara's, the gal on the TV commercial about detergent who had Cara's slightly husky voice.

There was no getting away from her.

He decided he had been alone for too long.

When Mary Jo, Sam Travers's secretary, batted her eyelashes at him for what must have been the fiftieth time that week, he decided to ask her out to dinner. It was probably just what he needed, he thought, a chance to take his mind off Cara.

It was a disaster.

Mary Jo was everything he had thought she would be— and he didn't want any part of it. He tried, though, God knew. He looked deeply into her eyes over their candlelit dinner—and imagined Cara looking back at him. He set about to charm her with witty remarks, and found himself listening for Cara's laugh and not the high-pitched trill of Mary Jo.

But the worst was when he kissed her.

It was the least successful kiss he had ever given anyone. At fourteen with braces he had kissed better than that! Disconcerted and embarrassed, he had scowled at his feet while Mary Jo tried to pretend that her feelings hadn't been hurt.

"I don't suppose you'd like to come in," she ventured when they stood just outside her apartment door.

And compound the disaster? God, no! Owain rubbed a hand behind his neck to loosen his shirt collar. "I don't think I ought to."

Mary Jo looked miserable.

"It isn't you," he hastened to assure her. "It's me. It's..." But he couldn't finish the sentence. He didn't know what to say.

They stared at each other awkwardly for a long moment. At last Mary Jo said, "It's been interesting," and shook his hand, as if he had just sold her a set of encyclopedias.

"Yeah," Owain muttered, mortified. He fled down the stairs without looking back.

He told himself it was a fluke, not Cara. So the next night he had tried another date. He asked Shelly, a backup singer whom Dougal had introduced him to, to go out to the movies with him.

It was a dreadful movie, not worth watching in the least. And Owain wouldn't have minded a bit if Cara had been with him. He would have loved an excuse for devoting his entire attention to her in the darkened theater. With Shelly he had simply been bored.

Every minute made him long for Cara more.

Obviously finding another woman wasn't the answer.

But sitting alone, stewing about the mess he had made of his life wasn't good either. He needed people. So when the phone call from his mother came, offering him an invitation to Thanksgiving dinner, it sounded like a gift from heaven.

"I'll be there," he promised.

And he was. Early in the afternoon he pulled up in front of the story-and-a-half white stucco Spanish-style house that was perched high on a hill overlooking Laguna Beach. His mother was waiting on the front porch.

She threw her arms around him and hugged him tight. "Owain, love, I'm so glad you came. You've been away too long."

Owain kissed her, then held her out at arm's length to smile into her eyes. His breath caught at the sight of the same smoky brown irises that his daughter had. His throat tightened.

"Evan's already here. It's so good to have both my boys home for once." She hurried him into the living room where his father was lying on the couch watching a football game. "A real family holiday it is, isn't it, Tom?"

Owain's father grunted in agreement, never taking his eyes off the game. "Come sit yourself," he commanded. Owain sat and was joined moments later by his younger brother, who handed him a beer and took a long swallow of his own. Owain leaned back and tried to will himself into the simple enjoyment of the afternoon. It had been several months since he had even seen his parents, let alone simply relaxed around them. But his mind kept wandering.

"What'll you do without UCLA to root for, Dad?" Evan asked his father.

Tom O'Neill folded his hands behind his head and contemplated his impending move back to Britain. A smile flitted across his craggy face. "Rugby," he murmured. "Soccer." He gave Evan a disdainful look. "Better you should ask what I've been doing here all these years!"

"He'll find himself plenty to keep busy," Owain said, knowing that, like him, his father never sat still. "But what about you, Mum? Going to take up knitting?"

Bronwen O'Neill had been a secretary at one of the law offices locally for fifteen years. She had worked as a volunteer at one of the hospitals, and every summer she worked at the art festival. Owain had been kidding about the knitting; he knew she would find plenty to do in Wales as well.

"I never gave up knitting," his mother reminded him as she set a bowl of mashed potatoes on the dining room table. She gave him a hard look over the tops of her owlish spectacles. "I'm only lacking someone to knit for. A grandchild perhaps?" she hinted none too subtly.

It was as if she had hit him in the stomach. He wondered what she would say if she knew she already had two. He could guess. It made him grimace and feel guilty at the same time.

"You're thirty-one years old, Owain," she went on. "Your dad and I were twenty-four when we got married. Twenty-five when we had you."

The same age I was when Hugh and Bronwen were born. Owain took a long draught of beer, hiding his expression from her. "Mum, I've heard it all before," he said, but his voice cracked as he said it. He got up hastily and left the room.

"Owain!" His mother came after him, coming up behind him where he stood in the kitchen, staring mindlessly out the window, seeing nothing except a future shot to hell. She touched his arm, then gave it a gentle squeeze. "I'm sorry, love." She gave a half laugh. "It must be hormones or something. Here you are, home for the first time in months, and I go on the attack."

"It's all right, Ma."

She gave him a hug. "Gloria Anderson's daughter just had a baby. That must be what set me off. Forgive me?"

Owain gulped. Forgive her? Would she forgive *him* if she knew that Hugh and Bronwen were out there—had been out there for six and a half years now—grandchildren whom she could knit for, spoil and otherwise love?

He turned and wrapped his arms around his mother, hugging her ample form hard against him, drawing in the soft warm smells that he associated with childhood and comfort and unstinting love. "Yeah, Ma, I forgive you," he managed.

"If it'll take the heat off big brother here," Evan said, coming in after them and giving his mother a sunny smile, "I just thought I'd mention that Shanna and I are engaged."

Owain's mother gave a little shriek. "Oh, Ev!"

The announcement did everything Evan expected it would. Owain's uncharacteristic reaction to his mother's perennial lecture on grandchildren was forgotten, and talk turned at once to Shanna, the red-haired nurse who'd snared Evan. Both parents were thrilled.

"When's the wedding?" Bronwen O'Neill demanded.

"December twentieth."

"But we're leaving on the twenty-second!"

"I know." Evan's arm went around his mother. "That's why it's the twentieth. It was as quick as we could get things arranged. You do want to see us tie the knot, I gather."

There was no question, of course, about that. Still, it didn't stop his mother from lamenting throughout most of the meal. But it was exactly the sort of lamenting she loved—the sort that made her "too happy." It made Owain's throat ache with envy for his brother.

The meal, as good as it was, tasted like cardboard in his mouth. He moved the turkey from one side of his plate to the other, picked at the cranberry sauce, nibbled a green bean. Mostly he just felt ill.

He had pinned a lot of his hopes on coming home. It was supposed to make him feel warm and loved, a part of things—a part of a family.

Most of what he felt was distance. These people were his family, yes. But he had changed, grown up. And ultimately they were not his primary family anymore. He sat there in the bosom of his parents' home and felt more homesick than he had ever felt in his life. He needed Cara, damn it. He needed Hugh and Bronwen.

He pushed his chair back and stood up. "It was great, Mum. I think I need to take a walk. To settle it all, you know?"

His mother took one look at all the food left on his plate and stopped in midsentence, her forehead wrinkled with concern. "Are you all right, lovey?"

"Fine." And before anyone could call his bluff, he was out the door and down the steps.

It was only five blocks to the beach. And though the wind was raw, it was nothing compared to the Wisconsin wind he had left behind him. It did have, though, a touch of savageness, something that ripped away the sense of careful balance that he had been trying to get the hang of for the past two weeks.

It was no good trying to pretend that he could get on with his life and forget Cara. She had woven herself right into the fabric of his soul. There was no way to tear her out without tearing himself to shreds in the process.

He sat on the sand, watching the wind-whipped breakers crash against the shore, hurling bits of driftwood against the sand. He felt as battered as the driftwood, at sea with his emotions.

Had Cara succeeded in getting over him? Had she been able to turn around and get on with her life just as she had been before he had walked into it? Or did he dare hope that she felt as awful as he did?

Was it fair to hope she might?

Suddenly he couldn't wait any longer. He needed to talk to her. To hear her voice. He needed to test the waters again, to see if she might have forgiven him.

He scrambled to his feet again and walked back up the beach, climbing the steps to the road two at a time. By the time he got to his parents' street he was almost running, driven by the same desperation that had driven him when he had begun to seek his child in the first place.

His mother was waiting when he walked in the door.

"Owain?"

He frowned. "What?"

"Are you all right? You seem so...so...distracted, somehow."

He nodded. Distracted. That was a good word for it. "I'm okay."

"I was afraid I'd hurt your feelings, going on and on about a grandchild, then getting so excited when Evan said he was marrying Shanna." She gave him an awkward, almost embarrassed smile. "You do know that I don't expect you to marry just to give me a grandchild, don't you?"

Owain shut his eyes. "Yeah, Mum, I know it." He spoke softly, his guts twisting. "I...I guess...it hit a sore spot because I...I might like that, too." He gave a faint smile.

She reached up and brushed a lock of hair off his forehead. "When the right girl comes along, love."

"Yeah." He ducked his head. "May I use your phone?"

His mother gave him an assessing look, one that told him that no matter what she professed, she still hoped the right girl was in the wings at least. "Of course, dear," she said at last.

He used the extension in the bedroom. His fingers trembled as he dialed Cara's number. They had half dialed it a hundred times, maybe more. But his hand never got it all the way done. Most times he had barely let himself start.

But this time he dialed it all, then clenched his fingers tightly when the call went through.

The phone rang six times. Eight times. Ten. Twenty.

No one answered.

He hung up deflated, depressed. He hadn't even considered that she might not be there.

Evan poked his head in the door. "Can I use the phone now? I want to call Shanna."

Owain stood up and handed his brother the receiver. "Go ahead."

He should have said, "Make it brief." But he didn't, and young love paid no attention to long-distance rates. Evan and Shanna talked for almost an hour while Owain lurked outside the bedroom, pacing the length of the hallway, his fists jammed into the pockets of his khaki slacks while the soft chuckles, low murmurs and smooth seductive tones of his brother's voice made him grind his teeth.

"Touchdown!" his father hollered in from the living room. "UCLA is winning!"

Owain grunted. Everyone was winning but him. He sighed and went back to his pacing, pausing long enough once to open the door to the bedroom and give Evan a hard stare. Evan didn't notice.

Finally Owain gave up and went out to haunt the living room where at least he didn't have to hear his brother. It was at least twenty more minutes until Evan joined them. His face was slightly flushed, his hair disheveled. He looked as if he had been doing far more than talking on the phone. Owain gave him a scathing look, uncomfortably aware that it was due more to jealousy than to moral outrage.

This time when he got no answer he called directory assistance and got Cara's grandmother's number.

"Owain?" Mrs. Nute sounded cautiously pleased to hear his voice. He felt better at once. At least Cara hadn't turned her grandmother against him, whatever she might have said to explain his absence.

"How are you?" he asked. "How is she?" He didn't have to say who.

"I'm fine," Mrs. Nute answered. "Just fine. I had the children with me most of last week. Cara's father had a mild heart attack. She took them and flew to Michigan for a few days. Then she sent the kids back to be with me and she stayed on another two. But he's home now, so she's back. As for how she is, Owain..." There was a pause. His heart clawed the inside of his chest. "She's hurting."

"What did she tell you?"

"That things between you weren't going to work out."

"I wanted them to."

"For Cara?" she asked him gently. "Or for the children?"

"What?" He was stunned.

"You're their father, aren't you?"

For a moment he was speechless. She had said the words without any accusation at all. Just quietly, matter-of-factly. As if she had simply looked out the window and remarked that it was raining, wasn't it?

"I . . . I . . ." he stammered. "Yes."

"And she found out."

"Yes."

"I thought so."

"How did you know?"

"That she found out?"

"That I'm their—" he lowered his voice for fear his mother would walk by then "—father."

"Your eyes. They're Hugh's. The hair is Bronwen's. I'm an old lady, Owain. I don't have a lot to do except think and look. I do that a lot. It wasn't hard to put together two and two."

"Did you say anything to Cara?"

"No. It wouldn't matter what I said to Cara at this point. What matters is what she believes."

He sighed and rubbed his eyes with his fist. "That's sure the truth."

There was a silence on the line. Then Mrs. Nute said softly, "She's here now. She and the children."

"Can I talk to her?" If he could swallow the lump in his throat.

"Just a minute." She set down the phone and he heard her move away, calling, "Cara."

He waited, his fingers knotting around the receiver as he wondered what he could say. Would she even listen to him?

Had things changed? So she was hurting too. Good. He felt a flame of hope.

"Owain?" It was Hugh, high-pitched and thrilled. "Is that you?"

"Yeah, it's me." He felt lighter at the sudden reprieve. "How've you been?"

"Good. Except I miss you. You shouldn't have gone. We've got a lot of snow now. We could go sledding if you were here. That bonfire and the guy, they were really neat, weren't they? I told my teacher and she said—"

"Hugh! Hurry up!" he heard Bronwen say. "It's my turn."

"Not yet!"

Owain heard scuffling, then the phone thumped. "Hey," he said quickly. Cara's voice came over. "Bronwen Williams, stop that this minute!" The simple sound of it made him ache.

"You'll get a turn," Hugh said indignantly. "Gram said I get it till the hand is on the four. That is, if Owain wants to talk to me that long. Do you, Owain?"

"Of course, I do," he said.

"When are you coming back?" Hugh demanded.

Cara's sharp, "Hugh!" came through loud and clear.

"I don't know yet," Owain said.

"Soon?" Hugh pleaded. "For Christmas?"

Before Owain could answer that, there was another clatter, and he heard Hugh say plaintively to someone—obviously Cara—"I was only askin'" and then Bronwen was on the line.

"I got my swimming badge, too," she said. "Just like Hugh's. And Mommy went with me to my banquet. And my friend's dog had puppies and we might get one. And we went to see Grandpa 'cause he had a heart attack. I got an A on my spelling. What are you doing?"

Missing you. "Working," Owain told her.

"Can't you work here? You used to, didn't you?"

He started to say, "I probably could," when the phone was snatched out of her hand.

"Goodbye," Cara said.

"Cara, I—"

"We have to leave, Owain. It is snowing like crazy here. I have to get home while I still can. Thank you for calling. Nothing's changed." And she hung up on him.

"Damn."

He set the phone down. Then jerked it back up again, angry now. His fingers punched out Mrs. Nute's phone number.

The phone at the other end was snatched up when it had scarcely rung.

"What is it?" Cara sounded furious, and as if she knew exactly who it would be.

"Don't hang up!"

She did.

Owain slammed the phone back onto the cradle and stalked out into the living room.

"Somebody just sacked the quarterback for the second time running," Evan crowed.

Owain knew exactly how the quarterback felt.

"Got anything stiffer than beer?" he asked his father, hunting in the liquor cabinet in the dining room.

Tom O'Neill sat up and, for the first time since he had left the table, looked squarely at his older son. Owain stared back at him defiantly. Slowly Tom heaved himself to his feet, walked with great deliberation to the hall closet and took out his Windbreaker. He pulled it on, then tossed Owain's to him. "Come on," he said. "I'll buy you a drink."

Twenty years ago, when his father had finally made the decision to seek his fortune in America, he had gone out walking with Owain. They had walked for miles, ending up staring out at the lonely sea from the pier at Penarth.

His father had told him there, had asked how he felt, had listened to his fears, his hopes. Then he had taken him to the local pub where he had ordered himself a pint and Owain a shandy. Together they had sat in companionable silence, each with his own thoughts, but with the oneness that comes from sharing a momentous decision.

When Owain had made the decision to drop out of college and commit himself completely to Cardiff Connection, once more they had walked, talked and, finally, toasted Owain's uncertain future with a bottle of Irish whiskey.

They had done the same when Owain had quit performing four years ago and had gone back to college.

It didn't surprise Owain that Tom suggested it now.

Neither of them spoke for a long time; they just walked. Down the hill and through the narrow streets they went. Owain wondered what his father would say if he poured out the whole story.

Would he be surprised? Somehow that seemed unlikely. Nothing much surprised Tom O'Neill.

But Owain couldn't tell him this. This wasn't the sort of problem a son laid on a father. This was the sort of problem a son ought to be mature enough to sort out himself. Still, his father's presence helped. It steadied.

There wasn't much traffic. November had thinned the crowds who hit Laguna in the summer months. The holiday merrymaking with families had thinned it further. Few people sauntered along the sidewalks. The streets were almost deserted.

They walked side by side until Tom O'Neill stopped along one of the side streets and nodded at a small, dimly lit bar. It looked far more posh than the one Owain remembered going to back in Penarth. But he didn't care. He grinned when his father held the door for him and announced, "My local."

"You've come up in the world."

"No. Moved sideways is all," Tom said.

Owain found the thought comforting.

There were only three people inside besides the bartender, all men who looked as if they, too, were escaping from a holiday meal. One of them greeted Tom by name and waved him over.

Tom shook his head. "Not today. Got to talk to my boy." He nudged Owain into a chair beside a small table at one of the windows overlooking the sidewalk. "What'll you have?"

"Whiskey. Neat."

Tom looked at him a long moment, then walked to the bar and got the drinks. He set the whiskey in front of Owain, then set his on the other side of the table and sat down across from him.

"That bad, is it?"

Owain took a small swallow of the whiskey, feeling it burn all the way down, waiting for it to dull the pain. "Bad?"

"You don't usually take it neat."

Owain wrapped his hand around the glass and met his father's concerned gaze. "I guess I don't."

"Shall we talk about it?"

Owain sighed, knowing that if he didn't say something, his father would put a worse construction on things than already existed—if possible. "It's simple really. I want something and I can't have it." He managed a self-deprecating laugh.

His father wasn't fooled. "A woman." It wasn't a question.

"Mmm." Owain took another sip. The burning lessened. The hurt didn't.

"She doesn't want you?" Tom sounded shocked, as disbelieving as Suzy had.

Owain grinned faintly. "Not every woman wants me, Dad."

"Fools," his father snorted. "What's the matter with her?"

"Nothing," Owain said quickly. "It isn't her. It's—" He set the glass down and raked his fingers through his hair. "Oh hell, it's just . . . it isn't even that she doesn't want me. She just thinks she shouldn't."

Tom snorted. "Why not?" His brows came down in a suspicious stare. "She married?"

"No. She's a widow."

"Ah." Tom took a long swallow, let it settle, then spoke. "I get it. She thinks she's being faithful to the first one, does she?"

"Not exactly. I mean, she loved him. But she . . . but I . . ." He couldn't tell his father, couldn't explain the reasons. "She just doesn't think she should, Dad. She has her reasons."

Tom considered that, considered his son. "Good reasons?" he asked finally.

"She thinks so," Owain admitted.

"Do you?"

"No, damn it, I don't!"

Tom smiled. "Thought not. So how are you going to convince her?"

Owain blinked. "Convince her?"

"To change her mind," Tom explained as if Owain were not quite bright. "You love her, I gather."

"Yes."

"Well, then . . ." Tom looked at him expectantly.

"Well, I . . ." Owain stopped, unsure of himself.

Tom smiled and shook his head. "'Tisn't like you, Owain, dithering like this. Not like you at all. You wanted something, you went after it, boy."

Owain finished his whiskey and slapped his glass down on the table, annoyed that his father, who had always understood him before, couldn't understand him now. "She won't even talk to me, for God's sake," he snarled. "That was her

I called, you know. And she wouldn't even talk to me! She bloody hung up on me, Dad!"

Tom didn't bat an eyelash, his smile imperturbable. "Then I reckon you'll have to stop using the phone."

Chapter Nine

"Home for Christmas, are you?" the rental car clerk said to Owain when she handed him the key.

"Yeah." At least he hoped he was. If he even got there. Outside the window of the Madison airport thick new snow swirled madly. It was a far cry from the Los Angeles he had left.

"Lucky you got the flight you did," she told him. "Winter storm warnings are in effect. I'll bet the last flight tonight doesn't get in at all."

"Lucky me," Owain said and, wishing her a Merry Christmas, ducked his head and went out into the storm.

Common sense told him to stay where he was. At least in Madison he would have a warm dry hotel room to spend the night in, and he could always drive to Belle River tomorrow.

But as usual where Cara was concerned, common sense had little effect. He found the car that the clerk had indicated without too much trouble, and he set out.

Darkness fell early in December. It was dark by five o'clock, but it wasn't the pitch-dark of a clear night. Rather the whole sky glowed with an eerie pinkish tint. The snow reflected the light around it, making Owain feel as if he were in a surreal world. The headlights probed the darkness cautiously. He headed west.

Three hours later he arrived.

It hadn't been easy. But considering the rest of the month he had just spent, it was fitting, he guessed. Leaving L.A., even after his father's words had prodded him into thinking that going back was the only answer, hadn't been easy. Dougal and his album had demanded a terrific amount of time.

He wrote for Dougal, then he agonized, and wrote some more. Then Dougal sang, they both agonized, and Owain wrote even more. At last, though, the album was cut. Dougal was pleased. No, Dougal was more than pleased. He was ecstatic.

"It's the best we've ever done," he chortled. "Best since *Tangle of Roots* anyway. We're really sailing again!" He had danced around the studio in his elation.

All Owain had managed was a wan smile and a feeling of relief. That was one commitment out of the way at least. He had plenty of others. His dissertation director demanded some changes, which took quite a lot of time, and he was enthralled with the interviews Owain had done so far with Mr. Hill and Cara's grandmother. He wanted to see the rest of them. It was a nice excuse to go back, Owain thought. As if he needed one.

But he couldn't go back until after Evan's wedding. And then he had had to see his parents off to Britain. It had been Christmas Eve before he could get a flight out. And he was lucky to get one then, the airline ticket seller told him.

Owain had considered himself lucky—even when the plane had set down in what looked like a blizzard.

After all that it wasn't going to stop him getting to Belle River tonight.

Now as he drew up in front of Mrs. Garrity's house, he heaved a sigh of relief. It was ironic almost. Why should he be relieved? The hard part—dealing with Cara—was yet to come. He got out of the car and turned to look across the park at Cara's house. The light was on in the window, beckoning him even more strongly now than the first time he had seen it.

Since he had left he had been casting about in the darkness, unfocused, confused, groping. Now he had a sense of direction again, a sense of purpose.

He had come home.

He turned away and stamped through the snow up the walk to Mrs. Garrity's front porch. There he kicked the excess snow off his boots and shook his head, flipping snowflakes off his hair. He turned the doorknob and went in.

Mrs. Garrity was in the kitchen, and when she heard the door open she came into the entry hall to stare at him with openmouthed astonishment. Then a broad smile creased her weathered face and she flung her arms around him.

"I knew it!" She hugged him hard, not minding his wet coat and the bags he still carried in his hands. "Oh, Lord, I just knew it!" Then her arms dropped suddenly and she stepped back, assessing him warily as if she had just thought of something. "Or are you leaving again?"

Owain shook his head. "I'm staying. For good this time."

Then she really did hug him. "Come in! Come in! Look who's here, Norbert," she called into the front parlor. "It's Owain. Put your bags upstairs."

"You haven't rented my room?"

"I should have," she told him tartly. "You goin' off like that. But, well..." She shrugged expansively. "I sort of thought you might be comin' back."

Owain smiled and brushed a kiss on her cheek. "Thank God you were right." He went up the stairs quickly, his bags in hand. Mrs. Garrity followed him, telling him about everything that had happened since he had left. "Rosie is engaged to Jimmy. They're getting married in the spring. They went to his parents in Toronto for the holidays. And Suzy went home. So did Larry and Belinda."

"So who's here?" Owain dumped his bags on the floor. His eyes strayed to the window where he could look across the park. The light in the window at Cara's still shone brightly.

"Just Norbert and me." Mrs. Garrity looked fleetingly sad. "Weren't for Norbert I'd have gone to Camilla's."

"Camilla?"

"My sister. The one across town," Mrs. Garrity reminded him. "You remember, you fixed her iron."

"I remember. Doesn't she have room for both of you?"

Mrs. Garrity made a face. "I expect she would. But you know Norbert. He won't put anybody out."

"He's putting you out, isn't he?" Owain asked reasonably as he followed her back downstairs.

"Mmmph." Which was all Mrs. Garrity would say. They both knew that she tolerated more from Norbert than she would from any five of her other tenants. "Because he has no place else to go," she would have said. But Owain knew, too, it was because she had a genuine soft spot for the crotchety old man.

"Anyway," she said brightly, "now I have you, too."

She offered him a cup of coffee, which he took because he was freezing and his hands were shaking. Part of him wanted to go right over to Cara's. Another part of him wasn't willing yet to take the risk. As long as he hadn't gone yet, she hadn't turned him away yet and he could still hope. So for the moment at least he sat in the parlor and let Norbert's conversation glide over him, putting in an occasional word, nodding at the appropriate spots.

Mrs. Garrity chipped in now and then. From her Owain half hoped to hear some tidbit of information about Cara and the kids. But nothing was said. At last the coffee had gone cold and he could stand it no longer.

Getting to his feet, he carried the cup into the kitchen, then came back out, his hands tucked into the pockets of his jeans, his walk studiously nonchalant. "Think I might just take a walk."

"In this?" Mrs. Garrity's eyes went to the swirling mass of white beyond the window glass.

He shrugged. "Need to clear my head."

She looked skeptical. "Suit yourself."

He let himself out into a swirling maelstrom. The wind blew bitterly from the north, whipping the snow into tornadolike gusts across the park. He turned up his collar and set off around it, skirting the edges, avoiding the drifts. It was a measure of his besottedness, he decided, that he had left a perfectly warm, pleasant Southern California morning to come back to this.

He clumped up onto Cara's porch and rang the bell, remembering the first time he had done so. His hands had been clammy then. He had felt awkward, tongue-tied, unsure of what to say, how to begin.

Nothing much had changed.

Including the fact that Cara wasn't there this time either. But no one else answered the door in her place. He frowned. It wasn't a night to be outside, damn it. She had to be there. She simply *had* to be.

But she wasn't.

He walked around to the back door and pounded on it. Nestor stared at him implacably, warm and dry on the other side of the window.

"Where the hell is she?" Owain asked him.

Nestor blinked in response.

Finally Owain turned and sloughed back to Mrs. Garrity's, turning every few yards to stare at the house behind him, curious and worried. Had she gone to her grandmother's? Had she been in an accident? Lord knew the roads were terrible. Please God she hadn't been hurt!

He threw open the door at Mrs. Garrity's and stumbled, snow-covered, into the foyer. "I can't find Cara," he blurted, all pretense gone.

Mrs. Garrity looked up at him, then to the mantel clock and nodded her head. "I would imagine she's at church." Her voice was placid.

Owain sagged against the door frame. "Church?" His knees wobbled, his mind spun. Relief swam through his panic. "Church?" he croaked again.

"Norbert and I were going to go, but we don't do well out in the snow." She glanced at the clock again. "Services must be about half over by now. She ought to be home in about an hour if she walked. Want another cup of coffee while you wait?"

But Owain was already opening the door again. "Which church?"

"On High Street. Corner of First."

He nodded. "I know the one." And he was gone.

He couldn't have asked for a better place to stage meeting her again. She might well slam the door in his face if he walked up to her house. But he knew her well enough to know that she wouldn't freeze him out in the middle of a church congregation. Not on Christmas, anyway.

It was unfair, he told himself as he walked quickly up the hill toward High Street. But life was unfair. And if ever a man had needed everything on his side that he could manage, Owain was the man and the time was now.

The frigid air made him gasp as he hurried along. He got a stitch in his side. The cold seared his lungs. And when at last he arrived at the church to see the rainbow of light spilling across the snow from the stained-glass clerestory window, he slowed down long enough to feel his heart pounding and his ribs heaving. He sucked in one long last draft of icy air, then mounted the steps and eased open the heavy oak doors of the church.

The sweet clear sound of children's voices washed over him as he stood in the vestibule, getting his bearings. One of the ushers turned and saw him, then beckoned. Owain shook his head. He wasn't sitting just anywhere. He was going to find Cara. He came up behind the usher and began studying the backs of the members' heads.

"Follow me, sir?" the usher asked him.

Owain shook his head again, his eyes going up and down the rows looking for blondes. The hymn ended and the congregation sat down. That helped.

"Are you looking for someone?" the usher asked.

"Cara Williams."

The usher brightened. "Yes. She's—" he craned his neck and looked too "—about halfway up on the left. But I don't think you can reach—"

"Thank you." He spotted her when the usher did, and was striding up the aisle before the man could finish his sentence.

Heads turned to look at him. The pastor, who had launched into his sermon, gave him a wary look. Owain smiled and nodded.

The pastor camouflaged a grimace and went gamely on. "...what we've been waiting for this Advent season. At times we have all felt lost, abandoned, left out in the cold. No doubt the people of God felt the same way. At times they, too, must have wondered if the Lord had abandoned them. But does a father abandon his children?"

Owain reached the row in which Cara was sitting. "Excuse me." He climbed over the elderly lady sitting on the end, then edged past the gentleman next to her. The whole row looked over and began to shift. Cara turned.

"Of course, he doesn't," the pastor went inexorably on. "And that's what we celebrate at Christmas. A father's love for his children."

Cara stared at Owain, shock written on her face.

He stepped over the last person and squeezed in next to Bronwen, who flung her arms around him and hugged him with all her might. He hugged her back with one arm while he reached around Cara and tousled Hugh's hair with his other hand.

But his eyes never left Cara's. He gave her his heart.

Something flared in her eyes for a split second. Then it vanished before he could identify it.

"Merry Christmas, Cara," he said under his breath.

She swallowed hard. He saw her throat work convulsively. He wanted to let go of the children and gather her in his arms. He wanted to wrap her once and for all in his love.

"Merry Christmas, Owain," she whispered. Then she turned back to face the pastor, her hands knotted together in her lap.

She didn't glance his way again for the rest of the service.

It didn't matter. He did enough looking for both of them. He could scarcely take his eyes off her. He had been too long without her, and they seemed to need simply to be allowed to look.

Through the prayers, he traced her profile, his eyes following the line of her jaw, the curve of her ear, the loose fall of escaping tendrils of honey-colored hair. During the offertory they dropped to watch with agonized fascination as her fingers twisted the envelope in her hands. During Communion, when he followed her up the aisle, his eyes settled on the back of her neck, that warm, vulnerable spot that he loved to kiss. He wanted to reach out to her, to touch her, to feel her respond to him. But he didn't dare.

So he shoved his hands into the pockets of his jacket, clenching his fists, and deliberately forcing himself to focus on something else. Divine guidance was what he ought to be focusing on, he decided. He would need it in enormous supply once the service was over. He sent a prayer winging heavenward that once they were outside, the walls between them would come down.

It didn't look as if his prayer was going to be answered. When the last prayers were being said and Cara was struggling to slip her arms back into her coat, he reached over to help her. She spun away from him—at least as far as one could spin in a cramped church pew. Things didn't look encouraging.

Well, perhaps he could at least gain a truce. A cease-fire that would give him a chance to reinfiltrate her life. Because she had been right about one thing—he had deliberately done it once. And he was damned sure going to try to do it again.

The congregation was getting ready to sing the recessional. He saw Cara's mouth open. Her lips parted. He wanted to touch them with his. Bronwen thrust a hymnal into his hands and he fumbled madly for the correct page when she hissed it at him.

But for once neither words nor music registered. Nothing registered until the minister blessed them all and said, "The Lord be with you. Go now to new beginnings."

It was exactly the blessing Owain needed.

To the strains of "Joy to the World" he walked with Cara and the children out into the snow-covered world. Cara smiled at her friends, greeted neighbors, cooed over someone's new baby, while all the while she steered Hugh and Bronwen through the crowd, down the steps and onto the recently shoveled path.

For all the attention she paid him, Owain might as well have stayed in California. But Hugh and Bronwen didn't stint. Each hung on one of his arms, and they chattered a mile a minute all the way home.

Cara glowered at them, then at him. He met her hostility with more equanimity than he felt.

"How about a new beginning, Cara?" He kept his voice low so that the children couldn't hear.

Cara pretended not to hear either. She walked with her head in the air, her eyelashes catching the snowflakes. He saw her blink, and wondered if the dampness streaking her cheeks was a melting snowflake. Or a tear.

She walked on ahead of them, ignoring them all, and had the door to the house opened before he and the children even came up the walk.

"Hurry up," she said to the twins. Her eyes skated over Owain.

"Can Owain—" Hugh began but she cut him off.

"Say good-night," she commanded them. "The sooner you get to bed, the sooner morning comes."

"And Santa!" Bronwen chimed in. Cara obviously knew that Santa was going to do better than Owain in popularity. At least on Christmas Eve.

Hugh bounded halfway up the steps, then stopped and looked at Owain.

"Go on," Owain told him. "I'll be around."

He heard Cara draw in a sharp quick breath.

"See you, then," Hugh said, and went on indoors. Bronwen followed him, then turned long enough to say, "I'm awful glad you're back."

Owain watched them disappear, then turned his attention to Cara. She was standing by the door, her arms folded tightly across her chest.

"You're not glad, though, are you?" he asked her softly.

"What do you think?" Her voice was bitter.

"I think I love you."

She gave him a pained look and turned away.

"I had to come, Cara."

"Yes, I know. A father never abandons his children."

"It isn't that."

"Isn't it?" She stepped inside the door. "Good night, Owain."

"Cara?"

She paused, the door almost shut.

"Merry Christmas."

This time her only reply was to close the door.

He understood now what it was like to be shut out. He wasn't going to let it happen for long.

THE TEMPERATURE HAD FALLEN and the wind had picked up even more in the past three hours. It was five past one on Christmas morning. It was eight degrees above zero. The windchill, Mrs. Garrity had told him just before he'd bundled her and Norbert Hill into the cab that was going to take them to Camilla's, was thirty-seven below zero.

Owain believed her.

And if Cara was a heavy sleeper, he was in trouble.

He hammered on the door once more, stamped his feet on the porch and huffed great steamy breaths of air into the wind. "Damn it, Cara, come on!" he muttered. The tips of his ears were freezing. His face hurt. The snow squeaked beneath his feet. He hit the door again, harder than ever.

At last a light was flipped on upstairs. He pounded some more. Another light came on in the living room. Then, at last, he heard the sound of the night latch turning and the knob rattled.

Cara opened the door.

He gave her a hopeful smile. "Pardon me, ma'am, is there room at the inn?"

"Owain! For heaven's sake!" She glared at him.

"I'm not kidding. Really." He stamped his feet again. "Can I at least come in, Cara? It's getting damned cold out here."

She hesitated, then held the door open slightly wider, letting him pass. "What's going on?" she demanded. "What are you up to this time? Have you been lurking outside for the past—" she glanced at her watch "—three hours?"

"I was at Mrs. Garrity's, naturally. Her furnace went out."

"Tell her to call Claussen's."

"Can't call anybody. It's Christmas. And Claussen is in Florida. We checked."

"Well, I'm sure there must be someone. I'll look in the phone book." She turned and walked briskly into the family room, flipping on the light, hugging the ivory-colored chenille robe tightly around herself. Owain's eyes followed the curve of her hips. He sucked in his breath and shut his eyes until the surge of hunger he felt for her had quieted. Then he went after her.

"There must be someone," she was muttering as she scoured the pages of the phone directory.

"Doesn't matter now," Owain said easily. "Mrs. Garrity and Mr. Hill are at her sister's. I put them in a taxi about twenty minutes ago."

"Why didn't you go with them?'

"No room at that inn. Two was all Camilla could manage. Unless I wanted to share a single bed with Mr. Hill. I didn't. Neither did he," Owain added, trying to suppress a grin.

Cara glowered, obviously feeling maneuvered.

"Besides, I thought you might take me in. Mrs. Garrity thought so, too. And she wanted to have someone close by, to go back and check on the pipes periodically."

Cara muttered something under her breath.

"What did you say?

"I said, 'I don't believe this.'" She paced the family room, her arms hugging her chest, the robe swishing about her feet.

Owain didn't speak, just waited. Cara fumed.

Finally he said, "Hey, come on, Cara, it's Christmas. You gonna make me go sleep in a cold house?"

"Why didn't you just stay away?"

"You know why."

Her lips compressed into a tight line. "When can someone come and fix it, then?"

"Don't know yet. Marlowe's will have to come down from Prairie, she said. That's a long way. Police aren't encouraging people on the highways, I hear. Maybe the day after Christmas." He would have liked to say after the first of the year, but he knew Cara wouldn't buy that. He was lucky she seemed to be buying this.

"Humph." She paced some more.

Owain waited, trying not to look impatient, trying not to look as if it mattered as much as it did.

"So stay," she said ungraciously. "But don't you try anything."

"Try anything?" He couldn't stop the grin this time.

He heard her teeth snap together. "You know exactly what I mean."

He ducked his head. "Right."

She strode to the sofa and began flinging the cushions off onto the rug. "You can sleep down here. I'll get sheets and blankets." She went up the stairs without another word.

Owain opened the sofa into a double bed, then stacked the cushions that Cara had thrown aside into a neat pile. When she came back with the sheets and blankets, he took them from her outthrust hands without comment and began to make the bed.

Cara went to the other side and wordlessly began to work with him. Their movements synchronized as they spread the sheets and folded hospital corners at the bottoms. They stood and bent in unison. Just like making lo—

"I forgot the pillows," Cara said suddenly and vanished up the stairs again.

Owain sat down on the newly made bed and waited for his pulse to slow down. He was burning of the heat whereas moments before he had been too cold. He shed his jacket, then his sweater.

"You can wait to undress until I go back up, if you don't mind," Cara said starchily. She flung a pillow at him. He caught it just before it could smack him in the face.

"Thank you," he said.

"You're welcome." It was clear she didn't mean it. They stared at each other. The wind rattled the panes of glass in the family room windows. Upstairs the whole house seemed to creak. Owain saw a tiny pulse flutter at the base of Cara's throat. Her eyes dropped.

"How about a truce?" he suggested softly.

"A what?"

"A truce. You know—" he gave her a faint grin "—for the holidays. All the best wars have them."

Cara was not amused. "You seem to think this is a big joke."

He sighed. "No, damn it. It's not a joke at all. Or if it is, the joke's on me." He rubbed a hand through his hair. "I just meant that I don't want to spoil things for the kids. I wouldn't like our battle to wreck things for them. I would like their Christmas to be happy."

"It would have been," Cara told him pointedly.

"Would it?"

The tension roared between them, loud enough to make his ears ring. He saw the tiniest tremble in Cara's jaw. She hovered on the bottom stair, her fingers gripping the newel post, her knuckles white.

"Damn you, Owain." She bent her head, then lifted it, shaking her hair out of her eyes, thrusting her jaw out at him in defiance. "You'll have your truce then. For the children." There was no doubt that the emphasis fell on the last three words. "But that's all you'll have, Owain. Good night."

And she went back up the stairs, her back stiff, her posture rigid with suppressed rage. The light shut off when she reached the landing. He shut off the one down below, then sank down onto the sofa in the dark.

Footsteps creaked over his head. He stripped off his shirt, untied his hiking boots and kicked them under the sofa, then slipped off his socks. Standing up again he unbuckled his belt, popped the snap on his jeans and slid them down over his hips. He dropped them next to his shirt and slid under the covers. Upstairs he heard the bed creak. He remembered the times he and Cara had made it creak far louder and more insistently than that.

"Don't think about it," he mumbled to himself. He was in her house again. For now that was enough.

And it would be more than his life was worth if Cara ever found out that his electrical expertise extended to furnaces as well as irons and toasters. No one knew that except him.

And if Mrs. Garrity suspected how her furnace had developed a rather sudden malady a few hours ago, she wasn't complaining.

"Imagine that," she had said when she had looked at the thermostat. "Furnace must've broke down. We'll have to go to Camilla's after all." Owain ignored the broad wink she had given him as the taxi pulled away.

Owain lay back down and folded his arms under his head. It wasn't going to be easy—this evening had proved that. But he didn't want things easy anymore. He was no longer a child who expected all things wonderful to be handed to him on a plate.

Well, there would be no Cara on a plate. If he wanted her again, he would have to work at it. He would have to convince her that he loved her as well as the children. And chances were it would take time, patience and perseverance.

But looking around him—at the silhouette of the Christmas tree, tall and dark against the pinkish glow of the snowy night, at the three stockings hung above the fireplace, at the presents heaped beneath the tree, and Nestor prowling among them, sniffing out which one contained the catnip mouse—Owain knew he wanted it.

The bed creaked again. He heard footsteps in the hallway. The light flicked on for a moment in the bathroom, then off again. Footsteps approached the stairs. He felt a wild surge of hope.

"I've put a clean towel in the bathroom for you," Cara said.

He twisted under the blankets, in pain almost. "Thanks."

And like the ghost of Christmas past, she was gone.

A towel, for God's sake! He didn't need a towel. He needed Cara. Now. Desperately.

There was no other woman on earth he wanted so badly. She was, for now and for always, going to be his woman.

But as he lay there sleepless until the first gray streaks of dawn touched the horizon, he wondered if he would ever be able to convince her to become his wife.

Chapter Ten

Whoever thought that "Peace on Earth" had anything to do with Christmas obviously never spent it in the company of six-year-old twins. It was the noisiest, most beautiful Christmas that Owain could remember in his entire life.

It would have been perfect except for the coolness that existed between Cara and himself. It had not thawed by morning. But the twins' enthusiasm masked Cara's deliberate indifference. When they hurtled down the stairs at just past seven and found him lying on the sofa almost under the tree, they acted as if he was the greatest gift they could have received.

They both turned to their mother with shining eyes. Hugh even said thank-you. But Cara, still standing on the stairs behind them, shook her head.

"The furnace went out at Mrs. Garrity's," she explained in a careful monotone. "That's all."

"But I thought..." Hugh's smile vanished. His face fell.

"I know what you thought," Cara said evenly. "Don't think it."

"But, Mom!"

"Just be glad for the day." And she went past them all into the kitchen to put on the coffee.

Owain knew how hard it was for her. It was all too clear that Hugh and Bronwen wanted what he wanted himself.

Deep down, he thought, Cara still wanted it too. But she wasn't admitting it. At least not yet.

He and his son set about playing with one of Hugh's toys, a lunar lander, trying to ignore the tensions that had reared their heads between mother and children, tensions he knew were his fault.

Out of the corner of his eye he watched Cara. He still couldn't get enough of just looking at her. He had written a song about the way she moved, the fluid grace of her body. He could just imagine what she would say if he told her. A grin crept onto his face.

She was opening a can of frozen orange juice, biting down on her lower lip with concentrated effort. Then she dumped the juice into the container and mixed it with the requisite number of cans of water.

"Hey, look, Mom," Bronwen called. "See what Grandma and Grandpa Williams sent?" She held up a corduroy jumper and a turtleneck shirt to go under it. Then her eyes got round when she saw what was beneath them. "A doll dressed just like I will be!" she breathed. And she pulled out a doll, obviously lovingly made, and dressed in a jumper and turtleneck just like the ones she had shown her mother.

Cara smiled. A real smile. The first true one Owain had seen all morning. "They're lovely."

"See?" Bronwen held them out to Owain. "My daddy's mom and dad gave them to me."

"They're great," he said and meant it. He could not be jealous of the love that Martin's parents showered on his children. He could only wish that Cara would let his own shower a bit too. But he couldn't say that. It would be just one more thing that would make her think that he was after the children and that she was the means to the end, nothing more.

He unfolded himself from the sofa and went into the kitchen. "Can I give you a hand?"

"No thank you." She didn't look at him.

"I could set the table."

"I said, 'No.'" The look she gave him was pure ice. "You've done enough, Owain. *More than enough*." She spun away, the spoon stirring like fury in the orange juice.

Taking the hint, he walked away. But after breakfast he didn't take no for an answer. The children had cleared the table at Cara's insistence, but then she sent them off to the family room to play with their new toys while she did the dishes.

Owain picked up the dish towel and leaned against the counter. "I'll help."

"I can do it," Cara said shortly.

"I know that. I want to help."

Her jaw tightened and she glanced over her shoulder at the children as if she were trying to judge if they were able to overhear what she might say. She must have decided that they were for she managed a forced smile. "Suit yourself."

She washed, making an unholy clatter with the silverware and the plates. Owain dried.

"Thanks for letting me stay," he said under cover of the noise.

Cara shrugged, scouring the frying pan like mad.

"I've enjoyed it. I haven't spent a Christmas with kids in years. Since I was a kid, I guess."

She shrugged again, rinsed a stack of plates and thwacked them into the drainer. Owain dried them carefully, then tried again. "Is it always this snowy at Christmas?"

"Some years."

He smiled. "Ah, progress."

She gave him a sharp look. "What?"

"You spoke to me."

She rinsed off the bacon platter, redirected the spray and soaked the front of his shirt. "So sorry," she said with false sweetness. "You go change. I'll finish up here."

Owain knew enough to make a strategic retreat. For the moment at least. Actually he knew enough—he thought—to take a bit of perverse hope from all the coldness he was getting. If she truly didn't give a damn about him anymore, she would be a lot more relaxed around him than she was.

He came back with a dry shirt on just as she was hanging up the dish towel. "Be careful," he told her. "I owe you one."

She gave him a wary look, then went into the other room as if by avoiding him nothing would happen.

She was wrong. He got his own back an hour later.

He had gone outside with Hugh and Bronny to build a snowman. The snow had ceased at last and the wind had dropped, leaving the park a winter wonderland just right for eager hands to roll gigantic snowballs to make snowmen. It didn't take much urging to get Owain outside to help make one.

It also, he figured, preserved the truce in a more palatable way than he and Cara were managing in the same silent room. But he felt a little guilty while he was out there rolling around in the snow, as if he were depriving her of her children on the holiday.

When she was dragged out of the house by Bronwen so she could admire their finished snowman, he said so.

"I didn't mean to take them away from you, Cara."

She just stared at him, her expression indecipherable. The cold air had reddened her cheeks, and blond tendrils of hair were escaping from beneath her blue-and-white Norwegian snow cap. Owain thought she looked like an angel.

"It's all right," she said somewhat stiffly. "They're enjoying themselves."

Owain watched them rolling in the snowdrifts like red and blue puppies, giggling and laughing as they pelted each other with snowballs. "Yeah, but they'd have enjoyed this just as much with you."

"Mmm." She ducked her head, refusing to look at him.

"Cara?"

But he never got to speak, because at that moment Hugh smacked him in the back with a snowball. "Gotcha!" his son cried.

Instinctively Owain scooped up a handful of snow and packed it. Turning, he flung it lightly at Hugh. It hit him in the chest.

Seconds later Bronwen hit her mother and Hugh hit his sister. The sides were drawn.

"Come on, Bron," Owain said. "Let's get 'em." He started flinging handfuls at his son while Hugh, turning himself into a miniature tornado, churned through the snow, scattering it all over everyone.

"Hey!" Owain reached for him, squinting against the snowfall he was being inundated with. He grabbed the boy and held him over his head, spinning him around and then pitching him lightly into a drift. Straightening up, he grinned over at Bronwen, only to be hit hard in the back by a snowball thrown by Cara.

He stared.

"Got you," she said and he saw her smile.

She had got him, indeed. Every bit of need and desire that he had carefully suppressed surged through him. He felt as if he had been hit by lightning, not by a fistful of snow. "Did you now?" He moved toward her, a smile on his face. He bent and scooped up a handful of snow, beginning to pack it as he walked.

"Owain!" Cara began to back up, scooping up snow herself, packing it furiously, dropping it accidentally in her haste, then scooping more. "Owain!"

"Ye-es?" he drawled.

Hugh had floundered out of the drift and was running toward him. Bronwen shouted a warning, then launched herself and dropped her brother with a flying tackle. Not a bad idea, Owain thought, and picked up his pace.

Cara was almost running backward now. She floundered when the snow got higher around her knees. Catching herself she heaved the snowball at him. This time she missed. He grinned and started to run. Cara's eyes widened and she spun and began to run, too.

Owain tossed the snowball lightly, catching her between the shoulders. It hadn't been meant to hurt, only to disarm her, and it worked. She turned to grin and taunt him when he caught her, plowing her over in the snow and going right down on top of her.

"Got *you*." His mouth was only an inch from her own.

It was a mistake. The feel of her body, warm and yielding beneath him, sparked an instantaneous response. If the snowball that caught him in the back had been a lightning bolt, this was a full-fledged forest fire. God, how he wanted her! Wanted to touch her again, to love her again, to feel her loving response to him.

He couldn't help himself. Her eyes were dark jade, the deep green of a forest pool, and he wanted to drown in them. He wanted to drown in her. His lips descended, touching hers. They didn't ask this time. The answer would have been no.

They took, they tasted, they persuaded. And he could feel a response. He could feel the need in her the same as he felt it in himself, warm and trembling, aching for fulfillment.

And then she was shoving hard against his chest, pushing him over onto his back in the snow. She bolted to her feet, her shaking hands brushing down her jeans to rid them of the snowflakes. The color flamed in her cheeks.

"That wasn't funny," she snapped, and she strode back to the house without another word.

Owain—the ache of arousal mingling with the sting of loss—quite agreed with her. It wasn't funny at all.

NOR WAS IT FUNNY late that afternoon when he was sitting in the chair by the fireplace reading about Paddington Bear to the children and there was a quick tap-tap on the back door and Greg Christopher walked in.

Who was the more surprised would have been hard to say. But Greg's surprise was certainly the more obvious. He stopped dead, his arms full of Christmas packages, and simply stared. He didn't seem to like what he saw.

"You!"

"And a merry Christmas to you, too." Owain closed the book slowly and wrapped his arms around the slender shoulders of the children, drawing them against him instinctively.

Greg stood where he was a moment longer, then dredged up a smile for the kids and held out the packages to them. "Merry Christmas, gang."

Owain couldn't blame them for scrambling off the chair and descending on Greg.

"For us?" Bronwen asked, taking the one Greg handed her. And Hugh dodged behind her to grab a package from beneath the tree, which he held out to Greg.

"Thanks. This one's for you. From all of us." He turned and bawled up the stairs. "Hey, Mom, Greg's here!"

Greg had hunkered down to watch the kids open their presents, but he looked up again when Cara came down the stairs.

Owain looked, too, trying to gauge her reaction. It made his stomach knot.

She came down quickly and held out her arms to Greg. He swept her into his and gave her a sound hug. And a kiss. Owain's teeth ground together. He cleared his throat and stood up, then strode across the room, practically knocking them over on the way to the door. He opened it and shut it again.

"The cat wanted out," he said. "Excuse me." And he crossed the room again to the chair, careful to cut between them.

"So much for civility," he heard Cara mutter.

He gave her a tight smile. If she wanted civility, she had got the wrong man. He remembered one time when he and Mike and Dougal had been on the road. Some local yokel had been jealous of the time Owain was spending with his girlfriend. He had chipped Owain's tooth. Owain had broken his nose.

He would break more than Greg's nose if it came to that. And he knew Cara sensed it. But apparently she didn't mind playing with fire, for she stepped closer to Greg and took his hand, drawing him into the kitchen.

"How about a glass of wine?"

"Sounds wonderful."

She glanced over at Owain, who was leaning against the mantel glowering at her. "D'you want one?" she asked offhandedly.

"That would be nice." He gave her a polite smile, one that said he could keep his caveman tendencies under wraps if he had to.

But it wasn't easy.

Particularly when Bronwen and Hugh were simply thrilled with the kits to construct their own model dinosaurs that Greg had brought them. Owain wished Greg had brought something inappropriate, rather than being so on target with his gifts. What was worse was the blue lamb's wool sweater he gave Cara. It was elegant, and Owain could see at once that the soft drape of the cowl neckline would suit her as well as the color did. He was jealous as hell, particularly when, with very little urging from Greg, she agreed to go try it on.

He had given her a sweater, too. One that his mother had knitted over the past month, just to prove to him that she still could. It was gorgeous, a rust-and-gold wool that would heighten Cara's natural color. And she had said how nice it was in a very well-brought-up voice that seemed to betray no emotion at all.

She certainly hadn't volunteered to try it on.

He was hurt.

Cara took Greg's sweater and went upstairs. The moment she was out of the room, Greg turned to him, frowning. "I didn't think you'd be back."

"Why not?"

Greg shrugged. "Too small a pond for too big a fish, I'd have thought."

"What's that mean?"

Greg's blue eyes were wide and innocent. "A big star like you..."

Owain scowled. "That's past."

Greg looked skeptical. "Really?"

"Yes, really." Owain's voice was firm. "Anyway, who told you?"

"Cara, of course. She said you had to go back to L.A." He gave a polite smile. "Commitments, I think she said."

Owain didn't reply.

"So why don't you go back to those commitments?" Greg went on, his voice taking on a tougher note.

"Because now I have commitments here."

"Here? What commitments?" Then, as if he guessed what Owain would say, he said sharply, "Cara? Don't make me laugh."

"What's funny?"

"Not a damned thing. You stay away from her. She doesn't need you."

"A matter of opinion," Owain said more mildly than he felt.

"I mean it."

"And if I don't?"

Greg sidestepped that. "Why would you want to hurt her again?"

"I don't want to hurt her."

"You did."

"Not intentionally."

Greg glared at him, a muscle in his jaw working. "What is it about you?" he muttered. "Why you?" He spoke more to himself than to Owain.

"Well, what do you think?"

They both turned to see Cara standing on the bottom step, the new sweater hugging her breasts and curving over her hips, the blue of it somehow making her fair hair look even blonder and her green eyes like the depths of the sunlit sea.

"Gorgeous," Greg breathed.

Owain didn't say anything. Couldn't. His breath caught in his throat. He swallowed hard, trying to relieve the pressure. But it only got worse, for Cara stepped down from the stairs and came over to Greg, put her hands on his shoulders and went up on tiptoes to give him a kiss.

"Thank you." Her voice sounded breathy, slightly hesitant. Owain's fists clenched.

Greg smiled down at her, almost dazed. Then, clearing his throat, he shot a triumphant glance at Owain. "I was wondering," he said to Cara, "there's a concert tomorrow at Ellison Hall. Baroque music. Would you like to go?"

There was a second's pause. "I'd love to," Cara said. She looked over at the children, then back at Greg. "But we'd better make it a tentative acceptance. Suzy's out of town, and I don't know if I can get another baby-sitter on such short notice."

"Why not me?" Owain said.

Cara's head jerked around. Greg frowned.

Owain gave them a thin-lipped smile. "Since I'm going to be here anyway." It killed him to make the offer. The last thing he wanted was to see her go out with Greg Christopher. But the last thing *she* wanted, he figured, was to let him infiltrate the children's lives. And he knew by the look she gave him that he was right.

Cara was obviously torn, her eyes skittering from one thing to another in the room, as if she might light on the perfect answer out there somewhere. But she didn't seem to, because a moment later she drew away from Greg and twisted her hands together in front of her.

"Let me call Jenny Fielding down the street first," she said. "Then, if I can't get her..."

"Why not let O'Neill do it?" Greg put in easily. "It might be just the thing for him. Let him see what kids are like."

"Yeah," Owain couldn't help goading her. "Why not?"

Cara looked from him to Greg, annoyed. "All right," she muttered.

Pleased, and uncertain as to why Cara wasn't, Greg bent and brushed a kiss across her lips. "I'll pick you up about seven-thirty." He zipped up his jacket again and wrapped the muffler around his neck. "Merry Christmas."

"Merry Christmas." Cara sounded wooden when she spoke.

Greg went to the door and turned around as he opened it. "Merry Christmas to you, O'Neill. When are you going back to L.A. this time?"

"I'm not."

Greg stared, nonplussed.

Owain smiled.

Cara said something softly to Greg, something Owain couldn't hear. He nodded briefly, but he still gave Owain a wary look that lasted a few seconds before he went out into the waning winter light.

Cara shut the door behind him and leaned against it as if it were all that gave her the strength to stand at all. She glanced at her watch, then at Owain. He wondered if she were trying to calculate how many hours until she would be rid of him. He didn't imagine she would like the answer to that.

Finally she pushed herself away from the door and let out a deep breath. "Well," she said briskly, "I've got to get ready to go to my grandmother's now. Are you going to Mrs. Garrity's sister's for supper?"

Owain shook his head. "No."

"Oh, well, I'm sure there are several good buffets open. I know that—"

"I'm going to your grandmother's," he cut in before she could make it any more apparent that she didn't want him along. "She invited me."

Cara looked as if she had spent all morning adding a column of figures and it had just come out wrong. "How nice," she said.

The children saved the day. They chattered incessantly in the car, commenting about one present or another, then speculating about whether Gram would like what they were going to give her, then demanding that Owain tell them about Christmas in Wales.

He did, and Cara's frosty silence was not as noticeable as it might have been otherwise. And it seemed to be swept away altogether once they arrived at Mrs. Nute's.

She was clearly delighted to see Owain, and she made it plain without exactly clubbing Cara over the head with it. Her enthusiasm was natural, and since the kids' was, too, Owain felt better all the time.

As the evening wore on, Cara seemed to soften a bit as well. She smiled more, relaxed a bit. She didn't object when Owain held her chair for her at dinner, or when her grandmother suggested that he carve the turkey because he was the man of the house.

She even seemed to begin to enjoy herself by the time the dishes were done and put away and Owain had thrown another log on the fire. Her grandmother and the children were snuggled together in the love seat, and Cara was curled in the corner of the sofa. Owain debated going and sitting down next to her. But he was afraid to break the spell, so he sat in the armchair opposite and contented himself with simply watching her while he listened to her grandmother's Christmas stories.

The stories were reminiscences of Mrs. Nute's own childhood Christmases and, just as she had done with the story of her first experiences in America, she made these times come alive too. For a while he even forgot Cara was there. He let himself go, relaxing and listening, remembering what it was like to be a child again and have dreams.

"Didja have snow?" Hugh asked her, inching even closer.

"Now and then. Not like here." His great-grandmother shook her head. "I couldn't believe all the snow when I came here. That winter I thought it would never stop. My mama said it was God shaking the feathers out of his pillows at night."

Bronwen giggled. "She didn't."

"Oh, yes, she did."

"Did you believe her?" Hugh asked.

"I wanted to. I wanted a little magic then. All children do, I think. And when Christmas came that first year, I got my magic."

"What was it?"

"A Christmas tree."

Both children stared at her, astonished. "What's magic about a Christmas tree?" Hugh wanted to know.

"I'd never had one," their grandmother said simply. "It seemed heavenly to me. And I was absolutely amazed when my dad brought one home that he'd cut in the woods."

"Didn't you cut 'em in England?"

Gram shook her head. "No. We didn't have any land to speak of. All the land was owned by big estates. Nobody had Christmas trees there anyway. At least no one I knew," she amended. "But I'd seen one. That's why I thought they were so wonderful."

"Where'd you see one?" Bronny asked.

"It was on a big estate near where I grew up. It was Christmas Day, and my grandfather had taken me for a walk, to get me out of the way so my mother and grandmother could prepare the dinner. My dad had already gone to America," she added. "And we walked and walked. I had little short legs and I could hardly keep up. Finally my grandfather carried me, and he said he'd show me something special if I was good. We cut through the grounds of this estate, close enough to the house to see. And there it was in the window, all lit up with candles." Her eyes shone at the memory. "A Christmas tree."

The children, who had always taken Christmas trees for granted, looked with new eyes at the small one across the room.

Gram shook her head. "I haven't thought about that in years," she said. "I wonder whatever happened to that place. I wonder if it's still there." She looked over at Owain as if, by having grown up in the same country, he might know.

He shrugged. "Where were you from?"

She told him. It was a small village in Essex. He frowned. "And your dad was a miner?"

"Yes. Everyone here was."

It was Owain's turn to shake his head. "Not many miners from Essex, I wouldn't think. Farmers and fishermen there."

Gram lifted her shoulders. "Well, my dad mined." She smiled again and Owain knew her mind was still busy with memories of times past, people remembered.

"You ought to go back sometime, you know," he said easily.

Gram looked startled. "To England?"

"Why not?"

She didn't say anything for a moment. Then she tilted her head to the side and pursed her lips. "Interesting thought."

"I don't know, Gram," Cara put in suddenly. "You might rather you hadn't."

Her grandmother gave her a curious look. "Why is that?"

Cara looked faintly uncomfortable. "Sometimes raking over old coals does more harm than good." She gave Owain a hard stare. The words, he knew, were meant for him.

"Sometimes," her grandmother agreed, but she didn't sound completely convinced.

Cara got to her feet and straightened the blue sweater that she had left on when she'd got changed to go to her grandmother's. "Come on, kiddos." She held out her hands to the twins. "It's been a long day and we've got a ways to go before we sleep."

"Ah, Mom." The protest came in unison. They looked at Owain, as if expecting him to take their side.

He stood up and stretched, lifting his arms high over his head and locking his fingers together. "Time to go, your mother said," he told them. "Get your jackets on."

They stared at him hard a moment, then gave in and scrambled to their feet, still grumbling. Owain looked over at Cara. She glared at him.

"I suppose you'd have preferred that I undermine you," he said in an undertone as he helped her on with her coat.

"I'd rather you weren't here at all."

"You've made that more than clear," he told her, and she had the good grace to look abashed. Her fingers fumbled with the buttons on her coat even though she ducked her head and stared at them with the greatest of concentration.

"Merry Christmas," her grandmother said to them both as they stood in the doorway. She leaned toward Cara and kissed her cheek.

"Merry Christmas, Gram."

"Merry Christmas, Mrs. Nute," Owain echoed.

She lifted her hand and touched his jaw. "Not Mrs. Nute," she chided him gently. "I'm just Gram."

He heard Cara suck in her breath sharply, but her grandmother just clicked her tongue as if to discount what was obviously an objection. "Gram," she repeated.

"Merry Christmas, Gram," Owain said. His voice cracked.

She kissed him, too, her lips dry and whisper-soft against the roughness of his cheek. She smelled of lilacs and springtime and he felt a wave of homesickness overcome him—a memory of his own grandmother so strong it made his throat ache.

She waved to them from the door as they drove off into the night.

"Neat, huh?" Hugh said drowsily from where he was curled in the back seat.

"Great," Bronwen mumbled. And they were both asleep.

Owain wished his own dreams were as easily fulfilled as a child's.

THE MORNING TURNED into a nightmare.

It started shortly after breakfast when Cara, having gone for a walk, ran into Junior Claussen just as he was coming out of Mrs. Garrity's house. The conversation she had with him, she told Owain moments later, was "enlightening to say the least."

He looked up from the breakfast table where he was reading the morning paper and drinking a cup of coffee, enjoying the domesticity and wondering how to prolong it, when he felt an instant chill in the air. "You don't say," he said mildly.

"I damned well *do* say." Cara flung the door shut, almost catching Nestor's tail in it, and came to stand on the opposite side of the table, placing her palms flat on it while she glowered down at him. "Junior thinks," she went on in a precise, well-modulated tone, "that those automatic ignition wires didn't just move themselves."

Owain tried to manage a modicum of interest. He felt slightly sick. "Really?"

"Really. He says someone must have moved them. Separated them, he said."

Owain lifted his eyebrows. "You think Mrs. Garrity is messing with her furnace?"

Cara slapped both palms hard on the table. "No, by God, I do not think Mrs. Garrity is messing with her furnace! I think you are!"

"Were," Owain corrected absently. Then outraged, "Me?"

"Oh, Owain! Don't give me that injured innocent stare. Don't give me your butter-wouldn't-melt-in-my-mouth look. I know you! You are the most manipulative person I have ever met. You manipulate everyone! Everything!"

"Cara—"

"Don't 'Cara' me! That furnace was just one more subterfuge, wasn't it, Owain? You knew I wouldn't let you in the front door otherwise, so you had to resort to that."

"That's right."

She looked positively apoplectic. "You admit it?"

"Of course I admit it. I knew you wouldn't let me in the front door, isn't that what you said?"

"Yes."

"And I was right, wasn't I?"

"Yes," she said through gritted teeth.

"And I wanted in, so..." He spread his hands. "What're you gonna do, call the cops?"

"I'd like to," she flared. "But you'd probably think of some way to talk your way around them, too."

"Probably."

"Oh!"

He smiled at her over the rim of his coffee cup.

"Well, it won't work," she informed him. "The furnace is fixed. So you can just go away now. Go on! Get out!"

Owain took another sip of his coffee and stayed right where he was.

Cara strangled the chair rung. *"Go on!"*

"No." He said it quietly, but with every bit of force he could muster. It was considerable. Cara simply stared at him. Her fingers clenched and unclenched.

"I love you, Cara. I want to be part of your life."

"You want your children and I'm standing in your way."

He didn't even dignify that with a response. "And you love me, too," he went on doggedly.

"I don't!"

"That's a lie."

"I'm not the liar around here, Owain O'Neill," she spat at him. "You're the liar. All those days you pretended to care about me, infiltrating my life, worming your way into my—" She stopped abruptly and bent her head. Her hands, gripping the chair back, shook.

"Into your heart?"

For an eternity he didn't think she was going to answer. Her shoulders trembled, her fists tightened. Then she lifted her head and glared at him, her eyes brimming. "Yes, all right. You want your pound of flesh? Into my heart, damn you! I did fall in love with you, and you betrayed me!"

"I did not!"

"What do you call it then?" she demanded bitterly.

He stood up and came around the table, reaching for her. But she avoided him, crossing the room and folding her arms across her chest, taking refuge behind the chair in the family room.

"Cara, it was a mistake."

She snorted. "I'll say it was. A doozy." She gave a brittle laugh. "But not as big a one as I made when I fell in love with you."

Owain jammed his fists into the pockets of his jeans. Outside in the snow he could see the twins hurling snowballs at each other, not a care in the world. Damn it, why wouldn't she believe him?

"Cara, listen, I've said I'm sorry. I handled it badly. But I explained all that already. It's over. What matters now is what happens between us from here on out."

"Nothing."

"What?"

"I said, 'nothing.' Nothing is going to happen between us. There isn't any 'us' anymore. So just leave, will you? Forget you ever knew us. It shouldn't be that hard." She was staring out the window, too, and the light caught the tears along her eyelids. She swiped at them, then sniffled and muttered, "Damn it."

"I can't forget you. I *won't* forget you."

"Well, I'll forget you."

"No, you won't. You can't either. Besides," he told her, "there won't be any more possibility of 'out of sight, out of mind' now because I'm staying right here."

"Not here."

"Not in this house, no. But at Mrs. Garrity's. Me and Norbert Hill," he told her grimly.

Cara gave a quick disbelieving laugh. "I'll believe that when I see it. You? Here? One third of the famous Cardiff Connection spend the rest of his life in Belle River, Wisconsin? There's a laugh."

"Well, the laugh is going to be on you." He crossed the room in three quick strides and grabbed her, hauling her into his arms just like the caveman he had been trying desperately not to become. "I will stay as long as it takes, damn it," he grated. And then he could help himself no longer.

His control snapped. His mouth sought hers and found it unerringly, kissing her hard, desperately. His tongue sought entrance, but was blocked by her tightly clenched teeth. She twisted, trying to get away from him, and only succeeded in infuriating him more. His arms tightened around her, holding her struggling body against his. He felt her shift, felt her mouth open slightly. An entrance at last, a yielding. He exulted. His tongue slid in.

"Ouch! Damn it!" He jerked his head back, spitting blood, wiping his mouth with the back of his hand. "What the hell...! You...you...*bit* me!"

"Yes," she said calmly, "I did." And she gave him a smile, exactly the same sort of smile that he remembered his mother giving him when, her patience tried to the utmost, she had finally given him a well-deserved smack on the bottom.

"But—"

"And I'll do it again if you ever force yourself on me. You can't take what you want all your life, Owain. You can't take me, and you can't take my children."

He sagged, tasting the bitter metallic blood. His heart pounded and his throat worked convulsively. The worst of it was . . . she was right.

"I'm sorry."

She looked at him, her green eyes doubting. He met them steadily. "I am," he said.

She pressed her lips together in a thin line. Then she gave a curt nod that accepted his apology but didn't go an inch beyond.

He sighed. "I—" But he never got to finish what he had intended to say, because just then the door flew open and Bronwen and Hugh thundered in.

"We need our sleds!" They shook snow to the four corners of the kitchen like puppies come out of a lake. Cara blinked, as if she didn't quite remember where she was. Then she nodded.

"I'll fetch them from the basement. You stay where you are." She took a step toward the basement door, then seemed to realize that she would have to pass Owain to get to it. Her consternation was evident.

Owain wiped a trickle of blood off his mouth and stepped back, giving her a slight bow as he did so.

She bowed her head and hurried past him.

"What'd you do to your mouth?" Bronwen demanded, studying him with undisguised interest.

"I . . . bit my tongue," he prevaricated just as Cara emerged.

Color flooded her cheeks. She thrust the sleds at the children, then turned away.

"You should get him some ice, Mommy," Bronwen said, "and a washcloth. Like you did Hugh when he got his bloody nose." And she stood right there and waited while Cara did exactly that.

"I don't know why you didn't think of it," Bronwen went on.

Owain, pressing against his mouth the washcloth she had shoved into his hands, gave her an interested look over the tops of the children's heads. She blushed even more furiously.

"I must've forgotten," she excused herself. Placing her hands on her daughter's shoulders, she steered her toward the door. "You go on now, both of you, before you drip all over the kitchen. And be careful."

"We will," Hugh promised. He halted on the doorstep to turn back to Owain. "Wanta come sledding with us?"

"In a little while," Owain said.

"You promise?" Hugh stood fast in the doorway.

"I promise," Owain said at the same time Cara said, "Hugh, stop badgering. You have your sister for company."

"Her?" Hugh grumbled. But his mother gave him a glare that sent him shuffling his feet out onto the porch and down the steps into the snow.

"You do not have to sled with them," Cara said firmly once the door was shut.

"I *want* to sled with them."

"I *don't* want you to."

"*They* do."

The two of them glared at each other.

"They're just children," Cara said irritably.

Owain bit his tongue before he said *My children*. Enough was enough. Instead he dabbed at his mouth again with the washcloth and said carefully, "Cara, they need more than just you and each other. They need someone to sled with, to go to father-son banquets with, to fly kites with. They need a father."

"They had a father. Martin is their father!"

"Martin *was* their father," Owain corrected softly. "But Martin can't do those things with them now. They need a flesh-and-blood father, not just memories. And you need a flesh-and-blood husband!"

"Maybe," Cara said to him, not looking at him. "Maybe I do."

He felt a moment's surge of hope.

"But if I did, you can be damned sure I wouldn't pick you. Greg is definitely more my style."

Owain groaned. "Don't be an idiot!"

"I'm not being an idiot!" Her hands on her hips, she lifted her chin and glared at him. "You want them to have a father, fine, they can have Greg."

Apprehension twisted his guts. "They have me."

"Greg can—"

"Greg can do whatever he damned well pleases. That's his business. And if you're a big enough fool to marry him, that's yours. But I abandoned those kids once, I'm not doing it again, Cara. Say what you want. Do what you want. But I'm *not* leaving!"

He snatched his jacket off the hook by the door and stuffed his arms into it, then yanked the zipper halfway up. "I'll pick up my gear when I get done sledding. I won't impose on your 'hospitality'—" he gave the word a bitter twist and was gratified to see her wince slightly "—anymore. But I want you to know, Cara, that no matter what, I am not leaving!"

"What if *I* leave?" she asked belligerently.

"Then I'll follow you." He turned and looked at her, his hand clenched over the doorknob. "Do you honestly think that there's anywhere you could go that I wouldn't find you?"

She gave him a look of loathing so powerful it wrenched his gut.

"I guess this is what they call a stalemate," she said at last.

Owain looked at her, his heart heavy. "Yeah, I guess it is."

Chapter Eleven

"I think I just might have to adopt you," Grandma Nute said when she opened the door for the cat and found Owain standing there for the third time that week.

Owain made a face, let the cat swish out between his legs, then stepped into the welcoming warmth of the kitchen.

"Or is that the wrong thing to say, under the circumstances?" Gram asked him, gesturing him toward the chair by the wood stove that warmed the room. At first Owain had considered it quaint. Now it was merely comfortable, and he looked forward to the hours he spent beside it. He didn't have much else to look forward to.

Shrugging off his jacket, he dropped it into the log box. "Under the circumstances," he said glumly, "it sounds about right."

"Still in limbo?" Gram put the kettle on and got cookies out of the cookie jar, put them on a plate and carried them to the table. Owain snatched one off, as he always did, before they ever got there. Not even Mrs. Garrity's cookies equaled Gram's. She batted his hand away, but with a smile.

"Limbo is a nice word for it," he said.

Nothing had changed really since the day he had walked out of Cara's house two weeks before, vowing to hang on forever. Of course, he had made such a hash of things that day, he could hardly expect things to change. He had done everything wrong. Kissing her in anger for one thing. Telling her in no uncertain terms that he was going to be there for the kids regardless of what she did or thought was another. Now she thought he was after them first and foremost without a doubt.

But however much he railed at himself in private, he didn't accomplish anything. Nothing seemed to accomplish anything. Not even the stiff apology he had made the next day.

There had been nothing to do but go on with his interviews and be there for the kids as he had said he would.

He felt like a divorced father. One with unlimited visiting rights. He made it a point to drop by most days after school to take the kids sledding or to hike through the woods in search of animal tracks. Once he had taken them to a Disney movie, and once he had taken them out for pizza. Each time he had invited Cara to accompany them. Each time she had refused.

The looks she gave him said she knew he was getting tired of it. But she thought it was the kids he was getting tired of, and that was where she was wrong. He loved the kids and he delighted in spending time with them. Their outings went far better than he had ever thought they would. What he was tired of was the cold shoulder he got from her.

As close as she came to a word of kindness was the morning that Bronwen dragged him off to be "shown" at show-and-tell since no one would believe that he was a bona fide former rock star. He had been wildly embarrassed, but he had gone. More to prove to Cara that he would hang in there no matter what than because he really wanted to go. And she had rewarded him with a halfway sympathetic smile and a "poor you," when he got back.

But beyond that, nothing had improved since the day after Christmas. If she no longer out-and-out objected to him when he came to get the kids, she was cool and resigned, determined, it appeared, to wait him out.

Well, she would have a long wait.

Owain reached for another cookie, nibbling on it, considering. "Has she always been this stubborn?"

"Always. Gets a notion in her head, and that's it."

"Once she had the notion that she loved me."

Gram gave him a gentle smile. "You'll just have to give her lots of time then, so's she can remember that."

Owain grimaced. "Hell could freeze over first."

Gram patted his hand. He noticed she didn't deny it.

"Plus there's Greg," he added irritably.

"Greg's a friend."

"Tell Cara that."

Gram looked taken aback. "You mean she's dating him?"

"She's dating him." He raked a hand through his hair and scowled fiercely. "The first time they went out, I got to baby-sit." He didn't bother to add that he had suggested it because he hoped Cara would turn Greg down.

Gram couldn't help smiling. "Bad for the old ego, was it?"

Owain grinned faintly. "Terrible."

"And she's still going out with him?"

"That's what Suzy says. She's the one baby-sitting now. Last night they went to some old Humphrey Bogart movie festival."

"Maybe she'll fall for Humphrey," Gram suggested hopefully.

"Anybody but me, I reckon."

"Poor Owain."

"Yeah." But feeling sorry for himself had never accomplished much in the past and Owain couldn't see where it was going to do a lot of good now. But he didn't know what was, either. "Enough of this," he said, flipping open his notebook and hauling the mini-tape recorder out of his pocket. "Let's get on with your interview."

That was the one thing that held him together—being able to interview Gram and Norbert Hill and two people he had met down at the Pleasant View Rest Home. Vicariously living out other people's lives gave him a small respite from his own.

Gram's saga had stretched out over the past two weeks, and Owain had found it endlessly fascinating. Cara's grandmother was a delightful storyteller, droll and amusing, with just a hint of self-deprecating humor that always made him want to hear more.

He had discovered early in his interviews that it often was best to work backward with his interviewees. To say, "Start at the beginning," never worked because they found it too daunting, and they often left important things out. But to start at the present and work back—even if, in this case, it took eighty years—was more thorough and gave him a better insight into how things developed.

He and Gram had worked their way back through her fifty-nine years of marriage, her six-week whirlwind courtship that had ended in Tom Nute's proposing and then whisking her off to New York City for a honeymoon.

"Halfway across the country," Gram told him, still starry-eyed at the thought. "And I'd only known him six weeks! My mother gave me three dollars," she confided, "to get home in case he left me."

Owain grinned. "Three dollars?"

"That's what Tom said when I told him. And I only told him because I lost it anyway when we were running to catch a trolley."

"I can't imagine anyone leaving you anywhere," he told her.

Gram rolled her eyes. "I'm sure there were times Tom was sorely tempted. I was a very opinionated lady. I never minded telling him exactly what I thought. Not unlike your Cara."

"I wish she was *my* Cara."

"Patience, my dear. Have patience."

Owain grimaced and thought there was nothing else he could have.

"Have you found someone to do the typing for you yet?" Gram asked him when they were finishing.

"I'm going to talk to a woman today. Someone called Marsha Saunders. I got her name off the bulletin board in the English office at the college."

"I know Marsha. She was one of the Kline girls who lived over Hazel View way. Married Loras Meecham when she was barely out of high school. They got divorced. Then she married Bobby Saunders. They're divorced now, too." Gram paused and gave Owain an assessing look. "She's quite a dish."

Owain grinned. "But can she type?"

Gram's eyes were sly. "Good question. I was thinking—" she gave a rock in her rocking chair, then planted her feet firmly on the floor "—you and Marsha might want to double-date...with Cara and Greg."

Owain sputtered with laughter. "You conniving old lady!"

BUT THE FOLLOWING AFTERNOON the idea didn't seem quite so funny.

Marsha Saunders was, as Gram had said, "quite a dish." And Owain was at the point of wanting to try anything. So when Marsha Saunders got the typing job, she got a dinner invitation, too.

Just to explain his dissertation, Owain told her. She gave him a look that said she doubted that. He ignored it. She batted her eyelashes to let him know what she thought they would be discussing. He gave her a quick smile. Nothing very committed. He didn't realize yet that it wasn't necessary to be very committed with Marsha. She could read love into a handshake.

"We could just go now, if you want to," he said.

"You don't think I should, uh, dress up more?"

He shook his head. "Not a bit."

Marsha shrugged, but went to the closet and got out a rabbit's fur coat that he helped her into. He tried not to think that Cara would have just put on her old down parka and not even asked. He tried not to think how much he preferred the parka.

"I've got to drop something off at a friend's house," he said casually as he slipped into the car beside her. "Hope you don't mind."

Marsha gave him a generous smile. "Not at all."

In the back seat he had a box of Legos that, put together, made a fantastic castle. He knew that both Hugh and Bronwen had been coveting it for ages. Cara had told them it was too expensive, and he had agreed with her. But yesterday on his way home from Gram's he had stopped in the local discount store to pick up some odds and ends. He had found it on the January clearance table at a price he knew even Cara wouldn't have balked at, so he bought it. Tonight seemed like a perfect time to deliver it. That Marsha was sitting next to him in the front seat was purely coincidental.

"I'll just be a minute," he told Marsha when he pulled up in front of Cara's house. "Would you like to wait here or come in with me?"

"Is that Cara Williams's house?"

"Yes."

She gave Owain a questioning look. "I'll wait."

He thought, judging from the tone of her voice, that he was glad she had made that choice. He gave her a quick smile. "Be right back."

Luck was with him. Cara answered the door. He gave her a bright smile and put the package in her hands. "It's for the kids."

She held it gingerly, as if it might explode in her hands. "What—" But the kids appeared behind her before she got any further.

"Whatcha got?" Hugh asked, peeking into the bag.

Bronwen had a better angle. "Hey, wow . . . it's the Lego castle!" She whooped once and flung her arms around Owain, hugging him hard. "Thank you! Thank you!"

Cara glared. "I told you that was too ex—"

"It was on sale. Cheap."

"But—"

"I wouldn't have bought it otherwise, Cara. Honest." He met her gaze sincerely.

Her eyes narrowed.

"It was sixty-five percent off."

Her brows lifted, then she gave a reluctant shrug.

"Can you help us put it together?" Hugh asked, taking the package from his mother.

"Hugh!" she remonstrated.

"Not tonight," Owain said quickly, glancing over his shoulder. It was the moment he had been waiting for. "I'm . . . going out."

Cara's gaze followed his. Her eyes got even narrower. Her spine stiffened. She gave him a tight little polite smile. "So I see. Do have a good time." And she turned on her heel and walked into the house. The door shut in his face.

He stood there staring at the closed door and congratulated himself on having made her jealous. And then what? he asked himself. For a split-second's reaction from Cara he had sentenced himself to an entire evening with Marsha Saunders.

"Way to go, O'Neill," he muttered and cast a longing glance back at the firmly closed door once more before he made his way back to the car and Marsha.

"Is Cara a friend of yours?" Marsha asked him.

"Yeah." He wasn't sure what Cara would say about that, but he wasn't going into it with Marsha.

"A *good* friend?"

He gave her a narrow look. "What difference does that make?"

"A lot," Marsha said frankly. "If she is, I want to know what you asked me out for."

Owain put his hands on the steering wheel, then rested his head on them. It wasn't so much that he was a jerk, it was that he was such an *incompetent* jerk! He couldn't even play one woman against another successfully. "To talk about my dissertation," he said dully.

"Good." Marsha folded her hands in her lap, obviously glad that everything was settled to her satisfaction, even though she did reach over and pat his knee as if to comfort him. "I might have enjoyed something more," she said consolingly, "but I don't intend to get dumped a third time, if you see what I mean. I want all the cards on the table."

Owain gave her a weary smile. He put the car in gear and slowly pulled out into the street. "I see what you mean," he said.

But if he and Marsha knew where they stood with each other, Marsha obviously hadn't filled things in for Cara. Cara threw him a daggerlike glance the next day when he dropped by to see how the castle was coming along, and when Hugh asked if he would like to stay and help out, she said bitingly, "I'm sure Owain must have better things to do."

"As a matter of fact, I don't," he told her. "I'd love to."

She didn't look any more pleased with that. And she was even less pleased half an hour later when the phone rang and it was Marsha wanting to talk to him.

"For you." She held out the phone as if it were contaminated.

Owain took it, listened, answered Marsha's question—a legitimate one about a piece of illegible handwriting—and then hung up, not even bothering to try to make the call sound like more of a romantic entanglement than it was. He didn't need to, he discovered. Cara's imagination was doing it for him whether he wanted it to or not.

"Hot date?" she asked him when he had set the receiver back down.

"Do you care?"

"Of course not!"

"Then why are you asking?"

Stymied, she spun away from him, going back to the computer and beginning to clack away on the keys. Owain followed her.

"Jealous?" he asked her.

"No!"

"I think you are. I want you to be."

She turned and glared at him. "Why? Why won't you just leave well enough alone? You see the kids. You see them more than most divorced fathers ever see them!"

"We're not divorced," he reminded her.

"We weren't married!"

"I'd like to be."

"To get the kids."

"To get you." He touched her shoulder lightly.

Cara jerked away from him. "Damn you, Owain. Get out of here."

"MAKING ANY PROGRESS?" Gram asked him when he went out to see her on the following Saturday.

"Progress?" Owain snorted. "Is there such a thing with Cara?"

Gram squeezed his hand sympathetically and offered him a freshly baked cinnamon roll. He got out his tape recorder and they went to work.

"OWAIN?"

He couldn't believe his ears. Cara? Asking for him?

That was a first. Since Christmas he had felt as if he were banging his head against a stone wall. It was Valentine's

Day, and if he weren't so stubborn, he probably would have stopped. He had certainly got no encouragement.

Cara was as cold as ever. Not that he had much of a chance to be with her. It was, he discovered, her busiest season. Tax forms and all kinds of affidavits had to be filled out. Figures had to be added, totaled, balanced and otherwise dealt with. He thought that one reason she might have just let him be with the kids was simply to keep them out of her hair while she worked. She never asked for his help, of course. But she didn't deny him access to the kids either.

And now? he wondered.

Perhaps she was calling to respond to his Valentine's Day card. It had said, "I'll always be here for you. I love you." He meant every word. And he had drawn a tiny rain cloud at the bottom instead of his name. He knew she considered him in that light. She would know well enough whom it was from.

"What's up?" he asked easily, leaning against the newel post as he spoke.

"I—I can't—I need—" There was a thread of panic in her voice, a desperation he had never heard before.

"Cara, what is it?" His own studied nonchalance vanished. "Has something happened to the kids?"

"N...no. It...it's not the kids. It's...my f-father."

"What happened?"

"Heart...attack..." She could barely get the words out. They seemed to be choking off the sound of her voice.

"Is he...?"

"Alive. He's alive. Holding...his own, my mother says." Cara didn't sound as if she believed it. "I—"

He didn't need to hear any more. "I'll be right over."

He hung up before she could say another word. "I'll be back," he told Mrs. Garrity as he sprinted through the kitchen, sliding his arms into the sleeves of his jacket as he went.

There were two inches of new snow on the ground and it was still falling, but he didn't pay any attention. He ran lightly through it, ignoring the way it slipped inside the loafers he wore, ignoring everything but getting to Cara as quickly as he could.

She must have been watching for him because the kitchen door opened the moment his foot hit the porch steps. She looked awful, her face blotchy with crying, her eyes red and swollen, her hair tangled, as if she had raked her fingers through it. He wanted to wrap his arms around her and hold her. He wanted to tell her everything would be all right. He wanted to say anything, do anything, that would ease her worry.

But she had a grip on her emotions by this time. She stood stiffly, like a soldier at Buckingham Palace, and as she stepped back to let him in, not even his jacket brushed against her.

"I'm all right now," she told him, but beneath the steadiness he could still hear the tremor that belied her words.

"Cara . . ."

"I'm all right. But . . . but I need to go there."

"To Michigan?"

"Yes." Her fingers wrapped around the dish towel, kneading it absently. "He's worse this time. My mother is alone. I . . . I would take the kids, but I can't help her and I can't be there at the hospital if I have to keep an eye on them. Besides, they were just there before Thanksgiving." Her voice trailed off. She let out a long breath slowly.

Owain opened his mouth, then closed it again. *I'll take them,* he wanted to say. *You go, I'll stay here.* But he didn't dare, did he?

"Will you stay with them?" Cara said.

For the second time that morning he thought his hearing had failed him. "Stay with them?" he repeated hollowly, his brain still trying to take it in.

"I wouldn't have chosen it," she said bluntly. "But I don't see any other option. I can't take them along. Gram couldn't handle the strain of it . . . I might have to be gone a couple of weeks . . . and Suzy has a crazy schedule this semester because of her student teaching and her ed classes."

"I get the point," Owain said dryly when she looked as if she might even find a few dozen more reasons why he was her last resort.

Cara managed the faintest ghost of a smile. "I'm sorry." Then her lips pressed into a thin line. "It doesn't change anything between us."

"I didn't imagine you'd think it would."

She fidgeted, her fingers knotting the towel, strangling it. "Well?"

"Well, what?" he asked, confused.

"Will you?"

Owain sighed. "You know I will. Go get packed, I'll make you a plane reservation now."

She started to protest, but then thought better of it. "All right. The sooner the better, I guess."

He got her a seat on the evening flight to Chicago. She had to change planes there, but she would be home before midnight. Then he went and picked the kids up from school.

"We're taking you to Madison," he told her when he got back with them in the car.

"You don't have to. I can take the car."

"If you got there," he said grimly. He had watched her for the past three hours as she had fumbled with the latch on her suitcase, spilled a carton of milk and dropped a glass that she was trying to set on a shelf in the cupboard. He could just imagine what a wreck she would make of the car—not to mention herself—if he let her drive to Madison alone.

"I'm driving you." His tone of voice didn't brook any arguments and Cara apparently realized it.

It took an hour and a half to drive to Madison. The snow had stopped, which made it easier than Owain had anticipated, and the kids helped by keeping the conversation relatively normal, but he noticed that Cara barely spoke.

He thought she looked as if she might break. She held herself stiffly, moved carefully, spoke almost without moving her lips. Was she remembering when Martin had died? Had she been like this then? He cast her a curious glance, but he couldn't read anything in her face. It was pale but composed. And the only time her composure slipped was when she bent to kiss the children at the airport. Then tears splashed down her cheeks.

"Mom, are you crying?" Hugh asked, aghast.

"It's all right to cry," Owain said. "It's better than not feeling anything at all." He looked directly into Cara's red-rimmed eyes, telling her with his that there had been plenty of times in the past six weeks when he had felt like crying himself. For a moment their gazes locked. Then she dropped her eyes and swiped at her cheeks with a tissue.

"Call tonight when you get in," he instructed her hoarsely. "Let us know how he is."

"But—"

He took hold of her hand—the first time he had really touched her since the day after Christmas. "Call."

"Yes." She looked down at their hands wrapped together and took a deep, shuddering breath. "Oh, God," she murmured, then dropped kisses onto the top of the children's heads and bolted through the doors to the boarding gate.

Owain took the children out to eat before they started back to Belle River. There was a delicatessen-cum-restaurant on the east side of Madison that seemed to contain every old-fashioned mechanical toy known to man. It also had a carousel and enough flavors of ice cream to tempt any child, even ones who had just put their mother on a plane. Both Bronwen and Hugh had cheered up considerably by the time they had eaten a sandwich and an ice cream and had inspected all the toys. They even fell asleep once they were in the car again.

It was an odd experience driving home with them. For all that he had been telling himself that he was behaving like their father over the past six weeks, he saw now that it had been more play-acting than anything else. Not that it wasn't sincere. It was. But it was also unreal. There had always been an out.

He could take them to the movies, he could play games with them or go for a walk in the snow with them. But Cara was always there in the background waiting to take over again.

Tonight Cara was in Michigan and he was a father for real.

His fingers tightened on the wheel. His foot lightened up on the accelerator, and he glanced over his shoulder at the children in the back seat. Bronwen was leaning against the car door, her coat bunched under her head, pillowing it. Hugh had slid over so he was lying against her. Asleep, they looked even younger than they did awake. More vulnerable. More dependent.

Dependent on him.

For a moment he was terrified.

For the first time in his life he was totally responsible for another human being—*two* other human beings. His life was no longer totally his own, his freedom to come and go, to do what he wanted to do when he wanted to do it— everything had changed.

The mantle of responsibility weighed on his shoulders. He felt it settle. It felt different. Odd. It would take some getting used to.

He wondered if that was why Cara had called him. Maybe she thought the responsibility would make him turn tail and run. He decided to ask her. The idea of her phoning pleased him. It was more than she had done in the past three months, really.

Progress of a sort, he thought with a wry smile. Now at least they were speaking.

He asked Cara about it when she called that night.

"Did you figure I'd panic?" he said when she rang up to report her safe arrival and said that, for the moment at least, her father was stable.

"Panic?"

"You know what I mean. Did you figure that I'd get a real taste of what it was like raising these two and vanish into thin air the moment you got back?"

"I suppose," she said slowly, "that I thought the possibility existed. But it wasn't uppermost in my mind."

"What was?"

"Having the kids well-taken-care-of while I was gone."

"Thank you for that, at least."

"You're welcome."

"I appreciate the vote of confidence."

"That's all it is," she warned. "Nothing else."

"I understand," Owain said.

But it didn't stop him hoping.

CARA'S FATHER'S HEART ATTACK was a serious one. He remained in the hospital for more than two weeks. He had good days and bad ones. He made progress, he slipped back. And every step—forward or backward—Owain heard about from Cara.

It got to be a habit—albeit an unconscious one, he was sure. But every night after she called to talk to the children, she would talk to him. Ostensibly it was to find out anything the children hadn't told her. In fact it rapidly developed into more than that.

Owain was the one who shared her concerns about her father. Her mother needed bolstering, so it was Owain who listened to her fears. He was the one she leaned on.

He felt vaguely guilty, as if he were taking advantage of a bad situation. But it didn't stop him from doing it. He needed the contact with Cara as much as she needed it with him. She was the adult in his life. He was the mainstay in hers.

They never talked about the way things were between them. He didn't care; she obviously didn't want to. But they talked about everything else. She told him about her father's careful steps from the bed to the chair and back again. He told her about the ballet recital and the peewee basketball game. She told him about her father's worries about medical insurance, and he told her about making a cabin out of Lincoln Logs for President's Day and about having to explain to Bronwen what Sadie Hawkins Day was. She told him that it was devastating to see the energetic father she had always known laid low, and he tried to imagine it. It was hard—his own father had always been the epitome of health and stamina. But he listened and encouraged and tried to help her the best he could.

"I just feel so helpless," she said one evening toward the end of the call. "I can't do anything for him. I'm not taking care of my kids. My work is falling behind...."

"You're doing what you have to do."

"Yes, I guess." But she sounded weary and unconvinced.

"Don't worry about the kids in any case," he told her. "Everything is fine here."

"That's what Hugh said." She sounded almost wistful.

"They miss you," Owain told her. "I do, too."

It was as close to a personal remark as either of them had come to making. It was followed by a long pause. In his heart and in his head, Owain heard Cara say, *I miss you, too.* But finally she just cleared her throat and asked, "How's Gram?"

"Fine. We go see her three times a week at least. She had us over for dinner last night. Told the kids all about planting out daffodils when she was a child."

"She loves daffodils," Cara said softly. "So do I. So did Martin." Her voice drifted off, as if she were remembering. "We were always going to plant some."

Owain's fingers tightened on the phone, jealousy of Martin pricking him again.

"When are you coming home?" he asked her.

"Dad should be home on Saturday if all goes well. I thought I might stay a day or two after to help Mom get him adjusted. Why? Are you getting fed up?"

"Not a bit."

"Oh." He couldn't tell if she sounded disappointed or not.

"We'll be looking forward to seeing you," he told her.

"Nothing's changed, Owain," she said quickly.

"Yeah," he murmured. "G'night."

THINGS HAD CHANGED whether Cara Williams wanted them to or not. Owain was the twins' father now. He knew it, Gram knew it, and if the children didn't know it in actual fact, they certainly seemed to feel the same way. So did almost everyone else. Even Greg, stopping by to see if he could help out, seemed to acknowledge that for some reason Owain belonged in a way he didn't. And Suzy came right out and said it.

She had come over to baby-sit for him so he could go finish up his interviews at the rest home, and when he got back they shared a cup of coffee while the kids played outside in the slush.

"Cara was crazy to dump you," Suzy said bluntly.

Owain was chopping tomatoes for a taco salad he was making for supper, and he didn't turn around. "She had her reasons."

"Greg?" Suzy said scornfully.

"Not just Greg," Owain said with as much honesty as he could.

"Well, she's going to have to change her mind after this."

"I hope so." But he had learned not to count on it. He took each day as it came, relishing it, and consigning worry about what would happen when Cara came home to the future that would come to pass when she did. Still, in private moments, he did hope.

Hugh and Bronwen, he discovered, hoped, too.

"You'd make a good dad," Bronwen told him one afternoon when he picked them up after school and took them to the library.

"Thank you," Owain said gravely, more touched than she could ever guess.

"You could marry my mother if you wanted to," she went on, sticking her tongue into the corner of her mouth while she considered the idea.

"It isn't only up to me," Owain reminded her.

"Well, Hugh and I would like it."

"It isn't only up to you two either."

"The problem is Mom, you mean."

He nodded.

"She loves you."

Owain looked down at his daughter and wished it were that simple. "Yeah," he said, his voice rough with emotion. "Come on, pick out your books. Hugh's almost got all his."

"Can we go for a walk before dinner again?" Bronwen asked.

"If you hurry."

She hurried.

The just-before-dinner walks were getting to be a habit. Owain put together a casserole early in the day, then stuck it in the oven just as they were about to go out the door. Coming home to a hot supper and a house redolent with wonderful smells was one of the real joys in life as far as he was concerned. It also prevented the before-dinner squabbling that the kids seemed to do. And day by day they were covering the whole town.

This evening, the meat, potato and cheese casserole beginning to bubble in the oven, they set out toward the west side of town.

Most of the snow had melted over the past two weeks. It was a far different world from the one Cara had left. Winter white had given way to the mud-brown of approaching spring. But the wind was still stiff and strong from the west as they set out. Scuffing through the park, Hugh said, "Remember when we met you? Remember the kite?"

Owain nodded. It seemed a lifetime ago. He felt like a different person.

"Think we could fly it again soon?"

"I think so." He tipped his head back, looking up at the still-bare tree branches, at the soft blue of the sky, and remembered the first day he had seen Cara. She had suited the autumn—her presence warm and golden like the brightly colored leaves, her smiling eyes welcoming him as a new friend. Were they friends again? Could they ever go beyond it?

Bronwen and Hugh ran on ahead. He watched them skipping up the street, darting around the trees that lined the sidewalk. A red ski cap and a blue one. A son and a daughter. He closed his eyes and tried to imagine going back to a life without them. He couldn't do it.

Nor could he imagine a life without Cara.

Fame, success, academic prestige, accomplishment. All very nice, but meaningless without love. Without someone to share it with.

They were passing the tall white clapboard church they had attended on Christmas. The children stopped and looked up the hill behind the church to the cemetery. Hugh leaned on the black wrought-iron fence and stared out across the brown grass to the higgledy-piggledy array of tombstones, and Bronwen, who had been chattering to Owain about her new books, looked over at him and fell silent.

"My daddy's there." Hugh's voice was low and laced with a sadness that no child his age should have had to know. It tore at Owain's heart. He hunkered down next to Hugh, seeing the rows of white, gray and reddish stones from the boy's perspective. The sight was even more daunting.

"Want me to show you where?" he asked. He turned to look at Owain, his blue eyes a mirror of the man next to him. Owain swallowed hard.

"If you want."

"Come on." Hugh took his hand.

Owain held out his other one to Bronwen. She looked at it, then at the graveyard beyond. Something flickered across her face that might have been reluctance. But then she squared her small shoulders and pressed her lips together. She took Owain's hand in hers.

Martin Williams was buried near the top of the hill that rose gently behind the church. A small, glass-smooth red granite stone marked the site. Owain stood beside it, looking down, reading the words. MARTIN H. WILLIAMS March 7, 1948–May 12, 1983. Barely thirty-five years.

Owain swallowed, remembering the pictures in Cara's kitchen of the smiling sandy-haired man with a twin on each arm. His throat tightened. It seemed unfair. And the most unfair thing of all was being caught envying Martin his children and his wife.

"I don't hardly remember him now," Bronwen was saying in a small voice. "Just the way he used to give us horsey rides around the living room, an' on Sunday mornings we used to get in bed with him and Mommy an' snuggle...." She blinked fiercely, her brown eyes suddenly swimming with tears. "I want to go now."

Before Owain could stop her, she took off running down the hill.

She was halfway home by the time he and Hugh caught up with her. Her cheeks were red from the wind and streaked from salty tears. Owain touched her hair, brushing it back behind her ears. She tucked her hands into her pockets and walked on. He rested one hand lightly on her shoulder, thinking perhaps that she might reach out and take it again. She didn't.

After dinner she was still subdued. Owain sent Hugh on up to take a bath and asked Bronwen to help him load the dishwasher. She did it silently, her normal line of chatter reduced to the occasional monosyllable in response to a direct question.

Finally Owain stopped asking. He was content to simply hover, wishing he could do something, but all at sea when it came to knowing what.

She was in the bath herself when Cara called later in the evening. Owain tapped on the door and asked if she wanted to talk to her mother.

"Not tonight," was all the reply he got.

She was in bed when he came upstairs to tell her to get out of the bath.

"Well," he said with a grin, "that was fast."

She didn't speak, just inclined her head slightly, her chin bobbing down to touch the down comforter on her bed.

Owain reached down and ran his hand lightly over her hair, letting the soft curls wind around his fingers, then stroking her cheek. Bronwen sniffled and bit down on her lip. Her eyes blinked.

He bent and kissed her forehead. For the first time, small arms didn't reach up and wrap themselves around his neck to tug him back down for a hug and a hard, smacking kiss. He paused, worried again.

"Bron?"

She rolled over onto her side facing the wall, curling up like a tiny bug and shutting her eyes. "Night."

Owain stood motionless watching her. How very like Cara she was—both of them hurting and shutting him out. "Night, love," he murmured at the doorway. Then he put out the light.

HE WAS SLEEPING in Cara's bed, and having trouble doing it as usual. For a time he had read Gram's father's diaries. Mostly they were day-by-day accounts of what happened. There was little introspection. Sam was not moved to philosophize about his life. But every once in a while he would comment about how different things were here from what he had been used to. It wasn't a complaint. Just a comparison. Immigrants' lives were like that, Owain thought, a melding of past and present. Old ways and new ways. And you didn't forget one just because you were now busy with another.

Just as Bronwen and Hugh hadn't totally forgotten Martin. He would always be a part of them, just as Owain's past was a part of him, just as Sam's was a part of his. And just as he couldn't regret his own past, so he couldn't regret Martin in theirs. He stared up at the ceiling and remembered the look on their faces when they had stood by Martin's grave. There had been a distant look in their eyes—a longing, a remembrance of things past—cloudy now, but still real.

The door to his room creaked and he raised his head. Bronwen stood in the doorway, her bear in her arms, sleepy and disoriented. Owain propped himself up on his elbows.

"Bron? What is it?"

She stood there a moment longer, then flew into his arms, sobbing as if her heart would break. He gathered her close, crooning to her softly, his arms rocking her, his hands stroking the small shoulders, the soft hair.

"Ah, Bron, shhh now." He brushed kisses over her hair, wanting to soothe her, to help her, flailing in his own inadequacy. "Bron? Bronny, what is it, love?"

She sniffled, then hiccuped. "Wh...what I said." She pulled out of his arms and buried her face in the pillows.

He leaned over her, saw her rub her eyes with her fist. "What did you say?" he queried softly.

"'Bout you bein'...my...daddy. Isn't fair," she gulped out between sobs.

Owain's guts twisted. "What isn't fair, Bron?"

"Isn't fair to *my* daddy," she wailed. "He...he wouldn't be my daddy anymore." She buried her face in the covers, her small shoulders shaking.

"Ah, Bron, no." He lifted her gently and turned her in his arms, cuddling her close, nuzzling his nose in her soft curls, kissing her hair. "No. That's not the way it works."

She sniffed, then scrubbed her face with her hand, staring up at him in the silvery moonlit room. "It's not?" she choked.

"No, it's not." He eased himself around so that he was propped up against the headboard of the bed, then he balanced her on his lap, hugging her against his chest, pulling the covers up around both of them. "You know," he began slowly, "your mother told me that you were adopted."

Bronwen tilted her head up so she could look at him. His mother's eyes penetrating his own, troubled but still listening. He prayed for a bit of her wisdom, then went ahead. "And that means that somewhere you have natural parents who—" he faltered for a moment "—who love and care about you even though you have adoptive parents, too. One doesn't cancel out the other. So, what you said—about me making a good daddy—doesn't mean that your...your first—" he struggled with the word, but got it out "—your first daddy, Martin, is going to be left out. It just means he loves you in a different way from now on."

He looked down at her, hoping he was making some sort of sense for her. She sat quietly, and he wondered if she understood at all what he had been trying to say. Then she chewed on her thumbnail for a moment and finally asked in a small voice, "Can I have you both, then? I m-mean . . . he was my daddy, b-but I l . . . love you, too." Her words ended on a tiny croaking sob, and the tears spilled down her cheeks.

Tears rolled silently down Owain's cheeks, too. He buried his face in her hair, breathing in its fresh flowery smell, its faint hint of Cara's shampoo. "I love you," he whispered brokenly.

He told himself that he would carry her back to her bed when she had gone to sleep. For now he would simply hold her close and give them both the comfort they sought. He leaned back against the headboard and closed his eyes, breathing in slowly and evenly as he listened to the shallower, shorter half sobs of his daughter. They quieted finally, gradually. She slept. And so did he.

It was dawn when, at last, he tucked her into her own narrow bed.

Chapter Twelve

"The kids took me to Martin's grave," Owain told Gram the next morning.

It was snowing—an early March, powder-puff sort of snowfall that dusted the muddy landscape and, like a powder puff, improved it cosmetically for a few hours. Driving had been touch and go, but Owain had taken a chance on it. He needed to talk to someone.

Once the kids had gone to school, he had rattled around the house, making beds, doing dishes, putting in the laundry, then trying to read Gram's father's diaries again. But he couldn't concentrate.

Not on that, in any case. His mind was totally preoccupied with images of Bronwen snuggling in his arms, sobbing over Martin and over him.

In the morning she had been a bit shy with him when she had first got up, as if wondering what he might say. He hadn't said anything, had just hugged her. And after a second's hesitation, she had hugged him back. Hard. And when the two children left for school and he waved goodbye from the door, Bronwen had got to the end of the walk, then turned and run back, throwing her arms around his waist and hugging him once again, then hurrying to rejoin her brother.

Owain hadn't been able to get it out of his mind. And as he sank down now into the love seat across from where Gram sat in the rocker knitting a sea-blue afghan, he was still running it over and over in his head.

"They go to the cemetery with Cara sometimes," Gram said now. "On Martin's birthday. Their anniversary. Just making sure he's still a part of their lives. I don't think that's wrong."

"No," Owain admitted. "She's done a good job with them."

Gram smiled. "She has." The knitting needles clicked away, soothing him even though it was Gram doing the knitting. "It hasn't been easy doing it alone."

"No."

"She did a lot of it alone anyway," Gram went on. "Martin was away on field trips a lot."

"Geologist, wasn't he?"

"Mmm." She shifted the growing afghan in her lap. The kettle whistled and Owain got up to make them a pot of tea. "He used to take his senior students on field trips once in the fall and once in the spring, two weeks at a time. And he was a consultant to one of the large oil companies. The university liked that. Got them a bit of prestige. Cara didn't much like it though," she added. "She thought him being gone on the field trips was enough."

Owain got the cups out of the cupboard and set them on the counter, adding milk to both. He looked at Gram over his shoulder. "Was he on a field trip when he got killed?"

Gram shook her head. "No. He was in Alaska for the oil company. There was a rockfall. Three men died, two of them instantly. Martin lived two days, but he didn't regain consciousness."

"It must have been terrible for Cara."

"It was."

He carried the cups of tea across the room and put one of them on the end table next to Gram. Then he sat down again and stretched his feet out in front of him, balancing the cup and saucer on his belt buckle, his fingers gripping the cup with a strength that he didn't even notice until his fingers shook from the force.

He didn't want to imagine Martin, broken and bleeding, living for two days, then dying. He didn't want to think about Cara, hoping, praying, loving, then losing. He shut his eyes and drew a deep breath, then let it out slowly. He took a sip of tea. He could have stood something stronger. Gram knitted on.

He thought back over the past five months. He remembered when simply seeing the child he had fathered was all the goal he had had. He remembered when the goal changed, when Cara found out who he was, when he stood looking down at the gravestone on the hill.

"Life's not as easy as it looks, is it?"

"Never," Gram agreed. She looked at him over the top of her glasses. "That's what keeps it interesting."

"Interesting?" That wasn't how he would have put it.

"At least."

"Yeah." He sighed and finished his tea, then carried the cup to the sink, rinsed it and set it on the countertop. Then he stretched and flexed his shoulders. "I better go."

"No tape recorder today?"

"No. Just a visit. I needed a friend." He went over and dropped a light kiss on her soft cheek.

"You're more than a friend, Owain."

"I'd like to be."

She squeezed his fingers. "You are."

He was almost out the door when something occurred to him. It had been in the back of his mind since Christmas, but last night, when he and Bronwen had come to terms with the past, the idea touched him again.

"Remember when we talked about going to Britain?" he asked.

"Of course."

"How about it?"

Gram stared. "Just like that?" she asked him. "Just hop a plane?"

"Well, I suspect it's going to be a tad more complicated than that. But why not? I mean, would you like to?"

"I'd love to, but I'm an old lady, Owain. I could never manage—"

"I could."

"What?"

"I'd come with you."

Gram's brows lifted.

"I mean it."

"You and me? Or you, me, Cara and the kids?"

"Don't tempt me." He shrugged. "Whoever. I just think it's a good idea. I'd like to do it. Would you?"

Gram stared off out the window for a moment, then her eyes went to the picture of her parents on the mantel. "Yes," she said. "Yes, I would. I'd love to go back. I'd love to see if anything I remember is still there. I'd love to go to London again. My grandfather took me once when I was little. We went to an enormous store and he bought me some lead soldiers. It's funny the things you remember," she said.

"Yes."

She looked up at him, her eyes bright. "You are a man of surprises, Owain O'Neill."

He smiled.

"I hope Cara comes to her senses soon and surprises you. She does miss you, you know."

"Did she say so?"

"She didn't have to say it. It's in her voice."

Owain sighed. But he would have liked the words. Any words. Some sign. Gram, he knew, meant well. But he also knew that she heard what she wanted to hear.

"It's a nice thought," he said, but he wasn't convinced.

"Don't worry, Owain. Everything will work out all right."

HE WISHED he felt as confident. But while he and Cara had worked out a truce on the telephone, he knew that in her mind it was only for the children's sake. He could feel the withdrawal in her tone the night she called to tell him when she would be coming home.

"I'll be in on Friday," she said without preamble. "I'm sure you'll be delighted. Fatherhood must be paling by now."

"No, it's not."

There was a long pause on the other end of the line. He knew she was wishing he had agreed with her, but he wasn't going to. He did add, however, "Fatherhood alone was never what I wanted, though, Cara."

"You say."

"It's the truth."

"And, of course, you always tell the truth."

It was the first sharp exchange they had had since she had left. It made Owain want to shake her. Instead he said flatly, "We'll be at the airport to get you. See you then." And he hung up.

"I wanted to talk to her," Hugh complained.

Owain grimaced. "Sorry. She was in a hurry," he said, as Cara's words echoed in his ears—*of course, you always tell the truth*.

Suzy, who was there using the computer for her dating service, gave him a skeptical look. Then she shook her head in sympathy. "Here's one for you," she said, turning back to the material she was typing into the file. "Five foot five, 113 pounds, red hair, green eyes, Ph.D. in English lit. Likes to water ski, swim and read poetry. What do you think?" She grinned.

Owain scowled. "I don't want a woman."

"He has Mommy," Hugh told Suzy.

"Does he?" Suzy asked.

Owain jammed his hands into his pockets. "No, I don't."

"Ah well, you have Marsha," Suzy said.

That was truer than he would have liked. Marsha was an excellent typist, he had to give her that. Regardless of what she had said earlier, she wanted more than just his typing, and she made no bones about it. She called him at Cara's on the flimsiest of pretexts—a question about a footnote, a query about the spelling of a word, something that was supposedly garbled on a tape—and then proceeded to invite him to stop over for coffee to discuss it. Once he was there, she managed to suggest that they check out the new movie at the cinema or the concert at the college. He tried to play it cool. His years of experience with groupies should have prepared him to, he thought. But then he had always had an advantage he didn't have here; he could always leave and go to the next town. Here he was stuck inventing excuses and feeling guilty because he was the one who had encouraged her in the first place.

While Suzy was there tapping away on the computer, Marsha called with another question. He hemmed and hawed, trying to decline the real reason for the call—an invitation to a church supper—as gracefully as possible. When he finished, Suzy grinned at him.

"Your ardent admirer?"

Owain grimaced. It never ceased irritating him how he couldn't do anything right where Cara was concerned or anything wrong with Marsha. "Maybe you could plug her into your computer," he suggested, not entirely facetiously.

"For a fee."

Owain knew enough about Marsha's straitened finances to know that she wasn't about to pay for a dating service. But there was no reason he couldn't. He grinned. "Sold."

"Only if you tell Marsha what you're doing," Suzy cautioned him. "This is a legitimate operation I run here."

"I'll tell her," he promised. After what he had run into with Cara by keeping quiet, he had learned his lesson.

The next morning when he went over to get his typing, he did. He thought he would have to argue with her, convince her. He expected her to throw his presumption in his face.

Surprisingly she did neither. She said, "You noticed that I'd set my cap for you, did you?" quite bluntly, so that Owain was more embarrassed than she was.

"Well, I . . ." he fumbled.

"Well, I did." She was completely matter-of-fact. "I don't like being alone. I never did. I like being in love. I believe in it, even though my track record isn't too hot."

Owain, whose track record was even worse, remained silent. He shuffled the papers she had just handed him and stared at the toes of his hiking boots.

"Well, it's not a bad idea actually, this dating service business," Marsha said, considering. "I might meet someone I've overlooked."

"You might," Owain agreed, privately thinking that Marsha, judging from what he had heard, hadn't overlooked many.

She gave him a what-the-hell smile. "So do it."

He did, and Suzy pulled a name out of the computer that very afternoon.

"It can't be that easy," he complained.

"It isn't easy. This is just the beginning. All the work is yet to come. But at least she has someone to start with now, someone who might be interested in her as well."

Lucky her, Owain thought grimly when he went to pick up the kids from school. In less than twenty-four hours Marsha had more going for her than he had after almost six months.

But then, Marsha's encounter with the mystery man wouldn't be fraught with complications from the start either. She would have no need to lie or omit things. Her courtship would probably be smooth and untroubled.

He wondered what Cara's courtship had been like with Martin. Had it been smooth sailing? Had they clicked immediately, felt an instant rapport?

He had almost an hour before he had to pick up the kids from school, and he found himself heading for the cemetery almost without realizing it. The day before's snowfall had all but melted, leaving behind it a world of brown grass and mud to squelch beneath his feet as he made his way up the hill.

He passed several bouquets of artifical flowers on his way. The mud-tipped plastic petals added a dull smudge of color to an otherwise grim landscape. But it was a real rosebush, heaped over now with straw to protect it from the winter cold, that drew his gaze. He could imagine it in the height of summer, laden with dark red roses, a living testament to the love between "JOHN CHAMBERS, 1881–1969 and his loving wife of 52 years, BESS, 1890–1974." Owain envied them their fifty-two years. Martin and Cara had had only seven.

He wondered, as he stood looking at the smooth granite tombstone, if he and Cara would have any at all.

A cold wind touched his cheek. He bowed his head and took a deep breath as he read the stark inscription again— the dates that spelled the beginning and end of Martin Williams's too brief life. He would have turned thirty-nine tomorrow. Would he have done things differently? Owain wondered. Would he have changed things if he could?

He had worked hard, according to Gram. He had loved well, according to Cara. By all accounts he had gone after what he wanted—in his work and in his life. He hadn't been afraid to tackle things head-on. He was a man Owain would have understood.

Well, Martin, he thought, *I want Cara now. I love her, too.*

He tapped his knuckles lightly on the cold stone, then turned and walked, chin up, back down the hill to the car. He thought Martin would have understood.

"Do you know what tomorrow is?" he asked the twins when they got into the car after school.

Hugh's face scrunched up in thought. "St. Patrick's Day?" he ventured.

"Not yet."

"Not Easter, either," Bronwen said. "And not Mom's birthday."

"Is it yours?" asked Hugh.

"Not mine," Owain said, pulling out into traffic. "Your father's." It wasn't as hard to say the word as he had thought it would be. He felt a kinship with Martin now, an understanding. "I thought," he told them, "that we might go and plant him a flower."

The date on the tombstone had nagged at him all the way down the hill. He remembered Gram telling him that Cara had taken the children there on Martin's birthday. He remembered Bronwen's tears, her loyalty to her father she could barely remember now. It seemed important to help her sustain that loyalty, to let her know that it was all right. Martin liked daffodils, Cara had said. They had been going to plant some. Well, he and the kids would do it now.

He had gone by the florist's before he went to the school.

The florist wasn't optimistic. "It's early for daffs in this part of the country."

"It doesn't have to be blooming yet. It just has to have a chance."

Skeptical, the florist shrugged. He disappeared into his greenhouse and returned with a large peat pot. In it were the green shoots of four daffodils—three inches of promise.

"You can put it directly in the ground inside the pot," the florist told him. "It's been hardening off outside for the past three weeks. Some people prefer them at Easter instead of lilies. In the house, that is. But if you want to try it outside, go ahead, though you ought to plant in the fall.''

"Can't wait till fall," Owain said.

"Well, go to it then. But remember, no guarantees."

Life didn't give guarantees, he thought now as he carried the pot of daffodils up the hill. Hugh skipped on his left and Bronwen walked more sedately on his right. If there had been guarantees they would have been out playing with Martin now and he would have gone on his way long ago.

"What'll we dig with?" Hugh asked when they reached the top of the hill.

Owain hadn't given it a thought. Typical, Cara would have said. Just one more example of his acting before he thought about it. He shrugged. "Our fingers, I guess." He dropped to his knees and dug in, scrabbling in the half-frozen mud to make a hole.

The twins fell to helping at once. Three pairs of hands dug hard, tossing aside chunks of mud and pebbles until they had a hole large enough to hold the peat pot full of daffodil shoots. Owain shaped the hole, patting the sides, then handed the pot to Bronwen. She held it in her hands a moment while her eyes scanned the smooth red stone. He could see her lips forming the words. Then she bent her head and slipped the peat pot home. Hugh began to fill in the dirt.

Owain settled back on his haunches to watch. Hugh hiked the dirt doggy-fashion, then scrambled to his feet and began pressing it down with his boots. Bronwen smoothed it lovingly, carefully, with small mud-encrusted hands. When she finished, she stood up and came over to stand by Owain. He shifted his weight and reached for her, drawing her against him, between his knees, looping his arms around her loosely, clasping her hands in his larger ones.

The green shoots stood tall, sheltered from the wind by the red stone. A few feet away a robin pecked away at the ground trying to get hold of a twig to carry to his new nest.

Harbingers of things to come. The promise of new life. A future.

Around Bronwen's small hands, he crossed his fingers.

"Come on, sprouts, time to go. Pizza for supper."

"Whoopee!" Hugh tore off down the hill, his red jacket sailing behind him in the breeze.

Bronwen reached forward and patted the dirt a bit more firmly around the flowers with her toe. Then she lifted her eyes and met Owain's. The sadness he had seen in them yesterday, the tears of the night, the distraction of the morning were gone. He saw peace. She gave him a small smile and held out her hand to him.

Another harbinger of the future?

He could only hope.

"THANK YOU VERY MUCH," Cara said politely. "It was very kind of you."

Owain gritted his teeth and nodded. But when she offered to pay him, he'd had enough.

"Like hell you will!" He slammed his palm down on the kitchen table, making the salt and pepper shakers jump.

Cara's eyes flickered to the stairs. Sounds of Hugh and Bronwen getting ready for bed drifted down. They were singing, glad their mother was home. Owain had been, too, until a moment ago.

"Well, it's a great deal to expect of someone," she said lamely. "Two and a half weeks of child care..."

"Child care? *Child care!*" He stared at her. "You think that's what I've been doing here for the past couple of weeks?" He said an extremely rude word that made Cara's cheeks turn pink. Pleased with the reaction he got, he said it again. Louder.

"Owain!"

"Damn it, what do you expect me to say? I love those kids. I love you! I would have done anything I could for you over the past couple of weeks. And not because I was being paid for it!''

"Well, I—"

"And you're a fool if you don't realize it. In fact, I think you *do* realize it. You just don't want to!" He stormed around the kitchen, getting angrier by the minute. "Pay me!" he fumed. "And then what? Did you expect just to be able to dismiss me? Send me out of your life so you wouldn't have the inconvenience of dealing with me anymore?"

"I was only offering—"

"Don't offer."

She sighed and brushed a hand through her hair. "Oh, hell, I knew I shouldn't have asked you . . . I knew I should have asked . . ."

"Asked whom? Greg?" he sneered. "You think he would have done it? How? When? You think he would have taken them with him on his geology field trips or to his labs? You think he would have let them sit in his office while he graded papers?"

"I wasn't going to say Greg."

"Well, who then?"

"I don't know!" she snapped. "Somebody who did consider it just 'child care,' then."

"And that'd really be good for the kids, wouldn't it?"

"Oh, damn you, Owain! You always make me sound wrong."

"You are wrong."

They glared at each other across the kitchen. Upstairs the snatches of song accompanied by bumps and thumps went on.

At last Cara's shoulders slumped. "I'm very tired," she said. "I wish you'd just go away."

A bitter smile twisted Owain's mouth. "I know you do." He hitched a hip onto the corner of the table. "You'll be pleased to know then that I am. Next week."

Her head jerked up and she stared at him, her expression unreadable. "Wha—"

"I'm taking Gram to England."

Her jaw dropped. "You're not."

"I am."

She stared at him. "Why would you want to traipse around England with an eighty-year-old lady?"

"Because I like that particular eighty-year-old lady."

"Owain O'Neill, rock star?"

"Owain O'Neill, friend."

Cara snorted inelegantly. "Another manipulative maneuver?"

"What's that supposed to mean?"

"Trying to get to me via my grandmother this time?"

"God, you're suspicious!"

"You mean you weren't going to blithely suggest that I come along? Bring the kids?"

The thought had crossed his mind. He had rejected it because he knew how her mind worked. He knew she would think it was just one more trick. And damned if she didn't, anyway!

"You mean, maneuver you into marrying me yet another way?"

Cara flushed.

"Damn it, how do I prove to you that it isn't the kids I want, Cara? What would it take? Do you want me to go out and shoot them, maybe? Then come ask you to marry me?"

"Owain!" She sounded shocked. She ought to, he thought. He raked his fingers through his hair.

"If I asked you to come, Cara, would you?" he demanded.

"You know I wouldn't."

He nodded. "I know it."

"Well, then..."

"Tell me, *why* wouldn't you come?"

She waved her hands in the air. "A thousand reasons."

"Tell me one."

"Owain."

"Tell me."

"I wouldn't leave the country with my father in precarious health."

"Could you make him better if you stayed?"

"No, but—"

"Tell me another."

She scowled at him. He scowled back, waiting.

"You'd want to see your parents, no doubt," she said.

"Yes."

"And they'd probably recognize the kids as yours in a minute."

"Probably."

"Well, then, you must see that's another reason. Two of them in fact. I don't want the kids upset. And I don't want your parents upset."

"Bull," Owain said. "You don't want to upset yourself."

Cara blinked.

"Why don't you at least have the guts to admit it?" he challenged her. "Why don't you admit the real reason you won't go?"

"What is the *real* reason?" Her tone was scathing, challenging him back.

"Because you're afraid to. Because you're no more indifferent to me now than you were in November! And—" he started walking toward her "—if you really want to be honest with yourself—and with me—you'll admit you still love me just as much as I love you!" He loomed over her. "Don't you?"

She shrank away from him for a brief second, then stiffened, her back going ramrod straight. An inarticulate sound came from her throat.

Owain ignored her, needing to say everything, needing to spit it out once and for all. For too long he had held his peace, waited, hoped, prayed that things would get better, that she would come to her senses on her own. Well, she hadn't; and he couldn't take any more. Too many things had crowded in on him, hurting him, hurting them both. "You're afraid to let yourself come with me because you might get involved again. You might get hurt again. Well, damn it, Cara, people who are still alive do get hurt!"

She scrambled away from him, taking refuge behind the kitchen counter.

"It's Martin who's dead, Cara, not you! You're still alive and well, for God's sake! Don't bury yourself with him. I love you!"

"You betrayed me!"

"Martin betrayed you, too."

She went white. "He never!"

"He did, Cara. He died. And you haven't forgiven him that any more than you've forgiven me! Well, I give up. I've tried. I've done every damned thing I can think of to make you believe me, to make you trust me—and it hasn't worked. So I quit. You tell the kids whatever you like—whatever will assuage your conscience. And if you ever decide you want to marry me, you come after me this time! Because I'm done coming after you.

"I might not have told you the whole truth to start out with, Cara. But it isn't me who's lying now! It's you!"

Chapter Thirteen

A part of him—the part that, despite everything, still believed in miracles—hoped she would come after him.

The realist in him—which was to say, the other ninety-nine percent—knew she never would.

But he didn't stop hoping until the wheels folded up under the wings of the giant 747 as it lifted off from O'Hare Airport a week later. Then he turned his attention from the bright-eyed old lady who had clenched his fingers during the takeoff and who was now leaning past him to look out the window with all the excited curiosity of her great-grandchildren. Owain closed his eyes and slumped back into his seat.

"Hell," he muttered under his breath.

Gram heard him and wrapped his fingers in hers, giving them a conspiratorial squeeze. "Look for the joy, my love. You'll find it."

Owain didn't think so.

He had burned all his bridges the evening she had come back. He had created an enemy and he knew it. But he couldn't go on any longer just being some sort of pseudo-divorced father, never quite acknowledged, never quite a part of her life. Better, he had thought in the heat of the moment, to cut the ties once and for all.

And maybe, he had thought, she would come to her senses. Maybe she would come after him. But there hadn't been a word. He had had Marsha finish up his typing within two days. He had checked over all the information with the people he had interviewed. Then he had gone back to L.A., this time telling Mrs. Garrity that, except for picking up Mrs. Nute the following Friday, he wouldn't be back.

He hadn't been. He had held out a hope that Cara would seek him out when he came for Gram. She didn't. Obviously the ties had been well and truly cut.

And if he was having second thoughts now, it was just too damned bad. He would, as Gram said, have to make the best of it. He would have to "look for the joy" wherever it might exist.

It wasn't easy.

The England they landed in was damp and drizzly, a gray, sodden landscape that Owain thought reflected his mood precisely. It didn't daunt Gram.

She had energy enough for both of them—and she proved it over and over during the next several days. Whenever he was tempted to stay in their hotel room, bury himself in the papers and feel sorry for himself, Gram had other ideas.

"Let's go to the zoo," she suggested the third day they were there. She looked up at him from one of her several "about London" magazines, her eyes bright with interest.

Owain slumped farther into the chair in which he was sitting. "There's a zoo in Madison."

"But they don't have British monkeys."

"Gram!" he protested.

But it was no use. No amount of convincing would persuade her that the monkeys in Regent's Park Zoo were just as exotic to Londoners as they were to the people of Madison. She simply professed not to believe him. Annoyed, he roused himself out of his chair and shrugged into his jacket, then grabbed the umbrella off the dresser where it lay and pointed it at her.

"All right, come on then. I'll prove it to you."

Four hours later over afternoon tea in the hotel to which they had just returned after a long tramp around the zoo, he glared at her. "You knew damned well those weren't 'British' monkeys!" he accused her.

She took a tiny sip of tea, the lines around her eyes crinkling slightly as she smiled at him. It was an ingenuous smile, one he remembered seeing on Bronwen when she got her own way. "You don't say?" was all she said.

He gave her a wry grin, acknowledging defeat at the hands of a master, also acknowledging that for a few hours she had managed to make him forget the miseries that haunted him whenever he let himself stop and think.

"You win," he said.

She reached out and touched his hand. He knew she would have given anything to say that he would, too. He respected her for not offering him false hopes.

"It was actually kind of fun," he admitted. "I'm sorry I've been such poor company."

"Nonsense, you've been wonderful," Gram contradicted. "How many handsome young men would spend three weeks dragging an old lady all over Britain?" She leaned toward him and said conspiratorially, "I've got three dollars stashed away in case you ditch me."

He laughed aloud. "Not a chance. I'm an idiot to keep moping around. Things will change, starting now."

HE MADE AN EFFORT to be sure they did. And if Gram noticed that there were still times when he would lapse into silence—like when they saw some children running across one of the greens flying a kite, or when the couple walking in front of them on Oxford Street stopped midblock for a lingering kiss—she didn't say a word. She simply kept right on about what she was doing. And in a moment the pain subsided to the same dull ache he always felt these days, and Owain moved to catch up with her.

They spent a week in London, then traveled to Essex to the small village on the River Crouch where Gram thought she was born.

"Are you sure?" Owain asked her as he surveyed the landscape.

"My mother always said so. Why?"

He shrugged. "Funny place for a miner."

The land was flat or gently rolling, patched with forest or cropland, the narrow roads edged by hedgerows just coming into leaf. Owain drove carefully along the narrow road that wound down to the village that sat a ways back from the tidal river. Gram leaned forward in her seat, her eyes darting this way and that, taking in everything, not willing to blink for fear of missing something.

At last, at the far end of the village, a distance of only several hundred yards, he pulled over and stopped by a pub. Gram stared around her, enthralled. There were no more than three dozen houses in the village proper, a few new, but most more than a century old by the look of them.

"Do you suppose I was born in one of them?" Gram asked.

A faint smile creased Owain's face. "It's possible. Do you want to get out and look around?"

For a second Gram seemed to hesitate. Then, "Yes," she said firmly. "Yes, I do." And she was out of the car even before he could come around and give her his hand.

They walked down the narrow street. The few people they passed looked them up and down as if strangers weren't all that common here. Probably they weren't, Owain thought. This wasn't Maldon or Burnham-on-Crouch, where yachtsmen and other boating lunatics from London came on the weekends.

It was smaller, but not unlike Belle River. He was struck how similar being here felt to the way he had felt when he had first come to look for his child. Did everyone have a past that needed taking out and examining? he wondered.

Did everyone have some place to go back to? Something to come to terms with before going on?

"Aren't you coming?" He heard Gram's impatient voice and discovered that he had been standing there gawking at a boatyard while she had walked nearly a whole block ahead.

"Where are we going?" he asked when he caught up to her.

She pointed. "There." He followed the line of her arm to the church and the churchyard they had passed when they drove into town. "Anyone I knew," she told him matter-of-factly, "would likely be there."

She passed the church by and went directly to the small graveyard next to it. It wasn't large, but it was well tended, no doubt by the descendants of the people buried there. A row of daffodils lined the fence, and it made him think of Martin's daffodils. Had they survived the last cold snap?

Better than he had, he thought wryly. He had fond thoughts of Martin. He liked him. And he had more in common with him than ever. Now they neither one of them had Cara.

He followed Gram along the rather haphazard row of gravestones, some of which, he realized, could have been of *her* great-grandparents. It gave pause for thought.

"What was your maiden name?" he asked her.

"Trevithick."

"Well, it's Cornish, that's certain."

"Everybody around Belle River was at one time," Gram said absently. She had her head down, reading the inscriptions as she passed. Owain followed. They had nearly covered the whole cemetery without finding any Trevithicks at all when a voice behind them asked, "Just visiting or were you looking for someone?"

Owain turned to find a short man, slightly beyond middle age, smiling at them through National Health spectacles. The man wore a yellow open-necked shirt, a pair of corduroy pants and a wheat-colored cardigan, but something about him was distinctly vicarish. Owain hadn't forgotten the feeling. A few seconds later the man confirmed it.

"Thomas Kempe," he said, holding out his hand. Owain shook it. "I've been vicar here for seven years now. Know them all by heart." His other hand swept over the cemetery.

"I was born here," Gram told him. "My family went to America when I was a child."

"Which family?"

"Trevithick."

The vicar frowned. "None of them here, I'm afraid."

It was Gram's turn to frown. "Not here?"

"What was your mother's name?"

Gram thought a moment. "Mary. Mary Inskip."

The vicar brightened. "Now them we do have. Inskips by the dozen. Right over here."

He took Gram's arm to help her over the uneven ground as he led her to one of the last plots in the corner of the churchyard. As he said, there were nearly a dozen stones, several with more than one inscription, and two or three almost worn away by time.

Gram halted in front of the most recent one, though it was by no means new.

"Robert Charles Inskip," Owain read aloud. "1834–1913. Your grandfather?" he asked, remembering her story of the old man who had taken her walking on Christmas and who had given her the treat of a young girl's lifetime with the London jaunt. He turned to look at Gram and found her smiling, with tears running down her cheeks.

"Grandpa." She reached up and touched her lips with trembling fingers, then her hand dropped to touch the white stone. Rooks chattered in the trees overhead. The rain, which had abated, began in earnest again.

"Come in for a cup of tea," Thomas Kempe invited them. "And I'll have a look in the records for this Trevithick of yours."

He bustled them in, made them a pot of tea, settled them in the lounge and then ferreted out his record book. He asked Gram for her birth date, then proceeded to check.

"Yes, here it is. Right here." He held out the record book to Gram, and Owain leaned toward her to read over her shoulder the rather ornate hand that had written, "May Florence Trevithick, daughter of Samuel and Mary Trevithick."

"Me." Gram lifted her eyes and beamed at him, her memories justified.

"But why Cornish?" Owain wanted to know, the puzzle still nagging at him. "Clear over here."

"Migration," Thomas Kempe replied. He settled back in his armchair. Outside the rain sluiced down the windows. Gram bent over the record book, reading the names softly, her lips barely moving. Owain, caught by the word he had been chasing in its various forms for the past three years, leaned forward, his elbows on his knees, and listened.

"Cornwall's economy depended heavily on its mines for years. Besides fishing, it was *the* industry in the area. A real slump hit in the 1860s after some booming years. A lot of people left then, went north to other mining centers or emigrated to America. Some left mining altogether. Others weathered the slump, only to be hit by another before 1890. By then tin mining in Cornwall had virtually stopped. Again, some went abroad right away. But if I were a betting man," said Thomas Kempe, "I'd wager your Sam came here to try his hand at something else. Fishing perhaps. We've lots of them hereabouts. And they make a living, some of them. Or they did. But it wasn't lucrative by any means. Perhaps when he married the Inskip girl, he wanted to give her a better life." The vicar smiled slightly. "To try the American dream, as it were. To strike it rich."

A bell rang somewhere in the back of Owain's mind. A memory. And just when it did, Gram laughed and said, "Yes, he always said that, Dad did. 'I'm going to strike it rich, Mary. Just you wait.'"

"A lot of them thought it," the vicar said. "That's why people follow their dreams."

"But they don't always find them," Owain said.

"Goodness no." The vicar scratched his head. "But what do they say? 'It's better to have played and lost than never to have played at all.'"

"'Loved,'" Owain corrected softly.

"Right. Not precisely theological," said Thomas Kempe, "but there you are, the truth nonetheless."

Owain, thinking of Cara, hoped he was right.

The niggling memory that had pricked at his consciousness when Thomas Kempe had spoken of striking it rich came back to him late that night. He was lying in the small bedroom of the bed-and-breakfast in Burnham-on-Crouch that they had chosen for the night after they had left Gram's birthplace. He could hear her puttering around in the room next to his, humming softly, obviously still pleased with what she had told him was "one of the happiest days of her life."

"I feel," she had confided, "as if I had done what my dad always wanted—struck it rich."

"I'm glad," he had said. And he meant it, too.

He *was* glad for her and for all the people who chased their dreams and found them. He hadn't.

But what he remembered now was a notation in one of Sam Trevithick's diaries, which he had been reading each night before he went to bed. It had obviously coincided with his decision to go to America—a decision Owain understood better after today.

Sam had written, "I would not leave here if I didn't have to. But I must look to the future. Because I could not find a way to live here doesn't mean that I won't somewhere. Good has come of it—Mary and the girls. Now it is time to move on."

Time to move on. Time to let go of one dream. Time to begin dreaming another.

He wasn't the first person it had happened to. But now, like everyone else whose dreams had crumbled—like Sam Trevithick, who hadn't made it fishing but was willing to look for the mother lode, like Marsha, who had gone through two divorces and still wasn't afraid to try, like all those dream chasers who emigrated in the hopes of a better existence—he had to get on with his life.

IN THE MORNING HE CALLED his mother and told her they were on their way.

"You're in England?" His mother was astonished. "And you didn't even say?"

"It was spur of the moment," Owain excused himself. "But I'd like to come if you don't mind."

"Mind?" She sounded as if he'd lost his senses. "When can you get here?"

"Well . . ." He tried to calculate.

"Today?"

"Not today."

"The day after?"

Owain smiled, touched by her eagerness, grateful for the maternal display of love. "The day after," he agreed. "And, uh, Mum . . . I . . . I've . . . got someone with me."

"A lady friend?" The words simply dripped hope.

Owain grinned. "Well, yes. But not exactly what you think. She . . . she's a grandmother actually. A great-grandmother."

There was a moment's pregnant silence. Then Bronwen O'Neill said wisely, "I won't ask now. I'll wait to meet her, lucky woman that she is."

"Lucky?"

"She's a grandmother, Owain. A *great*-grandmother."

"Right." He hoped she didn't hear the hollowness in his voice.

OWAIN FELT oddly like the prodigal son.

Perhaps it was seeing the road jam-packed with cars all about his parents' house and the garden full of relatives he hadn't set eyes on in years. Perhaps it was his mother's aura of suppressed excitement when she flew out the door to meet him at the car. Perhaps it was just being back in Penarth, where he had started from with so many dreams so long ago.

But whatever it was, he was distinctly unnerved.

"Oh, Owain! Oh, love!" His mother threw her arms around him and hugged him hard, looking up at him with eyes that were suspiciously damp.

"Hey." He hugged her back. "Homesick for me already? Want to come back to L.A.?"

"No, it's not that. It's..." She stopped, seeming to notice for the first time the elderly lady just getting out of the car. "Heavens, how rude of me! Owain, introduce us." She went round the car and took Gram's hand.

"This is...Mrs. Nute." It felt awkward to say it. "She's..." What was she? He couldn't call her Cara's grandmother. His mother didn't know Cara. "She's...the friend I've been traveling with."

His mother, bless her, didn't bat an eyelash. "Do come in, Mrs. Nute. I'm afraid we already had a little party planned for this afternoon. A few relatives—" she waved her hand at the mob of milling children and adults, several of whom had turned and were grinning at Owain now "—and when Owain called, we thought, so much the better. Most of them haven't seen him in years. But now..." She still held Gram's hand as she walked with her up the walk.

"Now they can all overwhelm her at once," Owain said. He grinned at his cousin, Lloyd, whom he hadn't seen in five years at least. "New baby?" he asked, nodding at the toddler Lloyd was balancing on one arm.

Lloyd nodded. "Thomas, after your dad."

"Where're Gareth and James?"

"Out there." Lloyd nodded across the garden.

Owain's eyes scanned the half dozen or so children kicking a soccer ball in the field next to the house. The two little dark-haired boys would have to be his cousin's sons. The redhead was undoubtedly David's Lewis. And the blond one was . . .

"Welcome home." His Auntie Susan gave him a smacking kiss. Owain hardly noticed. He felt as if he had been hit in the gut by the soccer ball as he stared out into the field over Auntie Susan's head. The boy looked exactly like Hugh.

"Owain." It was his mother saying something to him, but he couldn't fathom what. "Come inside now. There's someone I want you to meet."

He allowed himself to be dragged, but he couldn't help one last glance over his shoulder at the running children. His cousin Rhys's son? Simon had been blond. But was he that young?

"Owain." His mother was hauling him through her new house with no regard to showing it to him, no pausing to let him examine each room, no encouragements to comment.

They went through the entry and into the kitchen where his Aunties Frances and Sian were still setting food out on plates.

"Oh, Owain, you're here!" they bubbled, but his mother hustled him right on past.

"In the sunroom," she said, hauling him through an archway into a small solarium. "Your dad added it on first thing when we got here. And I'd love for you to tell me what you think later. But just now there's someone here to see you."

She backed out through the archway as quickly as she had dragged him in. He stood there, dumbfounded, staring at Cara.

For a moment he wondered if he were mistaken, if perhaps this golden-haired lookalike were some lucky cousin's wife. Then she gave a tiny, nervous smile and bit down on her bottom lip, and he knew it was Cara and no one else.

His heart was hammering as hard as Mike had ever played the drums. Astonishment and disbelief made sounds, he discovered, and they were at that instant thrumming in his ears.

"I came," she said.

He could only look. Did she mean—? *Could* she mean...?

Did he dare hope?

He saw her swallow convulsively. She licked her lips, ducked her head, then lifted it again and met his gaze squarely. "Could we talk, please?"

His tongue felt like shoe leather. "Y-yeah. Sure. Of course. I—"

"How about a cup of tea?" Auntie Frances stuck her head around the archway to ask. "And a biscuit?"

Owain shook his head. "No, thanks. I—"

"You, dear?" Auntie Frances seemed also to require an answer from Cara.

"No, thank you."

Auntie Frances tsked. "Skin and bones, lovely. You need a bit of fattening up."

Cara gave her a bleak smile. Owain looked at her carefully. She did look thinner. Almost gaunt, and very pale. She was wearing the same jeans she had worn the first day he had met her in the park. Then they had hugged her hips. Now they seemed to hang on her.

"Come on," he said. He reached for her hand automatically, wrapping it in his. It was cold, icy almost. But for once she did not resist him. She allowed him to lead her through the kitchen. He paused and snatched a handful of cookies off the tray that Auntie Frances had just prepared.

"I'll fatten her a bit," he promised his aunt.

"Just mind *you* don't eat them all," she told him with a smile.

They passed through a throng of relatives. Owain didn't notice any of them. Only his parents and Cara's grandmother stood out from the crowd. He looked at them, still half-dazed, only vaguely aware of their smiling faces, still wondering if in fact he was dreaming.

Then out of the corner of his eyes he saw Bronwen come dashing across the field. She didn't see him, sailed right past him in fact and skidded to a halt in front of his mother. "Grandma," she said, "come see what I found! Little baby prickly things."

Owain stopped in his tracks. *"Grandma?"* he echoed.

It was Cara who tugged on his hand this time, leading him. "Come on."

He went. He bundled her into the car he had just got out of, jammed it into reverse and shot back down the road, turning into the lane. He drove automatically, weaving through the narrow streets, then heading toward the coast, not stopping until he was parked along the waterfront near the pier.

Cara didn't say a word during the whole journey. She must have known he would have been an accident about to happen if she had. But when he pulled to a stop and cut the engine, it was Cara who took the initiative, who opened the car door and got out, who came around and stood beside the driver's door, waiting for him.

She looked tight-lipped and nervous, but there was a light in her eyes that he hadn't remembered seeing in months. He got out and began walking toward the pier. Cara fell into step beside him.

"I don't quite know where to begin," she said. "I'm sorry. I guess that would be the best place."

Owain looked at her warily. He was still afraid to hope. Perhaps it was her turn to feel guilty, her turn to try to make amends. Maybe she had brought the kids to see his parents out of some misguided good intention.

"It's just that . . . that I was . . . so hurt."

"I know, Cara. I'm sorry. I—"

"No!" She cut him off. "You've apologized a thousand times over. It's *my* turn now. Please."

Owain nodded. He slid his hands into the pockets of his jacket, his fingers clenching together to keep from reaching for her.

They turned and walked down the steps to the shingle beach beneath the pier, walking side by side down to where the steel-gray water lapped the flat dark stones. Storm clouds hung overhead, but so far the rain held off.

"You have to understand how it was with me," Cara said in a low voice. "After Martin died I was devastated. I guess I had thought that sort of thing always happened to other people. When it happened to us, I was shocked. And, you were right, deep down I suppose I was angry at Martin for 'betraying' me and dying."

"I was angry. I didn't mean—"

"No. You were right. To a point. Anyway, his death taught me a lesson. It taught me to be pragmatic, careful. Always erring on the side of security. I played it safe. I didn't take risks. I didn't want to jeopardize what I had. And then I met you." Her voice dropped even lower and Owain bent his head close to hers to catch her words.

They leaned against one of the pilings and stared out at a passing ship. "You were perfect."

Owain groaned. He bent and picked up a stone, flinging it into the water.

"And that was part of the problem," Cara went on softly, a catch in her voice. "In my mind you were everything I wanted. And I thought you loved me."

"I did love you."

She lifted her eyes, the wind whipped her hair across her face. "Yes. But I wasn't dealing with real love in those days.

I wanted a perfect love—one that nothing could happen to, unlike the one I'd had with Martin. I don't know—" she shrugged helplessly "—maybe my disillusionment came too close on top of our going to the House on the Rock. Maybe I couldn't settle for reality when fantasy had seemed so close at hand."

She took a deep shuddering breath. Her eyes were bright with unshed tears. "I was so very wrong," she whispered. Her shoulders shook. And Owain could stand no more.

He reached for her, wrapping her in his arms, burying his face in the softness of her hair. "Ah, Cara. God, I love you."

She burrowed her face against his jacket, sniffling, her arms around him hugging him tightly. "Still?" She lifted her tear-streaked face to look into his.

"Always. Forever." He kissed the tip of her nose. "Believe me?"

She blinked, then swiped at her eyes with the back of her hand. "Yes. You don't even have to shoot the kids."

Owain shuddered. "That was an awful thing to say."

"Yes, it was. But after you said it, I started to think. I thought that I was asking the impossible. There really wasn't any way you could 'prove' your love to me. And you had never asked me to prove *my* love."

"I did make you prove it in a way, though," Owain admitted.

"Because you didn't tell me about what a rich and famous man you are?"

He nodded.

"It's funny, you know," she said. "I probably should have guessed you were their father when you told me about Cardiff Connection. The lawyer had said the kids' natural father was a musician. I never thought he was *that* kind of musician though."

"What did you think?" He smiled at her. His fingers stroked her hair, her cheek, needing to touch her just to prove that she was real, that she was there.

Cara shrugged. "A member of a Welsh choir maybe. Or at best a cellist in the London Philharmonic."

"Thank you very much," Owain said dryly. "Are you disappointed?"

"Not a bit." Cara laid her hand on his cheek. "You didn't tell me your mother's name was Bronwen, either."

"I didn't think you'd care much for the coincidence."

"I might not have once. Now I think it's marvelous."

"It's what made me stay," he told her.

"Your mother's name?"

He nodded. "Hearing you call Bron. I couldn't believe it. It was like fate." He shrugged, embarrassed.

"Perhaps it was fate," she said softly.

He kissed her gently then, savoring the taste of her lips, thinking that not long ago he couldn't imagine ever being allowed to touch them again. "I can't quite fathom it," he said finally.

"Fathom what?"

"This. You. Here." He fumbled, unable to articulate how this abrupt swing in his fortunes made him feel. "You were so angry."

"I was angry for a while," she admitted. "I was hurt and I was scared."

"Now you're not?"

"No. Now I love you and I'm not afraid to admit it."

"What made you change your mind?"

"The daffodils."

Owain stared. "What daffodils?"

"Sunday I went to the cemetery with the kids. I hadn't been home on Martin's birthday, so I wanted to go. I was restless, I guess. All the things you threw at me were hurtling back and forth in my head. One minute I was madder than hell at you still. And the next everything you'd said made horrible sense. I needed to get some perspective. So I went to see Martin. And I saw the daffodils. The kids told me . . . that you'd planted them. It made me cry."

"Cara, I didn't mean to—"

She shook her head fiercely. "I *needed* to cry. I needed to stop hanging on to the past, living the present because of it. I needed to go on. And the daffodils made me see that. I could have planted them myself, but I never had. Because if I did, it would have been like making a pact with the future. It would have been taking a risk. There could be a cold snap, a heavy frost. They could die."

Owain could hear almost physical pain in her voice when she spoke the words. He knew what they cost.

She reached for his hand and wrapped it in hers. "I'm ready to risk again, Owain, if you are."

He took her face in his hands, tilting it upward. Silvery sunlight broke through the clouds, gilding her hair. "Will you marry me?"

"Anytime you say."

"Will you have children with me?"

"*More* children?" She sounded surprised.

He paused. "If you don't want more, that's all right. These two are plenty. I just thought . . ."

"I would love to have any children you give me. I want us to be a family, whole and complete."

He kissed her then, a kiss that made up for all the days and weeks and months of uncertainty. A kiss that spoke of despair conquered and love renewed. And Cara kissed him back, giving him everything that was in her, offering herself, her life, her love.

A paper cup hit her on the head.

"Lookit 'em kissin'! Just like the movies!"

Owain jerked his head up and shouted at the two blond heads that peered over the pier railing above them. They giggled, then vanished. Feet thundered overhead.

"Cripes," he muttered.

"Just like home," Cara reminded him, laughing.

"They are about that age, aren't they?" He grimaced.

"Uh-huh."

"It's going to be a challenge getting you alone around them."

"Probably."

"But it's good to have a goal to strive for." He grinned at her.

"Indeed it is." She kissed his chin, then her lips moved lightly along the line of his jaw, finally nibbling his ear. He felt a delicious shiver slide down his spine.

"You're stoking fires that are going to be hard to put out," he told her.

"I warned you. I've decided life is worth a few risks. Why," she said as she looped her arm through his and began walking back to the car with him, "you should see the lingerie I bought just to make this trip."

"Oh, yes?"

She had his attention now. Her eyes were positively dancing with glee.

"You bet." She grinned. "You're not going to be the only one in this marriage with red underpants!"

Keeping the Faith

by
Judith Arnold

It renewed old friendships, kindled new relationships, but the fifteen-year reunion of *The Dream*'s college staff affected all six of the Columbia-Barnard graduates: Laura, Seth, Kimberly, Andrew, Julianne and Troy.

Follow the continuing story of these courageous, vital men and women who find themselves at a crossroads—as their idealism of the sixties clashes with the reality of life in the eighties.

You may laugh, you may cry, but you will find a piece of yourself in *Keeping the Faith*.

Don't miss American Romance #201 *Promises* in June, #205 *Commitments* in July and #209 *Dreams* in August.

Harlequin American Romance

COMING NEXT MONTH

#205 COMMITMENTS by Judith Arnold

In the seventies they'd have called it "bad karma." Andrew Collins, self-avowed cynic of *The Dream*, and Kimberly Belmont, its resident optimist, seemed destined to remain antagonists forever. But shortly after the magazine's anniversary bash, something extraordinary happened. They'd become lovers. Was it an accident? Or a mistake? Catch the second book in the *Keeping the Faith* trilogy.

#206 FAIR GAME by Susan Andrews

Being a winner on *Love Life*, TV's popular dating game, meant that Julie Turner had to spend a week in Atlantic City with Marcus Allen, TV's heartthrob. To publicity-shy Julie it seemed more like a chore than fun, but how could she resist a man who whisked her away from the prying eyes of the media to a seaside hideaway?

#207 CHRISTMAS IN JULY by Julie Kistler

Kit Wentworth was furious. How dared Riley Cooper call her a lily-livered coward! The time had come for her to go home. But that meant seeing her family, and confronting the man who had prompted her exodus four years earlier.

#208 A QUESTION OF HONOR by Jacqueline Ashley

Helping people was a matter of honor to Frances McPhee. But traveling with her cantankerous old uncle Fergus and his companion to his Oklahoma cabin was pure torture. With Ash Blair's penchant for gourmet foods and pricey hotels—and his devastating charm—would Frances bring Fergus home safely without first falling in the poorhouse—or in love?

ATTRACTIVE, SPACE SAVING BOOK RACK

Display your most prized novels on this handsome and sturdy book rack. The hand-rubbed walnut finish will blend into your library decor with quiet elegance, providing a practical organizer for your favorite hard-or soft-covered books.

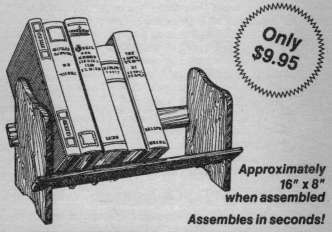

Only $9.95

Approximately 16" x 8" when assembled

Assembles in seconds!

To order, rush your name, address and zip code, along with a check or money order for $10.70* ($9.95 plus 75¢ postage and handling) payable to *Harlequin Reader Service*:

Harlequin Reader Service
Book Rack Offer
901 Fuhrmann Blvd.
P.O. Box 1325
Buffalo, NY 14269-1325

Offer not available in Canada.

BKR-1R

*New York residents add appropriate sales tax.